From Trumerica with Love

A Modern Retelling of George Orwell's 1984: A Dystopian Parody

Logan Emery Emerson

Contents

As retold by Logan Emery Emerson, *From Trumerica with Love* is a parody of George Orwell's *1984*.

***

"No book is genuinely free from political bias."
— George Orwell

***

"We're only getting started, and it's going to be beautiful."
— Donald Trump

PART 1: IN THE SHADOWS OF TRUTH

Chapter 1

It's a scorching day in July, and the Doomsday Clock is 88 seconds from midnight.

Liam enters the front doors of Plaza Residences, a swirl of dirt entering along with him.

In the lobby there's a massive poster fastened to a wall. It depicts the face of the country's supreme commander. The man is in his seventies and has wheat chaff-colored hair and ruggedly handsome features. He's Trumerica's Leader for Life.

Since the elevator rarely works, Liam takes the stairs slowly, resting several times on the way up, his hemorrhoids burning. On each landing, another Trufamily poster with an enormous face gazes from the wall. The eyes of each 3D poster follow you when you move.

On the third floor, he approaches a neighbor struggling to carry her bags. Liam offers to help. She declines, giving him a suspicious look.

I was just going to carry your heavy bags, he thinks. *I wasn't going to turn you in.*

He continues walking up the stairs, thinking, *To maintain your humanity, you have to be bifurcated. You have to have a split personality. You present your external self to all of Trumerica. That's you towing the line, mock-believing in impossibilities, and corrupting yourself in order to survive. But it is possible to have an internal self, a private life of thoughts and feelings that prove you're still actually human.*

Inside his apartment on the seventh floor, a harsh voice reads out stock market data. "The TASDAQ is up," the voice says, coming from a large screen built into the wall. "Every day, our improving economy proves that we're ending the theft of Trumerican prosperity."

Standing by the window, Liam's frail, meager body is hidden by the business attire that all members of the Organization are required to wear. He's thirty-eight with blond hair

3

and sunburned skin.

Outside, the world is a sweltering mess. Down in the street, wind whirls dirt and trash in spirals. Even though the sun is shining and the sky is bright blue, there seems to be no color in anything except the Trufamily posters placed all over the cityscape.

From his studio apartment, Liam can see approximately twenty posters. They're all placed in commanding positions. The Trufamily member depicted on each poster is different. Yet their dark eyes all look directly at Liam.

Each poster is captioned with the same words that fill up the bottom half of each poster—*Keep Trumerica Great*. Under each caption is the Trufamily Forty-Five logo with the double-headed eagle. One poster of Laura Ingraham is slightly damaged at the bottom, making the logo appear and disappear every few seconds.

In the far distance, a drone skims down between apartment buildings. It hovers for a while, then darts away. The Peace Police are always snooping into people's windows, always looking for something, anything.

Behind Liam's back, the newscaster on the Portal babbles on about the Organization surpassing its promises regarding the $55 trillion budget that's making Trumerica safer, stronger, and prouder.

The hundreds of millions of Portals throughout the country receive and transmit simultaneously. They pick up any sound above a low whisper. Also, when in their field of vision, there's a chance they'll read your feelings and intentions through your eyes, gathering your private and unconscious responses.

Liam wishes you could turn the abominable devices off, but you can't. The only time you get respite from them is between midnight and six. During those hours, the broadcasts turn off, but the monitors, like black mirrors, are still on. Nobody can completely shut off any Portal.

There's no way of knowing whether you're being watched at any given moment by an actual person. How often the police plug into any of the hundreds of millions of individual Portals throughout Trumerica is unknowable. It's even conceivable that the police officers themselves, not just their AI, watch everybody all the time. Nevertheless, they can access the Portals in your home whenever they want. You have to live assuming that your every sound and movement is scrutinized and cataloged.

Liam keeps his back turned to the Portal—it's safer. Though he knows even a back can be revealing.

He looks out his window at the grimy, sun-ravaged landscape of Lar-o-Maga Palm City, the biggest city of New Florida and the third most populous of the 379 states in Trumerica.

He tries recalling any childhood memory that could tell him whether Lar-o-Maga Palm City has always been like this.

Has there always been luxury apartment buildings with swimming pools on every terrace, and have those opulent private residential communities always been right next to ghettos with peeling paint on houses and questionably-hygienic food trucks parked beside bomb craters?

Has there always been Hyperloop hovertrains passing over slums and garbage dumps where kids forage for food scraps?

But it's no use, he can't remember anything. Not much really remains of his childhood except a bunch of unintelligible images that seem disconnected from everything.

In the distance there are four megatall skyscrapers that tower above all other buildings in the city. Three of these buildings are octagonal and soar up, floor after floor, exactly one mile into the air.

Those three buildings each house the headquarters of a different Trumerican bureau.

The Bureau of Facts produces news, entertainment, and the arts.

The Bureau of Legalism advocates for Trumerica at the Global Markets & Trade Barriers Organization.

The Bureau of Morality performs border control and maintains law and order.

There are one-hundred bureaus in Trumerica's moneyocracy. The other ninety-seven bureaus are in various cities throughout the country. They're also each housed in one-mile high octagonal buildings.

Liam knows a little about the Bureau of Facts, where he works. He knows even less about the other bureaus. He couldn't even name them all if he tried. Yet in his mind, they all pale in comparison to the fourth mega-tall building here in Lar-o-Maga Palm City—the Trump Tower.

Exactly two miles high, the Trump Tower is the headquarters for the Trumerica Freedom Organization. It also houses the penthouse condominium residence of the Trumerican President, Donald Trump. Frighteningly, excluding the top floors, the entire building has no windows.

Liam has never been up close to Trump Tower, nor even within half a mile of it. It's impossible to enter it except on official business. Even then you'd have to go through a maze of security posts with steel doors, sniffer dogs, face recognition stations, and x-ray systems. On the wide streets that lead up to the Tower, which double as tsunami evacuation routes, guards roam around in black uniforms, armed to the teeth with assault weapons.

Displayed on jumbotrons on the side of the three bureau cloudscrapers are this week's current slogans. From where Liam stands, it's easy to read them:

FACTS ARE ALTERNATIVE.

LAW WITHOUT STRENGTH IS CRIMINAL.

THERE IS ONLY ONE WAY TO LIVE—THE TRUMERICAN WAY.

Throughout the country, these one-hundred mega-structures are all constantly digitally displaying the Organization's mottos of the moment.

Liam turns around abruptly. With quiet optimism, he slightly smiles, which is advisable whenever facing a Portal. He goes to the kitchenette on the other side of the room. There's no food in his fridge except for a hunk of Trump steak that he's saving for tomorrow.

He opens a bottle of vodka. It gives off a sickly, oily smell. Liam pours out two fingers, prepares himself for a shock, then gulps it down. He cringes, his face turns scarlet, and his eyes tear up. The stuff is like acid. Swallowing TrumputinVodka initially feels like you're being pistol-whipped in the face. However, in the next moment the burning in your belly dies down and the world seems slightly less shitty. But it doesn't take away his pain. So he reaches for his dose pen and is upset to see that the vaporizer has just one hit of OxiQoxi left. He can't wait. He puts it to his mouth, inhales the vapor, and can almost instantaneously feel some of his pain ease away.

He crosses the room and enters his bathroom that's just big enough to fit a toilet and a tiny shower. The bathroom is to the left of the Portal. His Portal is in an unusual position. Instead of being placed in the end wall, as is normal, where it could command the entire room, including his bed in the corner, and the doorless bathroom, the Portal is embedded into the longer wall, opposite the window. To one side of it, the bathroom is like a shallow alcove.

Liam sits on the toilet with the toilet seat down and his pants still on. By sitting there he can remain outside of the Portal's view. He can be heard, of course. But so long as he stays in his present position, he's essentially invisible to the Organization.

He takes a thick, blank journal with a marbled cover out of a drawer under the tiny sink. It's a peculiarly beautiful book with smooth, creamy paper. These journals haven't been made in decades. He saw it in the window of a messy antiques store in a slummy part of the city. Instantly, he wanted to own it.

Members of the Organization aren't supposed to enter shops owned by the lower classes, the Subs. But the rule isn't strictly enforced because there are various things, such as micro-doses of OxiQoxi, that are often unbuyable via Walmart because of shortages.

He had glanced quickly up and down the street and then slipped inside and bought the journal. He carried it guiltily home in his backpack. Even with nothing written in it, it was a compromising possession.

Liam is about to start a diary.

If they find what I'm about to write, they'll consider me an enemy of the state. Most likely, they'll execute me. If I'm lucky, they'll only send me to a re-education camp.

The pen in his hand is also a relic of the past. Naturally, he's not used to writing by hand. Apart from short handwritten notes, he usually dictates everything into a microphone, which is of course impossible for his present purpose.

He holds the pen above the paper—then pauses. A tremor rumbles through his bowels. To mark the paper will be a decisive act. In small clumsy letters, he writes:

July 10, 2024.

Life doesn't have to be like this.

I can't wait to meet the new Trumerica—whatever and whenever that is.

He leans back and the toilet flusher digs into his back. A sense of helplessness descends upon him. He has no idea what the next version of this country could be, let alone should be. But he somehow feels that it can't possibly—shouldn't—keep existing like this forever.

He also doesn't know who his intended readers are. Yet right then, almost instantaneously, he decides that he's writing this diary for the people of the future.

The Portal starts playing advertorials.

For a long time, he just stares at the paper. It's as if he doesn't know how to express himself, as if he's forgotten what he intended to write. For weeks, he's been preparing for this moment. And all he figured he needed was courage. He predicted that the actual writing would be easy. He just had to transcribe some of the machine gun-like monolog that's always blasting away inside his head. At this moment, however, his internal dialogue is silent. Moreover, his hemorrhoids are itching unbearably. Not that he'd dare scratch them, because when he does they just become more inflamed.

The seconds tick by.

He's conscious of nothing except the blankness of the page in front of him, the irritating desire to scratch his ass, the blaring of an infomercial about a golf course, and a tipsiness caused by the shot of vodka and the hit of opioid.

Suddenly, in sheer panic, he begins writing. His handwriting is small and childish.

Last night at the cinema, I watched a documentary by Dinesh D'Souza. Somewhere along our southern border with Latineuropa, a fat family of illegal immigrants sprinted toward our border wall. The fat man, fat woman, and two fat children were about to try to scale the wall. But one of our drones shot them to hell and back, causing the audience to cackle with laughter.

The footage was amazing—the camera was mounted on the drone, and you watched it shoot the shit out of the illegals who had dangerous dreams of invading our great land so that they could steal our jobs and ruin our lives.

There was a lot of cheering and clapping from the section of the cinema for Organization members. But a woman in the Subs section bitched and complained that these movies shouldn't be shown to kids. The police escorted her out. I doubt that anything happened to her—nobody in the Organization really cares what non-Organization members say. Everyone knows that she's just another typical Sub. Overreacting. Always missing the point. Never standing up for Trumerica.

Liam reads over what he's written. He acknowledges that it's all crap. But then he remembers something that happened today that made him realize he had to start his diary as soon as he got home. It happened at this morning's Victory Rally, if anything so nebulous can be said to happen.

Liam writes.

I was sitting in one of the middle rows at this morning's rally, and I saw Gemma and Brannan ...

Chapter 2

It's nearly 11 a.m. and in the Information Security Department where Liam works in the Bureau of Facts, people leave their cubicles and walk into a massive room for the Victory Rally. Liam sits in one of the middle rows. Two people that he knows by sight, yet has never talked to, unexpectedly enter the room.

One of them is a woman named Gemma, this name being one of the most popular names for daughters of Trumerica. She works in the Public Relations Department. She's known around the bureau as the press release maven, though Liam thinks of her work being more about writing praise releases than what can really be called press releases.

This Gemma person always wears power suits. A bold-looking woman, she has thick hair, a freckled face, and swift, athletic movements. She wears a silver ring on her wedding finger, a symbol of the Making Abstinence Sexy advocacy group. Today, she's also wearing a red cap.

Liam disliked Gemma the first moment he saw her. Then, like now, she gives off a pungent vibe of being a fact-loathing loser and a race-baiting xenophobe. It's people like her who are the most bigoted adherents of the Organization. The swallowers of slogans. The snitches that squeal on anyone for any reason.

Once, months ago, passing each other in a hallway, she glanced at him. It filled him with terror. The idea crossed his mind that she might be an agent of the Peace Police. Though it's unlikely she's actually an undercover paramilitary agent, Liam continues to feel fear whenever she's anywhere nearby.

The other person is Brett Brannan, a member of the C-Suite. He's the Chief Operating Officer of Safeguarding Our Values, a team within the Bureau of Opposition Research and Counter-Disinformation. Brannan's job is so important that Liam only has a vague idea of its nature.

A hush passes over every regular Organization member in the room as they see the sleek suit of the C-Suite member approaching.

Brannan is a tall, powerful man with a thick neck and a coarse, humorous, brutal face. Despite his formidable appearance, he seems charming and charismatic. He has a habit of resettling his glasses on his nose, which is curiously disarming.

Liam has seen Brannan perhaps a dozen times in the past decade. He feels drawn to him because of a secretly held belief—or hope—that, deep down, Brannan is corrupt. Something in his face suggests it. He appears to be someone you could chat with—if you could somehow cheat the Portals and get him alone. Liam has never made the smallest effort to verify this guess. Indeed, there's absolutely no way of doing so without risking his life.

Brannan sits in the same row as Liam, two chairs away. Between them is a small woman who works in the cubicle beside Liam, and who Liam always thinks of as Short Liz. The woman with the freckles and wearing the red hat—the woman named Gemma—is sitting immediately behind them.

The next moment, a hideous noise bursts out of a massive Portal at the end of the room. It's a noise that jars your teeth and bristles the hair at the back of your neck. The Victory Rally has started.

Every day, each rally kicks off with a new ten-minute video. Each video focuses on an enemy of Trumerica.

Yesterday's video was about a racist traitor, Ilhan Omar, who wickedly wants to trick our police into using excessive force on Subs.

One of last week's videos featured Colin Powell, a prominent Illuminati member, saying, "Trump lies about things. And he gets away with it because people won't hold him accountable."

Another recent video featured Nancy Pelosi giving a press conference from her palatial mansion, Villa Les Cedres, viciously and falsely calling the latest worldwide pandemic the "Trump virus."

Today's video is about a crowd favorite. It's about Alexandria Ocasio-Cortez, their diabolical leader. Her haggard face flashes on the giant screen. Some of the audience hiss and boo at her. Short Liz's shriek is part fear, part disgust.

Alexandria Ocasio-Cortez—also known by her initials AOC—is a pedophile-defending and self-hating woman. Long ago, she assassinated several

Organization members, including Melania Trump, Mitch McConnell, and Sean Hannity. She then attempted—and failed, of course—to carry out a coup d'état against President Trump. She was caught and condemned to death. Somehow, she mysteriously escaped and disappeared.

AOC's face appears briefly in every Victory Rally video. But today, all Trumericans are fortunate to have ten whole minutes of her.

As the primal traitor and the earliest defiler of the Organization's purity, all subsequent crimes against the Trumerica Freedom Organization—all treacheries, acts of sabotage, sexual deviations—can be traced back directly to her teachings.

Somewhere, she's still alive and hatching her conspiracies. Most Trumericans suspect she's being protected by her foreign paymasters, probably Korchinpan's leader, Kim Jong-un. Others have a hunch she's hiding somewhere in Trumerica itself, just like how Obama and Osama hid out together for years in Chicago after their friends flew planes into the World Trade Center.

Liam's stomach tightens. He can never see Alexandria Ocasio-Cortez's face without a painful mixture of emotions. It's a trustworthy, yet wicked face. A clever, yet despicable face. A smiling, yet angry face. It resembles the face of a hyena, and her voice even sounds like a hyena laughing.

In the video, AOC delivers her usual venomous attack on the Organization. Her arguments are so exaggerated and perverse that a child could see through them. And yet, they're just plausible enough to fool less intelligent people.

AOC ridicules the great man she lost to and calls him an orange-faced demagogue.

She denounces the dictatorship of the Trufamily Forty-Five.

See claims that our representative democracy is really a kakistocracy.

She demands that Trumerica enter a new deal with Iranaqey.

She whines that President Trump is morally, intellectually, and temperamentally unfit for office.

She alleges that critical thinking and evidence is better than dogma or superstition.

She advocates for free speech, freedom of the press, and freedom of assembly.

She yells hysterically that the democratic socialist revolution has been betrayed.

Just in case you might doubt the reality of Alexandria Ocasio-Cortez's deceptive lies, behind her is footage of thousands of enemy soldiers marching. Sometimes they're Iranaqeyian soldiers. Sometimes they're Korchinpanian soldiers. The dull rhythmic

11

stomping of their boots form the background to AOC's high-pitched "hee-hee-hee" sounds.

After a few minutes of this video, many people in the room are already breaking out into uncontrollable exclamations of rage. Her self-satisfied hyena-like face on the screen, and the terrifying power of the enemy combatants behind it, are just too much to handle. Besides, the sight or even the thought of AOC produces fear and anger automatically. She's an object of hatred more constant than either Iranaqey or Korchinpan.

What's strange is that, although everyone hates AOC, and although every day her dumb ideas are refuted and ridiculed as the pitiful poppycock that they clearly are—despite all this, her influence never diminishes. There are always more libtards waiting to be seduced by her. A day never passes without the Peace Police finding treasonous spies in our very midst who are working for that corporate whore.

She's the commander of a vast shadowy army called the Illuminati. It's an underground network of conspirators dedicated to overthrowing the Trumerica Freedom Organization and then implementing her ludicrous ideas for a liberal, utopian, one-world government.

There are also whispered stories of a terrible collection of essays written by Alexandria Ocasio-Cortez and other liberals, anti-capitalists, and domestic terrorists. The book is a compendium of heinous heresies, human sacrifices, and violent rituals. It supposedly circulates clandestinely here and there. As far as Liam knows, the book has no title. People refer to it simply as AOC's book. But you only hear of such things via vague rumors. No Organization member would mention the book if there's a way of avoiding it.

Near the end of the video, the Victory Rally rises to a frenzy. People leap up and down in their places. They shout to drown the maddening bleating voice coming out of the massive screen.

Brannan's face is flushed. Sitting straight in his chair, his powerful chest swells and quivers as though he's preparing the assault of a wave.

The face of Short Liz turns bright pink. She chants, "Lock her up! Lock her up! Lock her up!"

In a lucid moment, Liam finds that he's shouting with the others and stamping his feet violently on the floor.

The horrible thing about Victory Rallies isn't that you're obliged to take part, but, on the contrary, that it's impossible to avoid joining in. Within minutes, any pretense is always unnecessary. A hideous ecstasy of fear and vindictiveness grabs everyone. A desire

12

to smash faces in with sledge-hammers seems to flow through the entire audience like an electric current. You're turned—even against your own will—into a grimacing, screaming lunatic that wants to flay people alive.

The rage that you feel is an abstract emotion that can be switched from one person to another, like the flame of a blowtorch. At one moment, Liam's hatred is directed toward Alexandria Ocasio-Cortez, immigrants, or welfare cheats. In the next moment, his hatred is against our commander-in-chief, the Organization, and the Peace Police. At such moments, his heart goes out to AOC, the lonely, ugly heretic on the screen and the sole guardian of sanity in an insane world. And yet, in the very next instant, he's at one with those around him and everything AOC says seems to him to be untrue. At those moments, his secret loathing of Donald Trump changes into adoration, and our Leader for Life seems to tower up, an invincible, fearless protector, standing like a giant against our enemies. In those moments, AOC, despite her isolation, her helplessness, and the doubt about her very existence, seems like some sinister enchanter, capable of destroying ou r way of life.

Suddenly, by the sort of violent effort with which you wrench your head away from the pillow in a nightmare, Liam transfers his hatred from the hag on the screen to the red-capped Gemma behind him. Vivid, beautiful hallucinations flash through his mind. *I'll beat Gemma to death*, he thinks.

The hate of the rally rises to its climax. The voice of AOC becomes an actual hyena's howling laugh. For an instant, even her face changes into that of a hyena. Then the hyena-face melts into an enemy soldier pointing a machine gun at you, making some audience members flinch.

Then, like a miracle, the vile warfighter fades into the gorgeous face of Donald Trump, an orange glow, full of power and mysterious calm, and so vast that it almost fills up the screen.

For the next hour or so, President Trump gives one of his inspiring, fascinating, immaculate, and frightening speeches, though Liam has a hard time believing one iota of it.

The part of his speech that gets the biggest cheers is Trump's last few lines. "If the righteous many don't confront the wicked few, then evil will triumph. The only way we can save Trumerica and our freedom is to fight this violence of lies with a clenched fist of truth."

After his speech, the live broadcast of our benevolent leader dissolves away. Yet the face of Donald Trump seems to persist for several seconds on the screen, as though the impact it made on everyone's eyeballs is too vivid to wear off immediately.

In bold capital letters, Trumerica Freedom Organization's new slogans for this week appear on screen.

PARANOIA IS PATRIOTIC.

POWER TRUMPS PRINCIPLES.

ILLIBERALISM IS THE FUTURE.

Gemma flings herself forward over the back of Liam's chair, almost touching him. She extends her arms toward the screen, and murmurs "Our hero."

The crowd breaks into a deep, slow chant of "D-J-T! ... D-J-T! ..." It's a refrain that's often heard in moments of overwhelming emotion. It's a hymn to the wisdom and majesty of Donald J. Trump. It's also an act of self-hypnosis, a deliberate drowning of consciousness by means of rhythmic noise.

Liam's guts seem to grow cold. At rallies he can't help taking part in the delirium. But the savage chanting of "D-J-T! ... D-J-T!" always fills him with horror. Of course he chants with the rest, it being impossible not to do what everyone else is doing. Mostly though, he has trained himself to conceal his feelings and control his face. But just as Liam senses his eyes might betray him, Brett Brannan takes off his glasses and glances at him.

In that fraction of a second, it's as if their two minds are open and thoughts flow from one into the other through their eyes.

I am with you, Chief Operating Officer Brannan seems to say telepathically. *I know what you're feeling. I know all about your contempt, your hatred, your disgust. But don't worry, I'm on your side!*

And then, like a flash, their connection breaks, and Brannan's face is as inscrutable as everybody else's.

Liam swings wildly between being uncertain about whether this significant event actually happened, and the belief—or hope—that some of his colleagues are indeed enemies of the Organization.

Perhaps the rumors of a vast deep state are true after all, he thinks. *Perhaps the Illuminati really exists!*

It's impossible—despite the endless arrests, confessions, and executions—to be sure that the Illuminati isn't simply fake news. Some days he believes in it. Some days he's certain it's a fictional conspiracy.

He decides that he probably just imagined the importance of that brief connection with Brannan. They just exchanged an insignificant glance, and that was the end of it.

Still, as Liam heads back to his desk and decides to write about this in his diary when he gets home, he's comforted in knowing that, in the locked loneliness in which he lives, even a fleeting glance registers as a memorable event.

Chapter 3

In his apartment, Liam Mateo Janz can't seem to remember much of what happened between today's rally and now. Between the moment he walked away from Brett Brannan and the moment he started sitting down here, in his bathroom where his Portals can't see him, is all a blur.

He sits up straighter. He burps. The vodka is rising from his stomach.

His eyes refocus on the page. He discovers he must have been writing, but not consciously writing, the words arising from his subconscious. And it's no longer the same cramped, awkward handwriting as before. His pen had slid automatically over the paper, printing in large neat capitals—

DONALD TRUMP MUST DIE.
DONALD TRUMP MUST DIE.
DONALD TRUMP MUST DIE.
DONALD TRUMP MUST DIE.
DONALD TRUMP MUST DIE.

—over and over again, filling half a page.

He feels a twinge of terror. It's perhaps silly, since the writing of those particular words isn't any more dangerous than the mere act of buying the diary. But for a moment, he's tempted to tear out the pages and abandon the whole thing.

He doesn't, however, because he knows it'd be useless. Whether he writes *Donald Trump must die*, or whether he refrains from writing it, makes no difference. Whether he continues or stops writing in the diary makes no difference. The Peace Police will get him all the same. He has committed the essential crime that contains all others—liberalism. Liberalism isn't something that you can conceal forever. You might dodge the police successfully for a while, even for years. But eventually, they'll get you.

They usually come for liberals at night. The sudden jerk out of sleep. The strong hands grabbing you. The lights glaring in your eyes. A dozen paramilitary personnel wearing facemasks and black hoods, all standing in your bedroom, looking at you.

In the vast majority of cases, there's no report of the arrest, and there's no trial. People simply disappear. Your name is purged from electoral rolls. Every record of everything you've ever done is wiped out. Your one-time existence is denied, deleted forever, and then forgotten. You're abolished. Annihilated. Vaporized.

For a moment, he's seized by a kind of hysteria. He writes in a hurried untidy scrawl:

They'll kill me. I don't care. They'll incinerate me. I don't care.

Donald Trump is a sexual predator and must die.

They always flame liberals. I don't fucking care anymore.

Donald Trump is a megalomaniac and deserves to die. I'm going to kill him. Someone has to. I'm going to assassinate the President of Trumerica.

He leans back and puts down the pen.

There's a knock at the door.

He thinks, *They've come for me already?*

He doesn't move, futilely hoping that they'll go away. But no, the knocking continues.

His heart thumps like a drum, but his face, from long habit, is expressionless.

He gets up and moves toward the door with the certainty of knowing that his life—his personal, internal life where he retains his humanity—will be over in a few seconds.

Chapter 4

About to put his hand on the doorknob, Liam realizes he left the diary open on the edge of his bathroom sink. *Donald Trump must die* is written all over it in letters possibly big enough to be legible across the room.

He rushes back, puts the diary in the drawer under the sink, and then opens the front door. Instantly, a wave of relief flows through him. It's merely Evelyn Tamariz, a crushed-looking woman with wispy hair and a lined face.

"Hi," she says in a dreary, whining voice. "Would you mind fixing my sink? It's blocked up." By way of explanation, his neighbor waves her stumpy left arm in the air.

Evelyn Tamariz lives on Liam's floor. Around thirty, she appears much older. Looking at her, you have the impression that there's dust in the creases of her face.

Liam follows her down the hall.

These repair jobs are a regular necessity. Their apartment building—like thousands of Plaza Residences around the country reserved for regular Organization members—was built decades ago. Now, they're all falling to pieces. Plaster flaking off walls. Pipes bursting. Roofs leaking. Repairs, except those you can do yourself, have to be approved by committees that often take years to do anything.

The Tamariz's apartment is bigger and dingier than Liam's. The place looks as though a large animal has trashed it.

A sharp smell of sweat permeates the living room. On the floor are a baseball bat and a burst football. There are dirty dishes and sweaty shorts on the table. On the main wall, above a Portal, there's a poster of the president, flanked by posters of Tomi Lahren and Antonio Sabàto Jr.

From another room comes the sound of children humming along to military music streaming from the Portal.

"My kids haven't been out today," Evelyn says, apprehensively glancing at the other room. "And of course—"

She has a habit of breaking off her sentences in the middle.

In the kitchen, the sink is full to the brim with filthy greenish water that smells of Bayer rice, a genetically modified rice that all Trumericans eat. Liam kneels down and examines the angle-joint of the pipe. He hates bending down—it always triggers some pain in the swollen veins in his anus—but it's a small price to pay to help his neighbor, who he's trying not to judge.

Evelyn looks on helplessly. "Of course, if Graham wasn't traveling for work, he'd fix it."

Graham is Liam's colleague at the Bureau of Facts. He's a man of paralyzing stupidity. A mass of imbecile eagerness. A completely unquestioning, devoted conservatard. He's exactly the kind of person on whom the stability of the Trumerica Freedom Organization depends.

When not working at the bureau, he's a leading figure in various Futurussia groups. Those groups organize spontaneous demonstrations, community service projects, and other voluntary activities. He'll tell you with pride that he has practiced his marksmanship at the local gun range at least twice a week for years. An overpowering smell of sweat follows him wherever he goes.

Using a wrench, Liam fiddles with the valves, washers, and nuts under the sink.

He's about to ask Evelyn if it's possible for someone like himself, who isn't in the Trumerican Reserves, to get a visitor's pass to her husband's gun club—

The Tamariz kids charge into the kitchen and watch.

Liam lets out the water and removes the disgusting clot of human hair that had blocked up the pipe.

"Hands up!" the boy yells savagely.

About nine years old, he menaces Liam with a toy handgun. A girl of about seven makes the same gesture with a spatula. The siblings are wearing blue shorts, gray shirts, and red caps that are the uniform of the Youth Counterintelligence Service.

Liam raises his hands above his head, but with an uneasy feeling, their vicious demeanours warn him that this isn't just a game for these two kids.

"You're a criminal-coddling liberal!" the boy shouts.

"We shoot pinkos like you!" the girl shouts.

They circle Liam.

"You're a traitor!" the brother yells.

"You're an Iranaqeyian spy!" the sister yells.

"We'll get you sent to our potassium mines in Berezniki!"

"We get free-market-fearing bedwetters like you vaporized!"

It's slightly frightening, like watching tiger cubs playing, yet knowing they'll soon grow into apex predators. In the boy's eyes, there's a calculating brutality and a quite evident desire to punch Liam, and a consciousness of being nearly big enough to do so.

Evelyn steps close to Liam and looks nervously at her kids. "They're upset that I'm too busy to take them to see the executions."

Up close, Liam notices that there actually *is* dust in the creases of the woman's face.

"Why can't we see the rescuing?" roars the boy.

"We have a right to see the executions!" the girl shouts, still circling. "It's an important rescuing!" she adds.

Liam remembers what they're talking about. Some Iranaqeyian or Korchinpanian prisoners—guilty of war crimes such as rejecting due process and spreading messages of hate and division—are to be executed by flamethrower tonight at the Trump Osprey Point Golf Club. This happens about once a month in all major cities throughout Trumerica. Children always want to go see them.

He says bye to Evelyn, nods tentatively to her son and daughter, and heads for the door.

Walking down the dark, dank hallway to his apartment, something hard hits the back of his neck. He spins around.

Evelyn drags her son, holding a slingshot, back into the doorway. There's a look of helplessness on the woman's grayish face, and Liam's heart goes out to her.

"AOC!" the boy yells at her as she closes the door.

Back in his apartment, Liam steps quickly past the Portal and sits on his toilet seat. He rubs his neck.

An advertorial playing on his Portal stops. A newscaster reads out a description of a new Floating Fortress that's now anchored between the English Isles of Trumerica and the Rhineland Bastard region of Iranaqey.

With those children, Liam thinks, *that unfortunate woman must lead a life of terror. Another year and they'll be watching her for any signs of becoming unpatriotic.*

These days, most children are members of the Youth Counterintelligence Service. Affectionately nicknamed the Deplorables, this youth group transforms kids into savages. And yet, none of them ever want to rebel against the Organization. On the contrary, they adore everything the Organization does and represents. The July 4th parades past the Winter White House, the morning military drills at school, the recital of slogans, the worship of President Trump—it's all a kind of glorious game to them. All their fury turns outward, against the enemies of the state—immigrants, traitors, leftists.

It's the new normal for parents to be frightened of their own kids. And with good reason, because hardly a week passes in which Turning Point Trumerica doesn't tweet about an eavesdropping little sneak—"conservative child hero" is the phrase the media uses—denouncing their parents to the police.

The sting of the slingshot pellet gradually wears off. He picks up his pen, wondering whether he can think of something more to write in his diary. Suddenly he thinks of Brett Brannan again.

Several years ago, Liam dreamed he was in a pitch-dark room. There was another man in the room that Liam could sense, yet couldn't see. "The truth will emerge where there's no darkness," the man said quietly, casually—a statement, not a command. In the dream, the words had made little impression on Liam. It's also only now that he realizes that the man speaking in his dream was indeed Chief Operating Officer Brannan.

Liam still can't figure out if Brannan is friend or foe. Maybe it doesn't matter. There's a link of understanding between them, more important than affection—maybe that's the sole thing that matters.

"The truth will emerge where there's no darkness," Brannan had said. Liam doesn't know what that means, only that somehow it will come true.

The voice from the Portal stops. There's a commercial for Syngenta soybeans, and then a short jingle plays, signifying the beginning of an important news segment.

"Your attention, please," the Fox Trunews host says raspingly. "Our forces in the Dahati Gulf have won a glorious victory. Military spokesperson Sarah Huckabee Sanders messaged me that this development might just bring the war to an end."

Liam listens to the rest of the newsflash. After a gory description of an Iranaqeyian battalion being blown to bits, it's announced that the Organization will be forced to increase the corporate tax rate from 21% to 23% in order to lower healthcare expenses and achieve greater income equality.

Liam belches again. The vodka and opioids are wearing off, leaving a deflated feeling. The Portal plays "God Bless Trumerica." Of course, you're supposed to stand at attention. However in his present position, he's invisible.

After the song ends, an infomercial for Trumerica University starts.

Liam walks over to the window, keeping his back to the Portal. The day is still sweltering and hazy. Somewhere far away, a missile explodes with a dull, reverberating roar. Over the past few months, about thirty missiles per week have been fired on Lar-o-Maga Palm City.

Down in the street, on the partly broken Trufamily poster, the logo for the Trufamily Forty-Five appears and vanishes. The forty-five people are the ones who rule the Trumerica Freedom Organization via the one-hundred bureaus. They, with objectives passed down by President Trump himself, decide the sacred beliefs and business strategies of the Organization. Then they disseminate them downward to the Organization's C-Suite—all the thousands of CEOs, CTOs, CFOs, CMOs, COOs, CHOs, CPOs, CSOs, etc., throughout Trumerica. Next, members of the C-Suite then trickle them further down to regular Organization members.

Trump's forty-five closest advisors are the ones responsible for the changeability of the past. They also brainwash Trumericans into believing that shadowy forces control everything and that Trump is our last chance to save Trumerica.

Liam feels as though he's walking on the bottom of an ocean, so far down that everything's pitch-black, the weight of the water crushing him. He feels lost in a monstrous world where he is the monster. He's alone. The past is dead. The future is unimaginable.

Is it possible, Liam thinks, *that a single person somewhere is on my side? And what about the Organization—will its control endure forever?*

He looks up at the skyline. The previous slogans have been replaced with new ones. They beam out like answers, all displayed on the three bureau buildings, all flashing at him:

TRUMERICA FIRST.

LIES ARE NOT ILLEGAL.

IT'S NOT A CONSPIRACY IF IT'S REAL.

He takes his cryptocurrency card out of his pocket. In tiny lettering, right there on the plastic card, the same slogans digitally scroll on the micro-screen alongside the face of Donald Trump. Even from the card, the President's eyes follow you.

Trump's face is on Happy Meal boxes, on the tiny chocolates placed on the pillows of

Trumerica Plaza Hotels. His face is also on the chips of Trumerica Taj Mahal Casinos. His eyes are everywhere. They're always watching you. Asleep or awake, working or eating, inside or outside—there's no escape. Nothing is your own except the gray matter inside your skull—but not even that's entirely your own because everyone's been brainwashed.

The sun has gone below the horizon.

Looking at the ginormous Trump Tower, Liam's heart trembles.

It's too strong, he thinks. *It can't be penetrated*. He even doubts that a missile could bring it down, architects having learned their lessons after the September 11 attacks.

He thinks again about who he might be writing his diary for. But no matter how hard he tries, he can't picture any of his readers.

In his future, there's a fate worse than death—it's annihilation. The diary will be reduced to ashes and himself to vapor. Only the Peace Police will read what he's written. Then they'll wipe it out of existence and out of memory.

How can you appeal to the future when not a trace of you, Liam thinks, *not even anonymous words scribbled on pieces of paper, can physically survive?*

"Janz," a woman on the Portal says sternly. "808337 Liam Janz, in five minutes you need to leave so that you can be back at work in time for your night shift."

With the diary, he feels like a lonely ghost that's jotting down truths nobody will benefit from. But maybe it isn't making himself heard but by staying sane that he can carry on the human heritage. He goes back to sitting on his toilet, grabs his pen, and writes:

From the age of authoritarianism—greetings!

From the age of Trumerican exceptionalism under Donald Trump—greetings!

To the future! To you!

That's who I'm writing this for. You.

A toast. To a time ...

When diversity is celebrated, not forbidden.

When truth will re-exist.

And when what is done can't be undone.

He puts the pen in the draw.

I'm already dead, he muses.

Now that he knows he's a dead man, it's important to stay alive as long as possible. He notices that some black ink from the pen is on his hand. It's exactly the kind of damn detail that could incriminate him. A pesky fanatic at work—like Short Liz or that Gemma

23

woman—might figure out that he's been using an old-fashioned pen to write something, then might squeal on him.

He puts the diary in the draw. It's useless to hide it. But he can at least confirm if it's been discovered. Putting a hair on it would be too obvious. With the tip of his finger, he picks up a particle of whitish dust and places it on the corner of the cover, where it's bound to be shaken off if they pick the journal up.

At his sink, he carefully scrubs the ink away, thinking of how he can steal a weapon from his neighbor's gun club, and thinking of ways he can get close enough to President Trump to assassinate him.

Chapter 5

In the morning, Liam is lying on his bed, trying to remember his family.

Liam's dad, tall and thin, always wore sunglasses and dressed in dark clothes. His mom was a statuesque woman with slow movements and magnificent blond hair. He doesn't remember much about his baby sister, other than that she was usually silent, and had large, watchful eyes.

In the late 1990s, when he was around ten years old, his dad was executed, and his mom and sister disappeared. They were swallowed up by different purges of deep state operatives, welfare queens, and supporters of the Trumerican Civil Liberties Union.

Liam remembers his dream from last night. In it, his mom and sister were somehow far below him. They were in a dark place, looking up at Liam. For a few moments, he thought they were maybe at the bottom of either a well or a deep grave. Whatever it was, it was moving downwards, further away from him.

Then he realized that they were in a glass-bottom boat that had been turned upside-down. They were trapped in an air pocket. Dark water surrounded them everywhere.

He was above the water, out in the light and air. And they were being sucked down to death, being circled by snapping bloodthirsty piranhas. Also, his mom and sister were down there *because* he was up here. He knew it and they knew it. There was no reproach in their faces, only the awareness that they must die so he can live.

He wondered why his mom didn't pound against the glass. But then he understood that breaking it would only kill them sooner—either by drowning or as piranha snacks.

Lying in his bed, staring at the ceiling, the thing that now suddenly strikes Liam is that their deaths, nearly thirty years ago, were sorrowful in a way that's no longer possible. Tragedy belongs to an ancient time when there was still privacy, love, and friendship, and

25

when family members supported each other without needing to know why.

He's not sure which particular purge scooped up his mom and sister, yet sometimes suspects that they were shipped off to Guantanamo Bay.

His mother's memory rips at his heart because she died loving him, a private and unalterable love, and he was too young and selfish to love her in return. Such emotional landscapes, he now realizes, can't possibly exist today. Today there's fear, hatred, and pain. But no dignity of emotion, no complex sorrows, no deep feelings.

He had a second dream. In that one, he was suddenly in a field standing on short springy, green grass. It was summer. It was the golden hour when, just before sunset, the daylight was redder and softer than when the sun was high in the sky.

This illuminated landscape around him recurred frequently in his dreams. In his waking thoughts, he sometimes called this dreamscape Libertopia. Other times he thought of it as Lah Lah Land. There were even times he liked to think that his subconscious was tapping into Lukomorye, the imaginary land created by the great Russian-American poet, Alexander Pushkin.

In it, there was a grassy field with a path wandering across it. On the other side of the field were hedges and elm trees. Nearby, though out of sight, there was a clear, unpolluted, slow-moving stream filled with herring and sunfish swimming in pools shaded by willow trees. Usually, the idea of being close to a body of water—regardless of whether it was a river, a lake, or an ocean—gave him nausea and a feeling of not being able to breathe. But for some reason, that particular stream in his dream didn't fill him with dread.

The woman with freckles and wearing the red baseball hat appeared in the field. She walked toward him. With what seemed like a single movement, Gemma ripped off her clothes and flung them disdainfully aside.

Her body aroused little desire in him. What overwhelmed him in that instant was admiration for how she threw her clothes on the grass. The graceful and careless gesture seemed to annihilate a whole culture, an entire system of thought, as though Donald Trump and the Organization could all be swept into nothingness by a single splendid movement of the arm.

An alarm coming from his Portal breaks Liam's reverie. It's seven o'clock. Time to get ready for his morning shift. Liam wrenches his body out of bed and reaches for a singlet and a pair of shorts.

If I lifted my middle finger at the Portal, Liam thinks, *and pulled down my boxer shorts and flashed my ass at whoever is watching, how long would it take for the police to barge into my apartment?*

Chapter 6

Liam puts on his singlet and shorts.

A violent coughing fit makes him bend over. This happens most mornings. Usually it empties his lungs so completely that he can only begin breathing again by laying on his back and breathing deeply. His hemorrhoids itch.

"Thirties group!" a woman yells. "Get ready, please!"

Liam springs to attention in front of a scrawny, muscular woman on the Portal.

She talks about how amazing her new sneakers are, then thanks today's sponsor, Under Armour.

"Bend and stretch," she sings in time with the music, "reach for the stars. There goes Jupiter, here comes Mars."

Liam, mimicking the fitness instructor, semi-remembers this song from his childhood.

"Bend and stretch," she continues singing, lifting her hands up and then touching her toes, "reach for the sky. Stand on tippy toes. Oh so high." She frowns. "Come on, put some effort into it!"

As he mechanically and stubbornly exercises, he manipulates his face into a look of grim enjoyment, which is considered proper during morning exercises.

He tries, yet struggles to think his way backward into the dim period of his early childhood. Everything earlier than the 1990s just fades away. When there aren't any records that you can refer to, even the outline of your own life loses its sharpness. You remember monumental events that probably never happened. You remember vague details of incidents, but little else. And there are long blank periods throughout your entire life.

Decades ago, everything was different. Even the names of places were radically different.

Lar-o-Maga Palm City, for instance, hadn't been called that back then. It had been called Palm Beach, Florida, which was part of a larger grouping of fifty states called the United States of America. And while the city of Palm Beach and the country called the USA no longer exist, the state of Florida still kind of does, it being an earlier version of New Florida, one of 379 states—and counting—in Trumerica.

Liam thinks back to when he was a kid. He can faintly recall that there had been a few years during his childhood when Trumerica peacefully traded with all the other authoritarian regimes. Excluding that one time, however, Liam can't definitively remember any other time when Trumerica wasn't simultaneously in a military war and a trade war with one or two of the other superstates.

He vaguely remembers some events that caused that harmonious period of global trade to end. One was a coordinated terrorist attack in Novosibirsk, Yekaterinburg, and Kazan. Another was hypersonic nuclear strikes that destroyed Dallas, Kuala Lumpur, Bogotá, and Johannesburg. And yet another was Trumerica obliterating the Gansu Wind Farm, the Jaisalmer Wind Turbine Park, and the Dumat Al Jandal Airtricity Project.

During the attack here in New Florida, he remembers his dad clutching his hand as they hurried to an outdoor sports stadium near their house, where the emergency announcements were telling everyone in his neighborhood to go. His mom carried his baby sister.

Liam and his family entered through the stadium gates. They followed other people navigating through some cement hallways. Eventually, they stood among approximately one thousand worried and horrified people, some in the stands, some on the field.

They found a place on the astroturf near an old couple who were crying. Liam could tell that they were suffering grief that was genuine and unbearable. In his childish way, he understood that something terrible must have just happened to them.

"We should never have trusted them," the old man said. "This comes from trusting the sons of bitches."

Which sons of bitches he was referring to, Liam can't now remember.

During the next few minutes, hundreds of paramilitary soldiers entered the stadium. Over the loud speakers came the command for all adult males to move to the sea-side part of the stadium. After a lot of fuss, the soldiers escorted all the men, including Liam's dad and the complaining old man, out of the stadium, guns pointed at them.

The men were hoarded onto Hydrofoil boats, taken miles out to sea, and thrown

29

overboard.

The official story was that it had been Iranaqeyians posing as Trumerican soldiers who had given the hundreds of adult men a sea burial. Liam wasn't so sure.

Since around that time in Liam's life, the military wars and trade wars have been literally continuous, though Trumerica hasn't always been fighting them against the same superstates. For several months during his childhood, there had been street fighting in Lar-o-Maga Palm City, some of which he remembers vividly. But to trace out the history of that period, or even to say who was fighting whom, would be impossible, since there are no historical records that accurately describe that period, and the media never mentions any other military alignment or business arrangement other than the existing ones.

At this moment, for example, in 2024—if it is indeed 2024—Trumerica is battling both a military war and a trade war with our enemies Iranaqey and Korchinpan, and is doing business with our friends in Latineuropa. In public or private, it's never acknowledged that the four dictatorships have ever been aligned any differently.

Actually, as far as Liam knows, Trumerica has been militarily and economically fighting Iranaqey and Korchinpan for just four years, and in an economic alliance with Latineuropa for that time. But this is all merely useless knowledge he possesses because—according to Organization doctrine—his memory isn't satisfactorily under control. Officially, the change of warring parties and business partners never happened. Trumerica is currently in a military war and a trade war with Iranaqey and Korchinpan. Therefore, Trumerica has always been at war with Iranaqey and Korchinpan. The enemy superstates—just like Alexandria Ocasio-Cortez and her liberal globalists trying to establish a one-world government utopia—always represent absolute evil, and it follows that any past or future agreement with our enemies is impossible.

The fitness trainer yells instructions. Liam and everyone else in the region watching this Portalcast copy the instructor, gyrating their bodies from the waist, an exercise that's supposedly good for your back.

The frightening thing, he thinks, *is that all of the Trumerica Freedom Organization's claims might be true.*

The Organization says that Trumerica has always traded goods exclusively with Latineuropa. Yet, Liam knows that Trumerica conducted business with Iranaqey and Korchinpan just four years ago. But where does that knowledge exist? Only in his own consciousness, which of course will soon be annihilated. And if everyone else accepts the lies that the Organization imposes—if all records and media tell the same fabrications of the truth—then those lies will become true.

Liam remembers something that the President said during a Victory Rally a few months ago. "Winners who control the past, also control the future," Donald Trump said. "Winners who control the present, also control the past, and losers control nothing."

And yet, the past, though alterable, has never been altered. Whatever is true now, has been true since the beginning. All that's needed is a never-ending series of victories over your own memory, this being one of the benefits of GreatSpeak—the ability to use words to obscure the truth.

"Take a quick break!" the fitness trainer barks.

Liam lowers his arms and breathes deeply. Over the years, he's thought long and hard about the psychological manipulation that is GreatSpeak. It is to know and not to know. To be conscious of complete truthfulness while telling carefully constructed lies. To believe simultaneously in multiple opinions that cancel each other out.

That's the power of GreatSpeak.

GreatSpeak is about using logic against logic. It's about both denying and demanding morality. It's about forgetting whatever is necessary to forget, then recalling it whenever it's needed, and then promptly re-forgetting it. All of this can be summed up into perhaps the most amazing mind-fuck of all—to consciously cause unconsciousness, and then to become unconscious of the act of hypnosis that you just performed.

"Ok!" the overly cheerful instructor shouts. "Who can touch their toes?" she says enthusiastically. "Let's do this! *One*-two! *One*-two! ..."

This exercise sends shooting pains all the way from Liam's heels to his ass and often brings on a coughing fit.

The past, he thinks, *hasn't merely been altered, it's been destroyed. How can you establish even the most obvious fact when there's no record of it outside of your own memory?*

He tries to remember when he first heard Donald Trump mentioned. He thinks it must have been at some time in the 1990s, something about a TV reality show. Or maybe it was something about a great modernization and beautification campaign that included getting rid of ugly buildings. Liam just can't remember.

In Portalcasts about history, President Trump is always the leader and guardian of Trumerica since its earliest days. His exploits had been gradually pushed backwards in time until they extended as far back as the 1970s when Black people supposedly owned their own businesses and even had their own version of Wall Street.

It's impossible to know how much of these legends are true and how much was invented. Sometimes, though, you can put your finger on a definite lie. It's not true, for example, as is claimed, that the Organization invented Facebook. Liam remembers seeing Facebook as a child, long before Eric and Don Jr bought it and kept Mark Zuckerberg on as CEO of the newly formed Bureau of Oversight. But you can't prove anything. There's never any evidence.

But once! Just once in his whole life Liam saw with his own eyes incontrovertible proof of the falsification of an historical fact! And on that occasion—

"Janz!" the instructor screams from his Portal. "Yes, *you*! Liam Mateo Janz! Bend lower, please! You can do better than that. You're not trying. Lower! *That's* better. Now, everyone, stand at ease and watch me."

Liam's entire body tenses. Yet he keeps his face completely inscrutable.

Never show dismay, he thinks. *Never show resentment. Never show defiance. A single flicker of the eyes can give you away.*

He stands watching the trainer.

She raises her arms, then bends over and tucks her fingers under her big toes. "*There*! *That's* how I want to see you do it." She rises, then bends over again. "Anyone under fifty is capable of touching their toes. We don't all have the privilege of fighting against our enemies, or doing business with our friends. But at least we can all keep fit. Remember our soldiers fighting for our freedoms! Just think about what *they* have to endure. And remember the C-Suite is doing deals on behalf of Trumerica! Just think how *hard* they work for our safety so that we can buy whatever we want. Now try again. That's better, *much* better."

For the first time in several years, and without bending his knees, Liam, with a violent lunge, touches his toes.

Chapter 7

At work, Liam stares into the retina recognition and iris scanning system. On his Portal, the following tasks appear:

On March 17, 2023, Breitbart News accidentally misreported the President's correct predictions. Correct his correct predictions.

On December 19, 2022, Fox Trunews unintentionally misprinted the President's justified comments on shit-hole countries in the undesired region of Africa. Reboot the comments.

On January 14, 2023, the Bureau of Pharmaceutical Quality unexpectedly misquoted OxiQoxi statistics. Improve the statistics.

On December 3, 2022, Glenn Beck, in a Blaze Media broadcast, inadvertently referred to a non-person who doesn't work for Trumerican Financing and Debt Forgiveness. Reorganize accordingly.

Liam's tasks refer to news items that the Organization thinks are necessary to alter or fix, though the code words most commonly used are *correct, reboot, improve,* and *reorganize.*

Liam tackles the first task. He speaks into his microphone and Siri displays the original Breitbart News broadcast. It's about Donald Trump talking in March at a rally attended by his supporters. The video shows the President predicting that there'll be no fighting in the Trumerican Caribbean, and that an Iranaqeyian offensive will soon be launched to take some of the disputed territories of South America.

The issue is, what Trump talked about didn't end up happening. Instead of trying to retake the disputed territories, traitors Ted Cruz and Omarosa Manigault, now generals of the Iranaqeyian High Command, attacked our Floating Fortresses in the Caribbean.

To fix this, Liam digitally alters Trump's lips and his audio so that the offending segment in the video now has the President predict what actually happened. Then Liam edits all the tweets that mention the data error.

To complete the task, he places his thumb on a thermal fingerprint reader, which sends his media files. Then he speaks a few commands about how this batch of files is ready for review, then drags the task on the top of his list into the digital trash can on his Portal. With an amiable rustle, all the old files associated with that task are deleted forever.

Of the thousands of people working on similar tasks to this one, the trash can icon displayed on Portals all throughout the Bureau of Facts represents the Organization's insatiable efforts to banish fake news and liberal bias from everywhere, no matter the effort, no matter the cost. Every morsel of defective data, every slice of inaccurate information, every chunk of invalid knowledge—you never know what is next up for deletion, nor what will take its place.

For his second task, Liam finds the Fox Trunews article from two years ago that needs adjustment. In it, Trump is quoted as saying that if immigrants don't want to contribute to the betterment of our country, then they should go back to Namibia, Somalia, or whatever shit-hole country they're from in the undesired territories. However, as of this morning, Namibia no longer exists because Korchinpan discovered lithium deposits there, and absorbed this formerly unwanted country into their superstate. Accordingly, Liam reboots the article by deleting the reference to the non-country Namibia and editing the article so that Trump now refers to Somalia and Kenya, which are still in the undesired territories and still shit-hole countries.

The third task refers to a simple error that Liam can easily fix. A few months ago, the Bureau of Pharmaceutical Quality issued a press release responding to false claims that drug makers flooded Trumerica with billions of opioid pills. The communique, tweeted out by Trump, counterclaimed that OxiQoxi overdoses are in fact forecast to decrease by 20%
.

The problem is, as Liam saw on several Portals on his commute via train to work this morning on the Hyperloop, OxiQoxi-related deaths are actually down 24%, thanks to the Organization's commitment to ending Trumerica's worst public health emergency in history, which is really now just a manageable crisis.

To remedy this, he merely edits the press release and does a find-and-replace on all tweets that refer to the figure.

The continuous alteration that Liam is engaged in is applied to news items, social media posts, books, posters, films, music, photos—to every kind of media, literature, or documentation that holds any political, economical, or ideological significance. Day by day, and almost minute by minute, the past is brought up to date. In this way, documentary evidence can show every prediction made by the Organization to have been correct. Also, no factoid or opinion that conflicts with the needs of the moment will ever remain on the record. All history is a palimpsest, scraped clean and re-inscribed as often as i s necessary.

Once done, it's impossible to prove that any falsification took place.

There are thousands of employees in the Bureau of Facts whose job it is to track down all instances of data, information, and knowledge that has been superseded and requires modernizing. Articles in the *Las Vegas Review-Journal* or the *Wall Street Journal* might—because of changes in political alignment, or mistaken prophecies uttered by Donald Trump because his aides gave him wrong information—have probably been rewritten at least a dozen times each, with no previous versions still in existence to contradict the current one.

Even the instructions Liam receives never state or imply that an act of forgery is to be committed. Instead, they always refer to slips, errors, misprints, or misquotations that need to be fixed in the interests of accuracy, democracy, and keeping Trumerica great.

But actually, he thinks as he adjusts the figures in the Bureau of Pharmaceutical Quality press release, *it isn't even forgery. It's merely the substitution of one mound of bullshit for another. And those of us who work here at the Bureau of Facts are simply information mercenaries.*

Most of the content that he deals with has no connection with reality. Statistics are just as much a fantasy in their original version as in their rectified version. Most of the time, Liam is expected to make them up out of his head—or, as he prefers to think about it, pull them out of his ass. For example, the press release by the Bureau of Pharmaceutical Quality, which is really a drug maker and distributor, referred to it as providing over 75 billion opioid pills in the past decade, which was complicit in over 400,000 Trumericans losing their lives in overdoses, and that these were all related to pills murderously tainted by Steve Bannon, Krista Suh, Serena Williams, and other Iranaqey conspirators. However, Liam knows that more pills were distributed than that, which resulted in even more overdoses. Still, in revising the press release, he marks the figures down to 68 billion pills and 350,000 deaths, thus enabling the C-Suite to claim that Trumerica is winning against our enemies who are trying to kill us.

It's quite possible that *hundreds* of billions of pills were distributed, leading to *millions* of overdoses, and that no Iranaqeyans were complicit in tainting any pills. Likelier still, nobody, not even Martin Shkreli, the Bureau of Pharmaceutical Quality's CEO, knew the actual figures, let alone cared. All we know is that, every year, we come closer to winning the war on drugs, even though almost every Trumerican is taking large quantities of op ioids.

And so it is with every fact, great or small. Everything fades away into a shadow-world in which, finally, even the date of the year is uncertain.

Liam glances across the office. In a nearby cubicle, a short man named Jake Sullivan works steadily away, his mouth close to his microphone. Sullivan has the air of trying to keep what he's saying a secret between himself, Siri, and his Portal. Of course, though, Liam can't read what's on his monitor because it's bio-linked with Sullivan's retinas and irises, and therefore solely viewable by him.

Just as Liam is staring at him, Sullivan looks up, meets eyes with Liam, and squints in a hostile manner.

Liam barely knows Jake Sullivan and doesn't know what he works on. People in the Information Security Department rarely talk about their jobs. In the long, drab office, with its dozens of rows of cubicles and its endless hum of voices murmuring into Sirimics, there are hundreds of people on this floor alone that Liam doesn't know by name, though he sees many of them hurrying through the halls or gesticulating during Victory Rallies.

He knows that in the cubicle next to him, a woman named Molly Myers labors all day solely at tracking down the names of people who have been vaporized—people who are now considered never to have existed and need to be deleted from everywhere. There's a certain derangement in this, since her husband was vaporized a couple of years ago.

A few cubicles away is a mild, ineffectual man named Connor Hughes, with hairy ears and a surprising talent for rhymes. He's engaged in producing new versions of songs that have become ideologically offensive, but for one reason or another, are to be retained.

This open plan office, with its hundreds of workers, is just one sub-section, a single cell as it were, in the hugely complex Information Security Department. Beyond, above, and below there are other swarms of workers engaged in an unimaginable multitude of jobs.

No, we're not information mercenaries, Liam thinks. *We're disinformation mercenaries.*

There are elaborately equipped studios for taking—faking—photos and making—also faking—videos. There are teams of writers, editors, actors, directors, and voice artists. There are teams of researchers who, all day every day, hunt down pieces of data, information, and knowledge that needs to be repaired. There are the vast Apple data centers where the corrected files are stored. There are the hidden furnaces where old hard drives are destroyed. And somewhere or other there are the directing brains—the CEOs, CTOs, CFOs, CMOs, CHOs, etc.—who coordinate the whole effort, formulate the policies, and decide which fragments of the past should be preserved, falsified, or rubbed out of existence.

The Information Security Department is merely one of hundreds of departments in the Bureau of Facts. And the bureau reconstructs not only the past. It also supplies Organization members with new films, videos, books, novels, music, plays, video games—everything from a country song to a stand-up comedy special, from a children's book to an adventure movie.

Then the bureau repeats the entire operation at a lower level for the benefit of the Subs who live on the outskirts of every Trumerican city. There are also hundreds of departments creating content for the pro-slavery, pro-LGBT rights, and pro-abortion Subs. Those departments produce superhero films, satirical news shows, and reality TV shows about sport, crime, cooking, home renovation, spouse-swapping, being rich and obnoxious, astrology, singing, and so on. They also write songs that are composed by algorithms, marketing experts, and Justin Bieber versificator bots.

Later that day, at the Victory Rally, the President only speaks for 40 minutes—a mercifully brief speech compared to normal. Sometimes, Trump can blah-blah-blah on for an hour or two. You never know when the verbal diarrheaist is going to prattle on and on and on until it feels like your ears are going to bleed.

After the Victory Rally, Liam returns to his cubicle, pulls in the bendable boom of the microphone, cleans his glasses, and settles down to his main task of the day.

Chapter 8

Liam's sole pleasure in life is his work. Most of it is tedious. Yet occasionally there's an intricate job that requires such deep concentration that he loses himself in it. Time seems to fade away, and it's almost like he himself no longer exists. These tasks are usually delicate pieces of forgery in which he's got nothing to guide him except his knowledge of the beliefs of the Trufamily Forty-Five, beliefs that change daily, making it hard to figure out what the Organization wants you to say.

Liam's good at this kind of thing. Sometimes he's even trusted with rectifying parts of the *Fox & Friends & Family* TV show, including its most popular segment, "Faith & Fame & Flag."

On his Portal, he rereads the task that he saved until last:

On December 3, 2022, Glenn Beck, in a Blaze Media broadcast, inadvertently referred to a non-person who doesn't work for Trumerican Financing and Debt Forgiveness.

Liam watches the offending video. It's mostly Beck ranting about homosexuality being a choice. It's also about him denying that he's a puppet of the homosexual agenda, which he says is the biggest threat to freedom and free speech in Trumerica today. In the video, Beck praises the work of a legitimately homophobic company, Trumerican Finances and Debt Forgiveness. This company provides affordable personal loans to sailors on Floating Fortresses. Beck also mentions an employee, Charles Kuurk, who recently won the company an Economic Medal of Honor. Kuurk is a prominent CFO in the C-Suite.

Or, *was.*

This morning Liam learned via the Fox Trunews playing on his Portal that Trumerican Finances and Debt Forgiveness is now closed. No reason was provided. Liam assumes—though this wasn't mentioned in this morning's newscast—that Charles Kuurk is probably the non-person who "doesn't work" for the company anymore, since he was indeed the only employee Beck mentioned by name.

Liam also assumes that Kuurk and many of his business associates, including CEO Richard F Smith, are now disgraced, discredited, and possibly already dead. That's to be expected. During bankruptcies and purges, political offenders and liberal socialists often aren't mentioned publicly before they're executed, let alone put on trial. These company closures and purges, presumably involving thousands of people, occasionally result in public trials of Untrumericans who confess their crimes and are later rescued—the term *rescued* being the Organization's way to refer to those it has executed. However, liberals who oppose the Organization usually disappear and they're never heard of again. Liam personally knows of approximately thirty people who have disappeared. He doesn't know what really happened to them. Sometimes, they might even still be alive.

Liam strokes his nose gently. In the cubicle across the way, Jake Sullivan hunches secretively over his microphone. Sullivan raises his head for a moment—again he flashes a hostile look toward Liam.

Liam wonders whether Sullivan is engaged in the same task as he is himself. It's possible. So tricky a piece of work probably wouldn't be trusted to a single person. It's possible that a dozen people are working on rival versions of what Glenn Beck said—or didn't say—about Charles Kuurk. And then later, a CEO in the C-Suite might select this version or that version, might re-edit it to their liking, and then set in motion the complex process of cross-referencing that would be required. Then, the chosen lie would pass into the permanent records and become the truth.

Liam will never know why Kuurk has been disgraced. Perhaps it was corruption or incompetence. Perhaps Donald Trump merely got rid of a too-popular subordinate. Perhaps Kuurk was suspected of heretical tendencies. Or perhaps—and this is the likeliest of all—the thing had simply happened because company shutdowns and purges, and the associated torture and vaporizations, are a necessary part of the mechanics of Trumerica's billionocracy.

The real clue is in the word "non-person," which indicates that Kuurk is already dead. You can't invariably assume this to be the case when someone is arrested. Sometimes they're released and allowed to remain at liberty for a year or two before being executed. Occasionally, but rarely, a person you thought had been long dead would make a ghostly reappearance at a public trial where they implicate hundreds of others by their testimony before vanishing, this time forever. Kuurk, however, is already a non-person.

He doesn't exist.

He never existed.

Liam decides it won't be enough to simply reverse the tendency of Glenn Beck's words in the video. It'll be much better to make it deal with something totally unconnected with its original subject.

He could turn Beck's words into the usual denunciation of mentally deranged traitors, privileged left-wingers, and global warming alarmists. But that would be too obvious. Liam could invent a new trade deal that Trump just brokered with Latineuropa and have Beck tout it. Or Liam could have Beck refer to Trumerica's energy dominance and how we're becoming less reliant on foreign energy imports. But he doesn't want to get cocky—if he concocted any of those options, there'd be a ton of work to corroborate and cross-reference them to existing events, people, and so on. What's needed is a piece of pure f antasy.

Suddenly, there pops into his head the fictional image of a certain low-ranking soldier, named Corporal Helseth, who recently died in heroic circumstances, fighting our enemies.

Sometimes, Liam thinks, *Glenn Beck devotes one of his shows to memorializing a humble Organization member whose life and death can be an example worthy of following. Today, why can't Beck commemorate this Helseth person on one of his shows? All I have to do in order to bring Corporal Helseth into existence is to set in motion the creation of a few fake news articles and a few minutes of deep fake videos.*

Liam pulls the microphone toward him and begins dictating. "At three, the patriot who would become Corporal Helseth refused to play with any toys that weren't tanks, military helicopters, or action figures. At seven, he joined the Boy Scouts. At nine, he moved on to the Deplorables Youth Counterintelligence Service. At twelve, he denounced his uncle to the Peace Police after overhearing him have an anti-patriotic conversation. At nineteen, he designed some nanotechnology for the Bureau of Weather Warfare that produced clouds of microscopic computer particles."

Liam pauses. Everything that he's inserted into this soldier's life so far is just backstory. What comes next will be crucial.

"At twenty-five," Liam continues speaking into the Sirimic, "working undercover in the Iranaqeyian state of Indonesia, Corporal Helseth infiltrated the Illuminati and encrypted the identities of key members onto an external drive. Pursued by enemy planes while flying over the North Pacific Ocean, he realized that there was no escape. So he pulled his F-18 up into a vertical, continued around until he was heading toward his foes, and clipped one wing of a Qaher-313 stealth fighter aircraft, sending it twirling into the ocean. Then he banked and smashed head-on into another enemy jet, taking it—and Corporal Helseth—out in a massive fiery explosion of patriotism over terrorism."

Again, Liam pauses. For this news item to really zing, he knows that he now has to bring it all home.

"On a recent episode of *The Glenn Beck Program*," Liam continues dictating, "Beck added a few remarks on the purity and single-mindedness of Corporal Helseth's life. Helseth was a total abstainer, he exercised for an hour every day, and had taken a vow of celibacy, believing marriage and the care of a family to be incompatible with a 24-7-365 devotion to duty. He held no beliefs other than those held by the Trufamily Forty-Five. He had no goals in life except defeating our foreign enemies, hunting down deep state operatives inside Trumerica, and helping the C-Suite maximize shareholder wealth for ordinary Trumericans."

Once again, Liam glances at his rival in the opposite cubicle. Something seems to tell him that Jake Sullivan is busy on the same job as himself. There's no way of knowing whose job will eventually be picked. But he feels a profound conviction that it'll be his own.

If one of Liam's supervisors pick his job, then Corporal Helseth, unimagined an hour ago, will become a fact. Corporal Helseth never existed in the present, but will soon exist in the past. Also, after the act of forgery is forgotten, he will exist just as authentically, and upon the same evidence as people who lived in previous centuries, such as the great Trumerican hero, Robert E. Lee, or the vile Trumerican traitor, Harriet Tubman.

Chapter 9

The following day, in the low-ceilinged cafeteria of the Bureau of Facts, the lunch queue jerks forward slowly. The room is totally full and deafeningly noisy. A metallic smell wafts up from the food serving stations.

Liam's friend, Shelly Adelsan, approaches. *Friend* is the wrong word. You don't really have friends nowadays. Yet there are some people whose company is more pleasant than others.

Shelly Adelsan is an agenda implementation specialist. She's a member of one of many teams responsible for carrying out the Trump administration's agenda. Her team works across many bureaus. Its goal is to make the entire moneyocracy more citizen-centered, market-based, and results-oriented.

Shelly is about five feet tall, with dark hair and enormous eyes that seem to search your face closely when she speaks to you.

"Hey," she says, "Do you have any female friends who might have some extra tampons they'd be willing to sell?"

Liam shakes his head. "Maybe there's a trade embargo on them," he says intentionally vaguely.

Several people have asked Liam recently about tampons. For months now, there's been a scarcity of feminine hygiene products. At any given moment, there's always some necessary item that Trumerica Freedom Organization shops are unable to supply. Sometimes it's toilet paper, sometimes it's butter. Currently, it's tampons. Women can only get hold of them, if at all, by scrounging through the Sub neighborhoods.

The queue jerks forward. Liam and Shelly each take a greasy metal tray from a pile at the start of the counter.

"Did you go see the executions yesterday?" she asks.

"I was working," Liam says blankly. "I'll see them on tonight's *Lana's Real News Update*."

"An inadequate substitute," Shelly says.

Her mocking eyes rove over Liam's face. *I see through you*, her eyes seem to say. *I know why you didn't go watch those prisoners burned alive by flamethrowers.*

"They were excellent flamings," she says. "After they were incinerated, their bodies were pulverized under a tank. Nice touch."

Shelly is venomously patriotic. She'll talk with gloating satisfaction of trials and confessions of liberals, of our drones attacking enemy cities, and of Donald Trump imposing tariffs on other superstates as a way of restoring Trumerican jobs lost because of massive trade deficits. Still, Liam finds it mildly interesting talking with her about the technicalities of implementing Trump's campaign promises.

"Next, please!" yells a white-aproned Sub.

Liam and Shelly push their trays forward.

The Sub swiftly dumps their lunches onto their trays. Clam chowder soup. DuPont soy cheese quesadillas. And today's pinkish-gray "mystery meat." Another Sub swipes their cryptocurrency cards.

They weave across the crowded cafeteria to where there's a bar. They buy vodka shots, then sit at a table that's directly under a Portal.

Liam holds up his shot glass, pauses for a moment to collect his nerve, and gulps the oily-tasting TrumputinVodka down. He eats some meat and guesses that it's possibly either genetically engineered salmon or lab-created chicken.

"How's the new book coming along?" Liam says, raising his voice to overcome the noise.

"Wonderfully." Shelly brightens up immediately at the mention of the book her team is working on to support Trump's agenda. "It's fascinating." She leans forward. "We're currently editing Sarah Palin's essay on Trump's brilliant business tactics. When he negotiates with our trade partners, did you know that he deliberately uses chaotic language with complicated grammar and an unrestricted vocabulary? His purpose—which is pure genius—is to incapacitate their ability to think freely and yet simultaneously encourage them to believe in various parallel multiverses of information, all of them spurious, contradictory, and self-defeating. That way, Trump ensures that the other superstates can't distinguish what's real, other than what they feel or believe, or what the President himself tells them."

One of these days, thinks Liam with sudden deep conviction, *Shelly will be vaporized. She's too intelligent. The Organization doesn't like people like her. One day, she'll disappear.*

He smiles, sympathetically he hopes, not trusting himself to speak.

"As Sarah Palin so eloquently wrote in her essay," Shelly continues, "this promises us all a better future. Why? Because Trump is reasserting Trumerican sovereignty!"

A sort of vapid eagerness flits across Liam's face. Nevertheless, Shelly detects a certain lack of enthusiasm.

She takes a bite of her food, chews briefly, and continues talking. "Can't you see that Trump's strategies will promote innovation and job creation here instead of in other superstates? That Trump taking a stand against foreigners will raise living standards for Trumericans?"

"Well, for everyone except—" begins Liam doubtfully, then stops. It was on the tip of his tongue to say the Subs. But saying that might be interpreted as being liberal-minded.

"The Subs aren't human," Shelly scoffs, deducing what Liam was about to say.

Liam suddenly isn't hungry. He swivels a little in his chair.

At a nearby table, a man and woman are talking rapidly, a harsh gabble of almost indecipherable words. Liam knows them. They work in the Cryptocurrency Media Department. The woman, Karen, wears glasses. Because of the angle at which Liam's sitting, Karen's glasses catch the light and present to Liam two blank discs instead of eyes. The man, Kyle, is about thirty, with a muscular throat and an enormous mouth.

Horrendously, listening to the sounds pouring out of their mouths, it's difficult to distinguish many of the words they're saying. Liam's only able to understand a fragment here and there. "Black Lives Matter is really just a fifth column that's promoting social radicalism," he hears Karen say. "Antifa is the hate group that's defacing statues and vandalizing monuments all across Trumerica," he hears Kyle say. "Traitors and foreigners are trying to illegally teach Trumerican children about white privilege," he hears Karen say. But the rest is mostly noise.

Yet, even though he can't understand most of what they're saying, there's no doubt about its general gist. They might be denouncing the Clinton Foundation, an international criminal organization and global slush fund. They might be demanding sterner measures against pedophilic liberals and sabotaging socialists. They might be fulminating against the economic atrocities of the latest trade deal proposed by

Korchinpan. They might be praising one of the Trufamily Forty-Five, such as Lance Armstrong, Elizabeth Holmes, or Bob Ney.

Whatever Karen and Kyle are actually saying makes no difference, Liam thinks. *Whatever it is, you can be certain that every word of it is pure patriotism and populism that aligns perfectly with the Trumerica Freedom Organization.*

Watching Karen and Kyle's jaws moving rapidly, Liam has a curious feeling that they aren't real human beings but are instead androids. Their brains aren't doing the talking. It's their larynxes. The stuff they're saying consists of words. But it's not speech in the genuine sense. It's a noise uttered in unconsciousness, like the beeping of a robot.

Liam wonders if Karen and Kyle have had partial lobotomies. But then realizes that they simply believe everything Donald Trump says. Nothing more, nothing less.

Shelly Adelsan is silent for a moment. With her spoon, she traces patterns in her soup. "Watching the videos played at Victory Rallies," she eventually says, "have you ever noticed that Alexandria Ocasio-Cortez has no factual basis to her accusations against us? It's as if she hates freedom for no reason. But what really pisses me off is how she tries to neutralize any legitimate charge that President Trump makes against her—that she's evil, a liar, a fascist—by using precisely those same words against our Lifetime Leader of the Free World."

Unquestionably, Shelly will be vaporized, Liam thinks again, this time with a hint of sadness. There's something subtly wrong with her.

There's something that she lacks—discretion, aloofness, a sort of saving stupidity. Nobody could claim that she's unpatriotic. She believes everything the Trufamily Forty-Five believes. She reveres Donald Trump. And she rejoices over cultural battles fought and won. A nativist to the core, she hates foreigners with a restless zeal. Yet a faint air of suspicion always clings to her, as if she's really just a TINO—a Trumerican In Name Only.

Shelly says things that should be left unsaid. She knows too much about too many topics. And she eats too frequently at McDonald's restaurants. There's no law against wining and dining at a McDonald's, which specializes in cocktails and chicken burgers, yet the restaurants somehow attract bad omens. The old, discredited leaders of the Organization often gather at them before they're finally purged. It's rumored that, many years ago, even Alexandria Ocasio-Cortez often dined at McDonald's restaurants, always ordering McPizza.

If Shelly somehow figures out Liam's secret opinions, she'll betray him instantly to the police, denouncing him as a deep stater.

She looks up. "Here comes Graham," she says. Something in the tone of her voice seems to add, *that moron.*

Graham Tamariz, Liam's neighbor in Plaza Residences, threads his way across the room. Blond hair. A froglike face. Mid-thirties. Fat neck. His movements are brisk. He looks like a little boy grown large. He greets them both with a cheery "Hi!" and sits at the table. Beads of moisture stand out all over his pink face. His powers of sweating are extraordinary.

Shelly pulls out a mini, portable Portal and starts thumbing through something on its screen that solely her eyes can see.

"Look at her working during lunch," Graham says, nudging Liam. "Such dedication! What are you working on? Something too brainy for me, I bet." He pulls out his cryptocurrency swiper. "Liam, buddy, can I get that donation off you now?"

"What donation?" Liam automatically feels for his card. About a quarter of your salary must be set aside for voluntary donations, which are so many that it's difficult to keep track of them.

"For the re-election. Well, your money will go to the Great Trumerica Alliance Super PAC. Same thing. What's important is that I'm the fundraiser for our block. And we're going to put on an amazing show. Seriously, it won't be my fault if our Plaza Residences doesn't have the biggest flags, flashiest lights, and best fireworks in the neighborhood. You promised me twenty Libras, remember?"

Liam hands over his card.

Graham swipes it through his LibraSwipaScana, types in twenty, then holds the device up to scan one of Liam's irises. "I heard my son got you," Graham says. "Sorry about t hat."

"It happens," Liam says.

"Disobedient little kid. His sister, too. But patriotic! All they think about are the Deplorables, the war, and the trade war. Do you know what my daughter did while hiking with her youth group around the perimeter of the NextEra Energy Golf Course? Mid-hike, she slipped away and spent the rest of the afternoon following a strange, guilty man. She tailed him throughout the city, then reported him to the patrols."

"Why?" Liam asks, somewhat taken aback.

Graham goes on triumphantly. "Amy made sure he was some kind of enemy agent—might have dropped in by parachute, for instance. But here's the point. What do you think tipped her off? He wore a pair of sunglasses that she'd never seen before. So she figured he must be a foreigner. Pretty cluey for seven, huh?"

"What happened to him?"

Graham shrugs. "I wouldn't be surprised if—" he mimes aiming a rifle and clicks his tongue.

"Good," Shelly says abstractedly, without looking up from her mini-Portal.

Liam nods. "We can't afford to take chances," he says dutifully.

"We're in the middle of a war," Tamariz says.

"And we're in the middle of the most important trade negotiations in Trumerica's history," Shelly adds.

As if on cue, a brief musical jingle comes out of the numerous Portals in the cafeteria. For a moment, Liam mistakenly thinks it's the jingle that always plays prior to an announcement by the Bureau of Creative Peacebuilding and Strong Superstate Defense about a military victory. But no, the music is a new version of the theme song for his very own Bureau of Facts.

"Attention!" the eager, smiling man on the screen says. "We have wonderful, important news for you. The economy is booming like never before. It's time that everyone has an opportunity to experience the Trumerican Dream. President Trump's agenda is driving an economic resurgence that's creating more and more opportunities for Trumericans. Over 5.3 million jobs were created this year, which is the 18th consecutive year that Trumerica's unemployment rate has remained below 1%. Unemployment is at its lowest—best—in the history of Trumerica."

Graham listens to the newsflash as if he's sedated.

Next, out of the Portals stream news about numerous public rallies across Trumerica that the C-Suite organized to thank Donald Trump for decreasing the corporate tax rate from 25% to 23%, thus increasing the productivity, innovation, and happiness of all Organization members.

And yet, it was just yesterday, Liam remembers, that it had been announced that the corporate tax rate would *increase* from 21% to 23%. *Is it possible,* Liam thinks, *that Trumericans could swallow this bullshit after only twenty-four hours? It appears so.*

Graham swallows it easily, with the stupidity of an animal. The android-beeping woman and man at the other table swallow it fanatically, passionately. If someone suggested to Karen and Kyle that last week the corporate tax rate was 21%, they'd probably beat them to death on the spot.

Liam thinks, *Am I the only person alive with a working memory?*

The fabulous statistics continue pouring out of the Portals. Compared with last year, there's more food, more clothes, more houses—more of everything except disease, crime, and insanity. Year by year and minute by minute, everybody and everything is rapidly improving.

As Shelly did earlier, Liam dabbles his spoon into his pale-colored soup, drawing a long streak of it out into a pattern. He ponders resentfully on the physical texture of life. *Has it always been this shitty? Has food always tasted like crap?*

He looks around the cafeteria. Dirt on the floors and tables. Grimy walls. Battered metal tables and chairs placed so close together that you sit with elbows touching. Always in your stomach and in your skin there's a sort of protest, a feeling that you've been cheated of something that you had a right to.

It's true that he has no memories of anything really that different. In any time that he can accurately remember, there's never been quite enough to eat, the next pandemic is always touted as being ten times worse than the current one, Hyperloop trains are always crowded, houses are constantly falling to pieces, coffee always taste like tar, and there's never anything cheap and plentiful except vodka and OxiQoxi.

In the cafeteria, nearly everyone is unattractive or downright ugly. Almost nobody embodies the physical ideals set up by the Organization—tall muscular men and gorgeous vital women.

"Hey, Shelly," Graham says, "Evelyn wanted me to ask—do you have any spare tampons?"

Shelly shakes her head.

"Just thought I'd ask."

Liam thinks of Graham's family. *Within two years, I predict that those obnoxious kids will denounce their dad to the police. Graham Tamariz will be vaporized. Also, Shelly Adelsan will be vaporized. I will be vaporized. Brett Brannan will be vaporized. On the other hand, Evelyn Tamariz, with her wispy hair and the dust in the creases of her face, will never be vaporized. The androids with the beeping voices will never be vaporized. And the Gemma woman from the Press Release Department—she'll never be vaporized either.*

He's dragged out of his reverie with a violent jerk. Gemma is at the next table. She turns partly around and looks at him in a sidelong way, but with curious intensity. A moment after they lock eyes on each other, she looks away again.

The sweat starts out on Liam's backbone. A horrible pang of terror splices through him.

Why is she watching me?

He can't remember whether she was already sitting there when he arrived, or sat there afterwards. Yesterday though, during the Victory Rally, she sat directly behind him when there was no need to. Her real objective was probably to check if he was shouting patriotically enough.

He thinks again that it's unlikely that she's a member of the Peace Police. But then again, it's the undercover paramilitary agents who are the greatest dangers of all. It's possible she's been studying him for several minutes, and it's possible that his features weren't perfectly under control. When you're in public or within range of a Portal, it can be fatally dangerous to let your thoughts wander. The smallest thing can seal your doom. A nervous tic, an unconscious look of anxiety, a habit of muttering to yourself—anything that suggests abnormality, of having something to hide.

Perhaps Gemma isn't following me. Perhaps it's a coincidence that she sat near me two days in a row.

Shelly puts her mini-Portal in her bag.

"Did I ever tell you two," Graham says, chuckling, "about the time my kids set fire to an old Sub? The old hag was dancing in front of Trufamily posters of Stephen Miller, Yevgeny Prigozhin, and Bill O'Reilly. My kids snuck up behind her and set her skirt on fire. Burned her quite badly. Not the nicest kids. But patriotic!" He pauses and licks his teeth. "Kids these days sure get better training than we ever got. And do you know the latest device every Deplorable kid is given? Kiddie-Portals! My daughter pointed hers out of our kitchen window and it picked up a man across the road. In real time, what he was saying appeared on her screen. Of course it's merely a toy, mind you. Still, it gives them the right idea, right?"

All of the Portals in the room let out a piercing beep, signaling that it's time to return to work. Everyone springs to their feet to join in the struggle around the elevators.

Chapter 10

Liam, sitting alone on his toilet, hidden from the Portal, writes in his diary.

About three years ago, I hadn't had sex in eight years, not since my wife and I divorced. I couldn't deal with the possibility of never having sex again. So, I visited a Sub neighborhood and—

For a moment, he doesn't know if he should actually write about the crime he committed. But then he realizes that writing about it or not writing about it won't ultimately make any difference, just like writing or not writing *Donald Trump Must Die* no longer makes any difference. He's a dead man, all the same.

Still, he wonders why it's forbidden for Organization members to have sex with Subs. Sure, he's familiar with the ostensible reason why the law exists—that it's criminal to promote any behavior that might result in the elimination of the distinct races, including a genetically superior group risking having their genes polluted by an inferior group. But he has a hunch that their rationale is just smoke and mirrors to cover up something else. What, though? He has no clue.

He decides to write about his sex crime another day. Right now, he wants to write about his ex-wife Chloe, not about the time he paid for sex with a Sub. He turns to a new page in his diary and continues writing.

My ex-wife had wide cheekbones, a pronounced jaw line, and a propensity to parrot pretty much any talking point she had seen on Newsmax Trumedia. She swallowed all the conspiracy theories the Organization fed her via one of its state-sponsored news networks. In my mind, I nicknamed her the "soundbite repetition machine."

Luckily, when we were together, she never became pregnant. After about eighteen months, we divorced. That was about eleven years ago. Generally, the Organization doesn't allow divorce, but it encourages it in cases where there are no kids, since repopulating Trumerica is every Organization member's responsibility.

It's possible I could have loved Chloe, right? ... If only she hadn't been hypnotized by the Organization ... If only I could have somehow stopped resenting her ...

Still, why was having sex with her always so annoying? More importantly, why can't I have a relationship with a woman I like, or even love?

The answer is actually quite straightforward—a real loving relationship is unthinkable because it doesn't benefit the Organization economically, politically, or militarily. By careful, early conditioning that's hammered into kids at school and in the Youth Counterintelligence Service, the natural urge to fuck and find solace in another person is polluted, though rarely entirely eradicated. My reasoning tells me that there must be exceptions. Yet my heart doesn't believe it.

Considered this way, the act of true love making—where two people indeed love each other—is therefore an act of rebellion.

For the next thirty minutes, Liam sits on his toilet and writes in his diary.

Chapter 11

The next morning, Liam writes in his diary:

If there's hope, it can only be found in the Subs.

It's only the Subs who have the power to destroy the Trumerica Freedom Organization.

Even though there are endless mentions of the deep state during Victory Rallies, Liam doesn't believe that the Organization could possibly be overthrown from within. Its enemies—if there indeed are liberals and terrorists within the Organization—have no way of identifying or meeting with other conspirators. Even if the legendary Illuminati exists, it's inconceivable that its members could ever assemble in groups of more than two or three.

But, Liam thinks, *the Subs! They make up around 80% of the population of Trumerica! If they can somehow become aware of their power, then they could rise up. They could blow the Organization to smithereens. They could take over and achieve economic, racial, social, and environmental justice for all. Surely, sooner or later, it must occur to them to resist the hate, bigotry, and white supremacy of the Trufamily Forty-Five. And yet—!*

He remembers once walking through a tawdry, dirty, and repulsive inner-city slum. Shouts came from around a corner. Inexplicably, he thought that the cries of anger could only mean one thing—that the Subs were finally rising up against the dictatorship!

He jogged to the corner and saw a mob of frenzied Subs pushing and shoving each other in front of a Walmart. There was a *Black Friday Sales* sign above the store's front doors, which were closed. The eager shoppers jostled each other to be the first ones to enter.

Liam approached slowly. It was 8:59. Inside, employees wore helmets and body armor, waiting to unlock the doors. The bargain-hunting shoppers yelled obscenities at each other, spat in each other's faces, and prepared to surge. The doors opened. In the ensuing mayhem, several Subs were knocked to the ground and an ambulance was called. Minutes later, as the crowds sidestepped around the injured, paramedics battled to save the lives of two shoppers badly trampled—but they both died, right there in the entrance. There was an announcement that everyone had to clear the Walmart. Several Subs refused to leave without first buying something on sale, complaining that they'd waited in line for hours.

In his apartment, Liam writes in his diary.

What might happen if these savages could care about something that actually matters? Until the Subs become self-aware, they'll never rebel.

Before Donald Trump came to power, easily winning both the Electoral College and the popular vote, Subs were hideously oppressed. They were forced to live off demoralizing food stamps. They were subjected to dangerous medical experiments. They were used as sacrificial pawns of war. Their kids were required to receive autism-inducing injections that vaccinated them against nothing.

The Organization claims to have liberated the Subs. And yet, the Organization teaches its members that Subs are naturally inferior and should therefore be deprived of the rights of full citizens, including the right to vote in Trumerican re-elections.

In reality, nearly all members of the Organization know very little about the Subs. It isn't necessary to know much. So long as they continue working, breeding, and consuming, their other activities are unimportant.

Left to themselves, like feral homeless kids let loose upon a bombed-out supermarket, they've reverted to a style of life that appears natural to them. They're born, they grow up in the gutters, they marry, pop out a few grotesque kids, trudge to work, learn the art of conspicuous consumption, rack up endless debt, and then continue working until they die. Films, sport, alcohol, and gambling consume their lives.

It isn't difficult to keep the Subs under control. A few agents of the Peace Police always move among them, spreading false rumors and eliminating those who might be capable of becoming unpatriotic.

No attempt is made to indoctrinate them with the Organization's ideology. It's undesirable for Subs to hold strong political views. All that's required of them is a primitive patriotism that can be appealed to whenever it's necessary to make them accept harsher living standards, to buy the latest device imported from Korchinpan, or to endure intolerably long wait times at hospitals. And even when they become upset, their discontent leads nowhere, because being unable to think rationally, they only focus on flippant, petty grievances. The larger evils invariably escape their notice. The majority of Subs don't even have Portals in their homes.

There's a vast amount of criminality in Sub neighborhoods of Lar-o-Maga Palm City, a whole world-within-a-world of thugs, drug dealers, and liberals who believe in same-sex marriage, big government, and a welfare state. But since it all happens among the Subs themselves, it's of no importance.

In terms of morals, they're allowed to follow their own invalid self-centered logic. It's insignificant, for example, if they don't believe in the proven link between abortion and breast cancer. Likewise, it's a trivial matter if they don't understand that the theory of relativity promotes moral relativism. The Organization doesn't even bother imposing sexual puritanism upon them. Promiscuity goes unpunished. Prostitution is permitted. As it was once written in a study conducted by Trumericans for Truth About Homosexuality: *Subs and animals are free.*

Liam's hemorrhoids throb. He shifts in his chair, but the pain remains.

The thing he invariably returns to is the impossibility of knowing what life before the Third Trumerican Civil War had really been like. Serendipitously perhaps, at that very moment a history show starts playing on his Portal. He decides to transcribe some of the narrator's words into his diary. That way, if someone reads his diary in the future, they'll be able to compare his notes with whatever version of history they're being fed.

He writes into the diary:

Before our Leader for Life was elected, Lar-o-Maga Palm City wasn't the dynamic, magnificent city it is today.

He struggles to transcribe as quickly as the narrator speaks. He misses the next sentence, but writes down the one after it.

It was a dirty, miserable place plagued by violent immigrants, homeless druggies, and gender traitors.

His writing hand can't keep up. There's a sentence from the Portalcast about how children were legally forced to ride buses to schools in other neighborhoods. Yet before Liam can even start writing it down, the next sentence begins. He decides to just listen to it, and to jot down the main points after it's finished.

"During the singing of our anthem at sporting events," the narrator says, "athletes knelt while criminals, rapists, and haters throughout the stadium would set fire to the Trumerican flag. Living standards were much lower than they are today, mostly because everyone had to pay hefty taxes to finance government health care, which never actually improved anyone's health. Every day, liberals committed hate crimes—such as slandering Rush Limbaugh—against patriotic conservatives who just wanted big government to stay out of their affairs."

Liam thinks, *How can you determine how much of it is lies?*

"Paradoxically," the narrator continues, "among all this lawlessness, poverty, and ignorance, there were thousands of ruling elites that lived in lavish houses overlooking lush lakes. Each house required hundreds of underpaid servants to cater to each pompous whim of these affluent oligarchs. The elites owned 99% of everything, and everyone else owned barely enough to survive. If a patriotic Trumerican accused a bureaucracy-loving elite of being insanely politically correct, the freedom lover would be labeled 'right wing' and thrown in jail. The main culprits were lowlifes like Hunter Biden, Vanessa Wruble, Sally Yates—"

He tries to stop listening, but the history show drones on. He tries to think of Gemma standing naked in his grassy dreamland, but he can't block out the show mentioning a long list of beliefs held by liberals. That white privilege is a scourge on society. That we should implement unconstitutional gun control laws. That spending on our military should be diverted to fund universal health care. That war heroes like George W. Bush are war criminals.

Then the show mentions something called "gay marriage," it being an attempt by homosexuals and lesbians to go against thousands of years of success that we've had with a one-man/one-woman marriage system.

Is it even possible, Liam thinks, *that the average person is better off now than they were before the Third Trumerican Civil War?*

The only counter-evidence is the prickling protest in your own bones, the feeling that your living conditions are intolerable, and that at some other time everything must have been better.

It strikes Liam that the truly characteristic thing about modern life isn't its cruelty and insecurity, but simply its falseness and meaninglessness. All you have to do is look around you. Life bears no resemblance to the lies streaming out of the Portals. Life isn't even close to matching up with the ideals the Organization is trying to achieve. For regular Organization members, every damn day is a matter of jostling with other commuters to get onto Hyperloop trains or onto Hydrofoil ferries, slogging through dreary jobs, and constantly going hungry. It's only the members in the upper echelons of the Organization—the C-Suite and the Trufamily Forty-Five—who seem to live comfortable lives.

The standards set up by the Organization are huge, terrible, and glittering. A world where machines, apps, and weapons can solve any problem. A country of warriors, fanatics, and consumers, all marching forward in perfect unity, all perpetually working, fighting, winning, clicking, buying, kowtowing. Everyone thinking the same thoughts, such as how fake Trumericans—Fauxmericans—should go back to the broken and crime-infested places from which they came. Everyone parroting the same soundbites, such as, "Korchies and Iranaqies will not replace us."

The reality is quite the opposite. Decaying, dingy cities. Underfed people trying to survive on Bayer rice, Monsanto milk, and Trump steaks. Sea walls regularly leaking and flooding entire Sub neighborhoods.

Day and night, the Portals pump out newscasts proving that people today have more scrumptious food, more opulent houses, and more exhilarating entertainment choices. That they live longer, work less, win more, and are healthier, happier, and more intelligent.

Not a word of it can be proved or disproved. The Organization claimed this week, for example, that more than 7 million jobs had been added to Trumerica's economy in the past three years, and that this year, unemployment reached its lowest level in half a century.

Even historical claims can't be confirmed with certainty. It's entirely possible that every Portalcast about history, even the things that you accept without question, is pure horseshit.

Liam starts questioning what he knows to be true.

Maybe global warming *isn't* just a Korchinpan hoax.

Maybe Elon Musk *didn't* build a tiny submarine that rescued those boys trapped underwater in a Thai cave.

Maybe Donald Trump *didn't* scale El Capitan without handholds.

Maybe Gertrude Baniszweski *isn't* Hillary Clinton's sister.

Maybe Don Jr. *wasn't* the first person to land a helicopter on the top of Mount Everest.

But it's impossible to figure out if these are facts or falsehoods because everything quickly fades into mist. The past is erased, the erasure is forgotten, and the lie becomes truth. However, there was just one time in his life, several years ago, when Liam saw with his own eyes unmistakable evidence of an act of falsification.

Back in the early 2010s, several purges—called Storms—wiped out all the original leaders of the Second Trumerican Civil War. By the mid 2010s, none of them were left—except Donald Trump. By then, all the rest had been exposed as liberal traitors, counter-revolutionaries, and globalists. Alexandria Ocasio-Cortez had fled and was in hiding, others had simply disappeared, while the majority were executed after spectacular public trials in which they confessed their crimes.

One of the most famous trials was of three Illuminati members named Julian Assange, Emma González, and Jeff Sessions, who were arrested in 2012.

Chapter 12

As often happens with C-Suite members who lose Trump's loyalty and are arrested, Julian Assange, Emma González, and Jeff Sessions vanished for about a year. Nobody knew if they were dead or alive. Then they suddenly reappeared in public and incriminated themselves in the usual way. They confessed to colluding with the enemy, embezzling government funds, murdering various members of the C-Suite, and committing acts of economic sabotage in an attempt to undermine our trade pact with Latineuropa. All three gave long interviews to *Fox Trunews*, repenting their defections and promising to make amends.

After they confessed, were pardoned, and were reinstated in the Organization, Liam actually saw all three of them in a McDonald's restaurant on Dixie Highway.

He remembers the terrified fascination with which he watched Assange, González, and Sessions out of the corner of his eye. Relics of the ancient world, they were the last great figures left over from the heroic days of the Organization. The glamor of the underground struggle and the two most recent civil wars still faintly clung to them.

Even though at that time facts and dates were already growing blurry, Liam had the feeling that he had known their names years earlier than he had known the names of many other C-Suite members. But also, they were outlaws, enemies, untouchables, doomed with absolute certainty to extinction within a year or two. No one who had once fallen into the hands of the Peace Police ever escaped in the end. They were corpses just waiting to be sent to the cemetery.

In the McDonald's restaurant, nobody sat at any of the tables near them. It was unwise to be seen sitting close to such people. They sat in silence, sipping glasses of vodka.

Of the three, it was Assange whose appearance most startled Liam. Assange had once orchestrated the hacking of various treacherous emails, dubious plans, and radicalized ramblings of Hillary Clinton. He then published them, undermining her attempt to regain power during a liberal uprising led by Alexandria Ocasio-Cortez. Back then, Assange was a dashing, clean-shaven young man with sleek silvery hair. Now, he had a long, unkempt, scraggly beard. He wore a shabby, wrinkled suit. His skin was sallow and pale. He was sagging, sloping, falling away in every direction.

The three of them sat in their corner almost motionless, never speaking. Uncommanded, the waiter brought fresh glasses of vodka.

Suddenly, all the Portals in the restaurant stopped playing an advertisement for Goya beans. Donald Trump appeared on the screen. Standing in front of an adoring crowd, the President smiled and pumped his fist in the air a few times.

Simultaneously, the faces of Assange, González, and Sessions brightened.

On the screens, footage of Mount Rushmore appeared for a few moments. Then, a close up on Trump.

"Our country is witnessing a merciless campaign to wipe out our history," Trump said, "Snitches and spies are defaming our heroes, erasing our values, and indoctrinating our children. Angry mobs shouting, 'No justice, no peace,' are unleashing a wave of violent crime in our cities. These Untrumericans are tearing down statues of me and defacing our sacred memorials. These deep staters are driving Trumericans from their jobs, shaming dissenters, and demanding total submission from anyone who disagrees. This is the very definition of totalitarianism."

Liam knew that it was risky to take his eyes off the President. But, for a brief moment, he glanced at the three former C-Suite members. All seemed to be on the verge of crying.

"They're trying to teach our children to hate their own country," Trump continued. "They're trying to trick us into believing that the people who built Trumerica weren't heroes, but were villains. This radical view of our history is a web of lies. All perspective is removed. Every virtue is obscured. Every motive is twisted. Every fact is distorted. And every flaw is magnified. Their goal is to purge and disfigure history beyond all recognition. Their so-called Black Lives Matter movement is openly attacking the legacies of every man on Mount Rushmore behind me."

Liam again risked a glance. Now, all three were openly crying. But they weren't tears of sadness or fear. They were tears of love—for Trump.

A few months later, Assange, González, and Sessions were re-arrested. It appeared that they had engaged in fresh conspiracies soon after their release. At their second trial, they confessed to a bunch of new crimes. They were executed, and their fate was recorded in the Organization histories, a warning to posterity.

A few years later, one day after Paul Ryan was vaporized, Liam was tasked with removing him from a page in the digital edition of a book titled, *A Day in the Life of Trumerica: Photographed by 200 of the Superstate's Leading Photographers on One Day, June 14, 2012*. His job was to delete the photo of Paul Ryan signing a budget proposal titled, *The Path to Prosperity: Restoring Trumerica's Promise*. Liam easily found the historical error and erased it.

Scrolling through the digital book on his Portal, Liam was stunned to realize that he was viewing a version that somehow hadn't been updated in at least a decade. As a result, it featured three photos of events that had since been expunged, annulled, forever forgotten.

One, a photo of Julian Assange skateboarding in the Trumerican state formerly known as England.

Two, a photo of Emma González crying while giving a speech in the now nonexistent Trumerican city that was called Washington DC.

Three, a photo of Jeff Sessions objecting to hate-crimes law in the Trumerican state of New Alabama.

But at their trials, all three defectors had confessed details that contradicted the photographic evidence that Liam had in front of him. They had admitted going to a secret Illuminati airfield in the Trumerican state of Saskatchewan. They had admitted flying to Tehran. And most importantly, they had admitted being in Iranaqeyian's capital on June 14, 2012 so they could sell intellectual property to the nefarious criminal group, the Consortium of Petroleum Exporting Corporations. The date—June 14—had stuck in Liam's memory because it was Donald Trump's birthday. But the whole corporate espionage story of these three liberal backstabbers had been featured in countless newscasts, vidlets, and speeches at Victory Rallies. There was only one possible conclusion—the confessions were lies and they never flew to Tehran on the President's birt hday.

Of course, this wasn't in itself a discovery. Even at that time, Liam rarely believed that the people who were wiped out during purges—elites, free speech haters, and deniers of traditional gender roles—had actually committed the crimes they were accused of. But the old, un-updated version of *A Day in the Life of Trumerica* digibook was solid evidence. It was a fragment of the abolished past, like a fossil being discovered in the wrong layer of rock in the ground, destroying a geological theory in the process. It was enough to blow the Organization to smithereens—but only if in some way its significance could be shared with all Trumericans.

As soon as he figured out what the digibook was, and what it meant, he clicked around the underlying media files and found that there were actually two versions of the digibook—the old one that had miraculously never been deleted, and an up-to-date one that seemed to correspond with the Organization's current version of historical fact.

He kept his face expressionless and his breathing controlled. However, his heart was thumping quickly. Worried that his Portal, which can detect heart palpitations, might expose him, he busied himself with other tasks for a few minutes. Then, acknowledging that there was nothing he could do with the old digibook without compromising himself, he dragged it to the digital trash can on his Portal.

Even though that was many years ago, having seen these photos with his own eyes makes a difference, regardless of the fact that the events they documented are now only fuzzy memories.

Today, if that digibook could somehow be undeleted, it might not even be considered evidence. Organization members would never believe that the past had changed. They wouldn't be able to comprehend that the past not only changes, but changes continuously.

Yet what most torments Liam is that he doesn't understand *why* the Organization undertakes the huge deception. Some of the advantages of falsifying the past are obvious. However the ultimate motive is mysterious.

He picks up his pen again and writes:

I understand HOW.

I don't understand WHY.

He wonders, as he has many times before:

Am I insane?

Perhaps a lunatic is simply a minority of one.

Centuries ago it was a sign of madness to believe that the Earth revolves around the sun. Today it's nuts to believe that the past is unchangeable.

I might be alone in thinking that the past is—or should be—unalterable. And if I'm the only one who believes that, then maybe I am batshit crazy.

Still, the possibility of being insane doesn't bother him. The horror is that he might be wrong, that maybe the past *is* changeable.

He pulls out his cryptocard and looks at the image of Donald Trump on it. The President's hypnotic eyes gaze into you. It's as though some huge force is pressing down upon you—something that penetrates your skull, bangs against your brain, bullies you out of your beliefs, persuading you, almost, to deny the evidence of your senses.

At some point, the Organization will announce that the Earth is flat, and you'll have to believe it—or be vaporized. It's inevitable that they'll make that claim sooner or later. The logic of their position demands it. Not merely the validity of experience, but the very existence of external reality, is tacitly denied by their philosophy. The heresy of heresies is common sense. And what's terrifying isn't that they'll hang, electrocute, or behead you for thinking otherwise, but that they might be right.

After all, he thinks, *how do I really know that the world is a sphere? How can I really prove that stars in the night sky aren't holograms? What proof do I really have that the past is unchangeable? If the past and the external world exist only in our minds, and if our minds are controllable, what then?*

But no!

His courage seems suddenly to stiffen of its own accord. The face of Chief Operating Officer Brett Brannan, not called up by any obvious association, floats into Liam's mind. He knows, with more certainty than before, that Brannan is on his side—the right side of history. He's writing his diary *for* Brannan.

The Organization brainwashes you to reject the evidence of your eyes and ears. It's their most essential command.

His heart sinks as he thinks of the enormous power arrayed against him, the ease with which any Organization intellectual could demolish his arguments in a debate, the subtle arguments that he wouldn't be able to understand, much less answer.

And yet, I'm right. They're wrong and I'm right.

With the feeling that he's communicating directly to Brannan, he writes:

Freedom is the freedom to say that a fact is a fact, the truth is the truth, and reality is real.

Chapter 13

At work, Liam walks past the office of a Chief Information Officer. The smell of roasting coffee—real coffee, not synthetic Covfefe Coffee—wafts out into the hallway. Liam pauses involuntarily for the briefest of moments. His hemorrhoids throb and he keeps walking.

He knows that he won't be going straight home from work tonight—a risky choice, since you can be certain that your commute time is carefully monitored. In principle, an Organization member has no spare time. It's assumed that when you're not working, eating, or sleeping, the loyal member is preferably participating in or watching a Portalcast. To do anything alone, even going for a walk by yourself, is dangerous. All throughout the Organization, individualism and eccentricity are frowned upon.

Tonight, however, as Liam exits the bureau, the balminess of the air and the soft, blue sky strengthens his resolve. He wanders off into the labyrinth of Lar-o-Maga Palm City. Losing himself among unknown streets, he hardly even minds where he's heading.

If there's hope, he had written in the diary, *it lies in the Subs*. Those words keep coming back to him, both a statement of a mystical truth and a palpable absurdity.

Now, he's somewhere in the Sub slums to the north of what had once been downtown West Palm Beach.

Liam spots a bulletproof luxury car in the distance. He stops walking. The Bentley, obviously occupied by a member of the C-Suite, drives by. Following behind the car are bodyguards on motorbikes and a prisoner van.

There's trash all over the ground. In dark doorways, and down narrow alleyways, Subs swarm in astonishing numbers, including ragged, barefooted children playing. Perhaps a quarter of the windows in the street are broken and boarded up.

Most of the Subs pay no attention to Liam. A few eye him with guarded curiosity. It isn't hostility. Merely a kind of wariness, a momentary stiffening, as at the passing of some unfamiliar animal. The business attire of the Organization isn't a common sight in a street like this. Indeed, it's unwise for an Organization member to be seen in such places, unless you're doing business here. The patrols might stop you if you happen to run into them.

Suddenly, there's a roar that seems to make the pavement heave. Shards of glass from a nearby window patter onto Liam.

He walks up the street toward where a bomb demolished some buildings. A black plume of smoke rises into the sky. There's dust everywhere.

As he approaches, on the pavement he sees a human hand severed at the wrist. He kicks the hand into the gutter.

To avoid the crowd forming around the ruins, he turns down a side-street. Within a few minutes, the sordid swarming life of the streets continues unabated all around him as though the fatalities behind him never happened.

In front of a bar, two Subs are standing close together, talking animatedly about something that seems important. Liam's a few paces away when the two Subs start yelling at each other. They seem on the cusp of blows.

As Liam passes them, he realizes that they're arguing about strategies to win the McDonald's Monopoly game.

The McDonald's Monopoly game is a grotesque marketing strategy that purportedly pays out enormous prizes on a regular basis. Millions of Subs obsessively play this game like it's the most important part of their day.

Every member of the Trumerica Freedom Organization knows that the game is rigged and that the prizes are mostly imaginary. Occasionally gift cards, Cineplex tickets, or Libras are actually paid out. Mostly though, the winners of big jackpots are non-existent persons. In the absence of any real communication between Subs in different regions of Trumerica, this is easy to arrange.

But if there's hope, Liam thinks, *it resides in the Subs. I have to cling to that. When I put it in words, it sounds reasonable. But when I actually observe them, that's when it becomes an act of faith.*

He walks on. The street runs downhill, turns, and then intersects with a broader street. Liam remembers this neighborhood. He walks some more. Sure enough, on a corner, there's the antiques shop where he bought his diary. Its windows appear frosted over, but really they're just coated with grime.

Liam remembers the proprietor. It occurs to him that the Sub, probably in her eighties, must have lived through the second and third Trumerican civil wars. She and a few others like her are the last links to a vanished world.

There aren't many Organization members left whose ideas were formed before the third civil war. After that war, older members were mostly wiped out in the great purges, the so-called Storms that removed criminals, anti-government extremists, and corrupt operatives of the deep state. The few who survived have long since been terrified into complete intellectual surrender. If there's anyone still alive who can give a truthful account of the country's early days, it could only be a really old Sub.

Suddenly, the passages from the history Portalcast that Liam tried to transcribe into his diary jolt back into his mind, and a lunatic impulse grabs hold of him.

He crosses the street.

What he's about to do is madness, of course. As usual, there's no definite rule against talking to Subs or going into their shops. But it's too unusual to go unnoticed. If the patrols turn up and question him, he could say that he's trying to buy tampons for his neighbor.

He opens the door. A twinge of fear slashes through him. As he enters the shop, a bell attached to the door rings. The shop has a musty smell to it. A light brown puppy sleeps in a corner under a bookshelf.

Liam again scans the room and confirms that there aren't any Portals.

The proprietor is frail and hunched. Her hair is almost white, but her eyebrows are bushy and still black. She's wearing a long, shapeless dress that's a cross between a shirt and a robe.

"I remember you," she says, her voice soft.

"I'm just browsing," Liam says.

"Take your time." She gestures with her hand. "There's no rush. There's not much demand these days for gorgeous, useless things. And there's not much of it left."

The shop is in fact uncomfortably full. Cluttered everywhere are shelves, crates, and display cases filled with everything from dusty boots to rusty bolts, from tarnished watches to wax flowers.

Liam picks up a mug with the following message written on it. *If we can send one man to the moon, why can't we send them all?*

"You must have seen some huge changes over the decades," he says tentatively.

The old woman's eyes move around the shop as though she expects the changes to have occurred here. "The weather was better. That was before the war, of course."

"Which war? The second or third civil war?"

"It's all war," the old woman says obscurely.

"People my age don't really know what it was like back then. And what they say in books and vidlets might not be true. I'd like to hear your opinion on that. They say that life was completely different then, compared to now."

The shopkeeper mumbles something, dodging the question.

Next, Liam asks if there was more oppression, injustice, and poverty back then. But the old woman picks up a Donald Trump bobblehead doll from a shelf, shows it to Liam, and tells him about how the President created the celebrity-fame-industrial complex. She adds that she doesn't really know what that is, but it sounds impressive.

Liam asks if people couldn't afford health care back before the wars. But the woman launches into a diatribe about how the health of our society is being threatened by a pedo-ring of global elites that traffic children for sex.

Liam asks if she can remember a time before the sea walls were needed to protect New Florida from the risen sea level. But the old woman steers Liam toward some tiny bottles. She tries to sell one of them to him, explaining that it contains powerful concentrations of various herbs and extracts to enhance male potency.

A sense of helplessness takes hold of Liam as he wanders away from her, down another crowded aisle. *This woman's like an ant*, he thinks. *She can see small objects in front of her, but can't see the mountain she's on. I could question her all day without getting a straight answer.*

The puppy is awake and checking out Liam. The shopkeeper waddles over to it and whispers affectionately to it as the puppy wags its tail.

Liam realizes that when all human memory fails and all records and media are falsified, the Organization's claims to have improved society will have to be accepted, because there doesn't exist, and never can exist, any standard against which it can be tested.

On a shelf, Liam spots a lump of glass gleaming softly in the amber light. He picks up the heavy hunk of glass. It's curved on one side and flat on the other, making it almost a hemisphere. There's a peculiar softness, as of rainwater, in the texture of the glass. Inside, magnified by the curved surface, is a strange, pink object that looks part rose, part sea anemone.

"What is it?" Liam says, mesmerized.

She leaves her dog in her cot in the corner and walks toward Liam. "Coral. It came from the Great Barrier Reef, before coral bleaching ..." the old woman trails off.

"It's beautiful."

She peers over the top of her thick glasses. "It's yours for four Libras."

Liam hands over a five Libra bill, the untraceable paper currency that all Organization members use when buying goods on the black market. "Keep the change," he adds, realizing that he can't remember the last time he ever tipped a Sub. He slides the coveted piece of coral and rainwatery glass into his pocket.

What appeals to him about it isn't just its beauty. It's also the fact that inside it is something belonging to a bygone era. He also likes that it's utterly pointless, though he guesses that it was one day maybe used as a paperweight. It's a bizarre, compromising thing for an Organization member to have. Anything old or beautiful is always vaguely suspect.

"There's another room upstairs," the old lady mentions off-handedly. "There's not much in it. Just a few pieces."

With bowed back, she leads the way slowly up the worn stairs, along a thin passage, and into a room. She turns on a lamp. Her gentle, fussy movements make Liam wonder if she's perhaps a bookworm or a musician.

Liam notices that the furniture is arranged as though the room is meant to be lived in. There's a rug, an armchair, a fireplace, an enormous bed, and a kitchenette in a corner. On the walls are an antique pendulum clock and a few pictures. There are no windows facing the street. Two windows look out onto the neighbor's backyard.

"We lived here until my husband died. I'm selling the furniture off little by little."

In the warm dim light, the place looks curiously inviting. The room awakens in him a sort of nostalgia, a sort of ancestral memory. It seems that he somehow knows exactly what it feels like to sit in a room like this, in a comfy chair, reading whatever took his fancy, absolutely alone, yet secure, with nobody watching him, no sounds except the friendly ticking clock and the calming crackling fire.

"There's no Portal," Liam can't help murmuring.

"Ahhh, I never got one of those things. Too expensive." She points. "Now that's a nice bedside table—six Libras."

Liam ignores her and walks over to a bookcase in the corner. Quickly he determines that it contains only Organization-approved books that have been published in recent years. The hunting-down and destruction of dangerous books had been done with the same thoroughness in the Sub neighborhoods as everywhere else.

The woman stands in front of a poster in a rosewood frame hanging on a wall. "Now, if you like old photos ..."

Liam comes over and gazes at the poster. The image in the poster is of an enormous golf ball-like geodesic sphere surrounded by fountains and trees.

"The frame's attached to the wall," she says, "but if you want to buy it, I can unscrew it. Three Li—"

"I know that building," he interrupts. "Where is it again?"

"It *was* in Orlando, or what's left of Orlando. It was called EPCOT Center. I don't expect that many people know this, but EPCOT stood for Experimental Prototype Community of Tomorrow. The whole theme park was dedicated to the celebration of human achievement. Imagine that! Ha! Talk about relics of times gone by! So, three Libras and this photo is—"

"No thanks," Liam says brusquely, a hint of rudeness in his voice.

The woman raises her hands. "Take it easy." She coughs, then smiles apologetically. "Life's too short to get cranky. 'Beware my friend, as you pass by'—"

"What's that?"

"Oh, that's just the first line of a creepy rhyme my friends and I used to say as kids when we walked past cemeteries. 'Beware my friend, as you pass by. As you are now, so once was I.' Huh, I can't remember the next two lines. The whole poem was inscribed on my husband's tombstone in Orlando, right near"—she points at the old photo of the EPCOT Center.

He squints. "I thought you and your husband used to live up here." He motions around the room.

"We did—fifteen years ago." She huffs and frowns at him. "Now, I'm selling the furniture off—"

"Little by little. Yeah, you said that."

Liam wonders when the EPCOT Center was built. It's always impossible to determine the true age of a building in New Florida. Here, you can't accurately learn history from architecture any more than you can learn it from vidlets. Statues, memorial stones, the names of streets—anything that might throw light upon the past has definitely been altered.

"You said it was built to celebrate human achievement?"

She nods. "And more. If I'm remembering correctly, EPCOT was built to instill a new sense of belief and pride in our ability to shape a world that offers hope to everyone on the planet."

Liam doesn't purchase the poster. It would be an even more incongruous possession than the glass paperweight. He lingers for a few minutes, though, talking to the proprietor.

Tiffany Murmidahn is sixty-three and has inhabited this building for thirty years, though now she lives down the street in an apartment she shares with her sister, who has Alzheimer's.

While they talk, the beginning of the rhyme, which Liam half-remembers from his own childhood, runs through his head.

Beware my friend, as you pass by.

As you are now, so once was I ...

Liam says thanks and goodbye to Tiffany Murmidahn and walks down the stairs alone. He decides that, after waiting a month or so, he'll risk visiting this antiques shop again. At that time, he'll buy more gorgeous, useless things. He'll buy the poster of the EPCOT Center, take it out of its frame, and carry it home concealed under his jacket. He'll also drag the rest of that poem out of Tiffany's memory.

Before leaving, he pops over to the puppy, which he's pretty sure is part labrador retriever, part poodle. As he pets the labradoodle, it licks his hand affectionately.

He opens the shop door and steps out into the late night and onto the sidewalk.

His heart turns to ice. A figure in a black dress about thirty feet away is coming toward him. It's the Gemma woman from the Press Release Department.

Chapter 14

Outside Tiffany's antiques store, Gemma looks Liam straight in the face, then walks quickly on.

For a few seconds, Liam is too paralyzed to move. Then he turns and walks in the opposite direction.

There's no way she'd be randomly walking on the same evening on the same obscure backstreet, miles from where Organization members live. Whether she's an agent of the Peace Police, or simply an amateur spy, no longer matters. She's definitely spying on him.

With each step, the lump of glass in Liam's pocket bumps against his thigh, and he's in half a mind to throw it away. He also desperately needs to shit.

Liam wonders what to do, then decides to retrace his steps. He turns and walks briskly. If he catches up to Gemma and they're still in a Sub area where there are few Portals, he'll smash her head in with his glass paperweight.

For twenty minutes, he walks frantically up and down various streets, yet can't find her.

Whereas killing Donald Trump still seems like an outlandish—and probably impossible—goal, killing this Gemma bitch would be a cinch.

All at once, a colossal sluggishness takes hold of him. All he wants is to get home, shit, and sleep.

It's after 10 pm when he gets back to his neighborhood, which is eerily dark. All electricity—except that which powers the Portals and Trufamily posters—has been shut off. He figures that the current weather conditions must present a high fire risk to the power grid.

He trudges up the stairs in pitch blackness.

In his kitchen, he lights a candle and swallows a shot glass of vodka.

From his Portal, a brassy female voice is prattling on in an infomercial about how to make a Trumptini, a cranberry-flavored Bacardi-based cocktail. Then there's a news alert with Trump saying, "Big government, big media, and big business are trying to shut you up, shut you out, and shut you down. We won't let them."

Liam sits on his toilet, takes the diary out of the drawer, and stares at the marbled cover of the diary, glimmering in the candlelight.

They always come for you at night. The best thing is to kill yourself before they get you. Undoubtedly, many members of the Organization do exactly that. Many of the disappearances are actually suicides.

He thinks of Gemma, and with a kind of astonishment, of the biological uselessness of fear and the treachery of a human body that freezes exactly when a special effort is needed. He could have silenced her—if he had only acted quickly enough. But precisely because of his extreme danger, he had lost the power to act.

It strikes him that in moments of crisis, you're rarely really fighting against an external enemy. More so, you're battling against your own body. Even now, despite the vodka, the dull ache in his belly makes even thinking clearly a difficult task. And it's probably the same, he guesses, in other seemingly heroic or tragic situations. On the battlefield, in the torture chamber, or on a sinking ship, the causes you're fighting become secondary simply because your body, your life, swells up until it fills the universe. Even when you're not paralyzed by fright or screaming with pain, life is a moment-to-moment struggle against something, be it hunger or cold, sleeplessness or an upset stomach.

He opens the diary. It's important to write something down.

Some people in the Portal start talking about the benefits of Trump Natural Spring Water. Their voices seem to stick into his brain like jagged splinters of glass.

He tries to think of Brett Brannan, his future reader. But instead he thinks of what will happen to him after he's nabbed. The thing is, the Peace Police rarely kill you straight away. Before death, there's the routine of confessing, the groveling on the floor, the screaming for mercy, the crack of broken bones, the smashed teeth, the bloody clots of hair.

Liam thinks, *Why do you have to endure it if the end is always the same? Nobody ever evades detection. Nobody ever fails to confess. And nobody ever escapes execution. So why don't they just kill you straight after they catch you?*

He again thinks of Brett Brannan, and knows what he's going to write. He writes:

Brannan, you once told me in a dream: "We'll meet where there's no darkness." I now

71

know what that means. The place where there's no darkness is the imagined future that we'll never see, but, with foreknowledge we can mystically share in.

Liam motions to stand, in order to get a much-needed dose of OxiQoxi, but then remembers that he's out, and he slumps down again, defeated.

The face of Donald Trump swims into his mind, displacing that of Brannan. Just as Liam had done a few days earlier, he takes his cryptocurrency card out of his pocket and looks at it. The face of Trumerica's Leader for Life gazes up at him, heavy, calm, protecting. *What the hell is going on behind that man's eyes?*

Abruptly, an advertorial that's vomiting out of the Portal stops and a certain jingle plays. It's the jingle that announces new mottos have been posted all around Trumerica. He leans sideways so that he can read what's on the screen. On his Portal are the Organization's triplet of new mottos blazing out at him—and simultaneously at hundreds of millions of other Trumericans.

THERE IS NO POLITICAL SOLUTION.
LOSERS FOCUS ON WINNERS. WINNERS FOCUS ON WINNING.
SEND THEM BACK.

Tomorrow, he thinks, *I'm going to have to kill Gemma before she gets me killed.*

PART 2: LOVE'S REBELLION

Chapter 15

Liam leaves his cubicle to go to the bathroom.

A solitary figure heads toward him from the other end of the long, brightly-lit hallway. It's Gemma. As she comes nearer, he sees that her right arm is in a sling.

Instead of the paperweight in his pocket, he has his old-fashioned pen. He brought it with him so that he could stab her with it. A knife would be preferable. But he could never risk bringing a knife to work. If he stabs her several times with the pen in her neck and eyes, he figures it will do the job.

But there are Portals every few yards in this hallway. He'll have to follow her home after work.

When she's about twelve feet away, she stumbles and falls almost flat on her face. She lands on her injured arm and cries out in pain.

Liam stops walking. In that moment, it's as if he feels her pain in his body. She rises to her knees. Her face is now a milky color against which her mouth stands out redder than ever. Her eyes are fixed on his.

A curious emotion stirs in Liam's heart. In front of him is an enemy that's trying to kill him. In front of him, also, is a person in pain.

Instinctively, he moves forward to help her. "You ok?" he says.

"It's nothing."

"Sure?"

Gemma nods and holds out her free hand, and he helps her up. She slips something small into his palm. He quickly transfers it to his pocket and feels it with the tips of his fingers. It's a folded piece of paper.

"Thanks," she says, then walks briskly down the hall as if the whole incident had really been nothing.

Even though they'd been standing directly in front of a Portal, Liam's positive that he hadn't revealed his surprise to be secretly slipped something.

Walking to the restrooms, he manages with a little fingering to unfold the paper. Obviously there's a message written on it. For a moment, he's tempted to go into a bathroom stall and read it. But that'd be stupid. The Portals on the ceiling see everything.

Later, he sits at his cubicle, eye-connects with his Portal, and yanks his microphone toward him. Fortunately the work he's engaged in is mere routine, the rectification of a long list of figures, not needing close attention.

His heart bumps in his breast with frightening loudness.

Whatever's written on the paper must have some kind of political meaning. One possibility is that she works for the Peace Police, just as he suspected. He doesn't know why an undercover paramilitary officer would deliver their messages in such a fashion. But perhaps she has her reasons.

Another, wilder possibility is that the message is from some kind of underground organization. *Perhaps the Illuminati exists after all! Perhaps she is part of it!*

Whatever the message is, it probably means death. Still, the unreasonable hope persists, and his heart bangs, and it is with difficulty that he keeps his voice from trembling as he dictates into his Sirimic.

After working for approximately ten minutes, he palms the scrap of paper in a way that he can just see it, yet it's still concealed from his Portal. On it is written in large handwriting:

You fascinate me.

For several seconds he's too stunned to do anything. Eventually though, he regains his composure. He can't resist reading it once again, just to make sure that the words are really there, then he fake sneezes, sneaks the paper into his mouth and, with some difficulty, smooshes it into small enough pieces to swallow.

For the rest of the morning, it's difficult to work. What is even worse than having to focus on a series of mind-numbing jobs is the need to conceal his excitement from the Portal. He feels as though a bunch of excited caterpillars are dancing in his belly, knowing that they're soon going to morph into beautiful butterflies.

Chapter 16

In the hot, crowded, noisy cafeteria, Liam hopes to be alone for a little while during the lunch break. But his imbecile neighbor flops down beside him.

The tang of Graham Tamariz's sweat is stronger than the stench of the food on their plates. Graham blabbers on endlessly about preparations for the re-election. He's particularly enthusiastic about a statue of Donald Trump, twenty feet tall, that his children and other neighborhood kids are making for the occasion.

Just once, Liam glimpses Gemma at a table at the far end of the room. She appears not to have seen him, and he doesn't look in that direction again.

After lunch, a delicate, difficult task is given to Liam that necessitates putting everything else aside. It consists in falsifying a series of 2022 production reports in such a way as to cast discredit on a prominent C-Suite member who is now under a cloud. This is the kind of thing that Liam excels at, and for two hours he succeeds in shutting Gemma out of his mind. Then the memory of her face and her words come back—*You fascinate me*—and all he wants is to be alone.

Later that night, at 11 pm when he's home and in bed, he's enveloped by the darkness, safe even from his Portal so long as he keeps silent.

He no longer thinks that Gemma's trying to trap him. All he thinks about is trying to contact her to arrange a meeting.

He remembers her naked body, as seen in his dream. A kind of fever seizes him at the thought that he might lose her! *What if I don't get in touch with her quickly,* he thinks, *and she simply changes her mind?* But the physical difficulty of meeting seems insurmountable. Everywhere are Portals, drones, and fellow patriots all willing to turn you in without hesitation.

Obviously the kind of encounter that happened this morning can't be repeated, he thinks.

If she worked in the Information Security Department, it might be do-able. But I have no valid pretext for going to where she works in the Press Release Department. I'll have to follow her home. Instead of killing her, I'll try to talk with her.

Suddenly, though, he realizes that to set this in motion, he'd have to loiter outside the bureau until she exited, which would be noticed.

Finally, he decides that the safest place is the cafeteria. *If I can get her at a table by herself, somewhere in the middle of the room, not too near the Portals, and with a sufficient buzz of conversation all around, we might be able to exchange a few words.*

On the next day, she doesn't appear in the cafeteria until he's leaving it. On the day after that, she's in the cafeteria at the usual time. But she's sitting with other people directly under a Portal. Then for three dreadful days she doesn't appear at all.

His whole mind and body seem to be afflicted with an unbearable sensitivity that makes every movement and sound an agony. Even in sleep he can't altogether escape from her image. He has no clue what happened to her. There's no one he can ask. She might have been vaporized. She might have committed suicide. She might have been transferred to the newest Trumerican state, the recently purchased state of Greenland. Worst and likeliest of all, she might simply have had second thoughts and decided to avoid him.

The next day, Gemma reappears. Her arm is out of the sling and she has bandages around her wrist. His relief is so great that he can't resist staring directly at her for several seconds.

On the following day, he enters the cafeteria and sees her sitting alone at a table. It's early, and the place isn't full yet. The queue edges forward until Liam is almost at the counter, then he's held up for two minutes because an Organization member in front complains to a Sub that he hasn't received his OxiQoxi tablet. But Gemma is still alone when Liam gets his tray and starts walking casually toward her. She's perhaps twenty feet away from him. Another two seconds will do it.

Then a voice behind him—"Liam!" He pretends not to hear. "Liam!" repeats the voice, louder. It's no use. He turns around.

A blond, young man named Wilsher, who Liam barely knows, invites him with a smile to a vacant spot at his table. It would be unwise and unsafe to refuse. After having been recognized, he couldn't sit at a table with an unaccompanied woman. It would be too noticeable. Liam gives his best warm smile and joins Wilsher, whose face beams into his. Liam imagines smashing a cleaver right into the middle of Wilsher's friendly face. A few minutes later, Gemma's table fills up. But she must have seen him coming toward her, and perhaps she got the hint.

The next day, he arrives early. Sure enough, she's at the same table and again alone. The person immediately ahead of Liam in the queue is a small man with a flat face and tiny eyes. As Liam turns away from the counter with his tray, he sees that the little man is heading straight for Gemma's table. His hopes sink again. With ice at his heart, Liam realizes that it's useless unless he can get her alone.

Liam stumbles forward and crashes into the little man's back. The little man sprawls onto the floor, his tray of food spilling everywhere. He gets to his feet with a malignant glance at Liam, who shrugs and looks around, baffled, as if to indicate that he too was pushed.

A few moments later, with a thundering heart, Liam is sitting at the table, and the little man is heading to the bathrooms.

Liam doesn't look at her. He begins eating.

I've got to say something before anyone else comes, he thinks. But now a terrible fear electrifies his spine. *She might have changed her mind! Also, it's impossible that we can ever be friends. Such things never happen in real life.*

He might have wimped out and stayed silent if at this moment he hadn't seen Connor Hughes, the hairy-eared songwriter, wandering around the room with a tray, looking for a place to sit. Hughes would certainly sit at Liam's table if he sees him. There's perhaps a minute in which to act. He's about to speak—

"What time do you leave work?" she murmurs without looking up.

"Six-thirty," Liam says quietly.

"Can you meet me at the Trump statue in Pruitt Park?" she says expressionlessly.

He nods slightly. "But won't that area be full of Portals?"

She spoons some watery soup into her mouth. "That won't matter. There's going to be a re-election rally nearby. President Trump himself will be there."

"How should—"

"Don't come up to me until you're sure that I'm heading toward the stadium."

"What time?" he asks.

"Seven."

"Ok."

Hughes doesn't see Liam and sits at another table.

Liam and Gemma don't speak again. For the rest of their meal, they don't look at each other. She finishes her lunch quickly and leaves the cafeteria. Liam stays, takes his OxiQoxi tablet, and, within moments, experiences a brief high marked by a sense of well-being, which is quickly usurped by a much stronger sense of dread.

Chapter 17

At the appointed time, Liam is standing below the huge gold statue of Donald Trump. The effigy is on top of an enormous concrete column. The sparkling President gazes eastward toward the skies where he vanquished the Iranaqeyian planes—a few years ago it had been the Korchinpanian planes—in the Battle of the Bahamian State.

At five minutes past the hour, Gemma still hasn't arrived. Again, a terrible fear seizes Liam. *She isn't coming! She changed her mind!*

Dozens of people are walking past the statue and heading toward a nearby stadium.

He sees Gemma. She crosses the road, heads toward him, then walks straight past him. Liam follows her and the crowd.

Along with hundreds of Subs and dozens of Organization members, they pass through extensive security checks to enter the stadium.

As best he can without appearing suspicious, Liam observes the security guards, wondering how he might sneak a weapon past them in the future.

At one end of the stadium is a huge stage adorned with flags. Most of the spectator areas are roped off, preventing anyone from sitting in three-quarters of the stadium. The one area where people can go is on the field itself, which is where Liam, Gemma, and maybe around one thousand people are currently standing.

At these kinds of rallies, Liam gravitates as much as he can to the outer edge. But this time, he shoves and squirms his way through the crowd, trying to get close to Gemma, who is maybe one hundred feet from the front of the stage. Soon he's within arm's length of her. But the way is blocked by a seemingly impenetrable wall of flesh—two enormous Subs, presumably husband and wife. Liam wriggles himself sideways, and with a violent lunge manages to drive his shoulder between them. He's next to Gemma. They're shoulder to shoulder, both staring straight ahead.

Kid Rock, wearing a fur coat, tank top, and loose pants, comes on stage. He starts performing his song, "Trumerican Bad Ass."

As Liam watches Kid Rock gyrate, his vision blurs—because Gemma's shoulder, and her arm right down to the elbow, are pressed against his.

Part way through the song, Gemma squeezes and holds Liam's hand. He explores her long fingers, the shapely nails, the soft palm. Merely from feeling it, he'd now know it by sight. In the same instant, it occurs to him that he doesn't know the color of her eyes. They're probably brown. But people with dark hair sometimes have blue eyes. And yet, to turn his head and look at her would be extremely dangerous.

"Can you get Sunday afternoon off?" she says just loud enough for him to hear over the music, and hopefully not loud enough for anyone else nearby to hear.

"Yes."

"Then listen carefully, you'll have to remember this," she says, her lips barely moving, her eyes straight ahead, never looking at him.

With phenomenal precision, she outlines the exact route he is to follow in order to meet her. She tells him to go to the Palm Beach Station; ride the Hyperloop south for about an hour; get off at the Golden Glades Station; head toward the McDonald's down the road; at the restaurant, turn left; follow that road for about a mile until there's a gate with the top bar missing; follow the path across the field; take the track between the bushes; look for the dead tree with moss on it.

"Can you remember all of that?" she asks.

"I think so."

At the end of Kid Rock's song, the Trumerican Freedom Kids singing and dancing group joins him on stage. Together they perform a rendition of "The Official Donald Trump Jam." Hundreds of people in the crowd sing the lyrics with them. "Cowardice—are you serious? Apologies for freedom—I can't handle this!"

"What time?" Liam asks Gemma during the chorus.

"About 3 pm. I'll get there by another way. So, I'll ask again—can you remember everything I just said?"

"Yes."

"Great. So, as soon as this freak show is over, get the fuck away from me."

It's almost imperceptible. But out of the corner of his eye he sees her flash a smile at him, just for a half-second.

Ten minutes later, Ted Nugent comes on stage to introduce the President. "Ladies and gentlemen," Nugent yells. "Our Lifetime Leader of the Free World!"

As the President comes out, the crowd goes absolutely wild.

Nugent raises his cowboy hat high into the air. "President Trump's message sings to Trumericans because he doesn't play politically correct brain-dead games!"

After the cheering and clapping subsides, Trump stares lovingly into the crowd. "You're going to look back on this rally for the rest of your lives," he says, grinning and nodding. "We will slay the warmongers. We will defeat the globalists. We will cast out the communists who hate our country. Trumerica was once ruled by freaks, neocons, open-border zealots, and fools. We're never going back to the party of Paul Ryan, Karl Rove, and Jeb Bush." Trump clenches a raised fist. "This is a movement like you've never seen before and you'll never see again. Believe me, it will never happen again."

Chapter 18

Liam decides to get to their arrival place a little bit early to check it out.

In general, you can't assume that you're much safer in the countryside than within Lar-o-Maga Palm City. There are no Portals in the country, but there's always the danger of concealed microphones that might pick up and recognize your voice.

In New Florida, it's difficult to make any substantial journey by yourself without attracting attention. For distances of less than 100 miles, it isn't necessary to get your ID swiped and your eyes scanned. But sometimes patrols at transport stations stop and frisk even Organization members, ask awkward questions, and detain those suspected of Untrumerican behavior.

Hyperloop trains are magnetic hovertrains that travel in air-free tubes. Due to lack of drag and friction, they're supposed to speed along at over 300 miles per hour. But for some reason, most of the time they go at around 30 miles per hour. Today, the train is full of Subs all in holiday mood, despite the oppressive heat. Seated around Liam is an enormous family, ranging from a toothless great-grandmother to a month-old baby, all going out to spend an afternoon in the country, as they explained to Liam.

Walking away from the Golden Glades station, Liam cautiously glances backward to check that he's not being followed.

After passing the McDonald's, Liam walks up a road dappled in light and shade, stepping out into pools of gold wherever there are gaps in the trees above. The air seems to kiss his skin. From somewhere deeper in the heart of the wood comes the soft coo-oo of doves. In a field to his left, there are hundreds of sunflowers. He somehow remembers that those flowers were once known for being "happy" flowers.

The sunshine makes him feel dirty and impotent, a sedentary creature of the indoors. It's like he can feel the sooty dust of Lar-o-Maga Palm City in the pores of his skin.

The road widens, and in a minute he comes to the footpath she mentioned, a track that plunges between some bushes. Eventually the track becomes so thin, and the sunflowers so plentiful, that it's impossible not to tread on some flowers. He kneels down and picks some so that he can give her a bunch when they meet.

He's smelling some of them in his hand when a sound at his back freezes him—the unmistakable crack of a foot on twigs. It might be Gemma, or he might have been followed after all. To look around would show guilt. He picks another flower. A hand lightly touches his shoulder.

He looks up.

It's her.

She extends the index finger of one hand vertically in front of her lips. She smiles, then parts the bushes and quickly leads the way along another narrow track into the woods.

Liam follows, still clasping his bunch of happy flowers. His first feeling is relief, and yet the sweetness of the air and the greenness of the forest are daunting.

They come to a fallen tree. She hops over it and forces apart some bushes where there doesn't seem to be an opening. Liam follows her into a natural clearing, a tiny grassy knoll surrounded by tall trees that shut it in completely.

Gemma stops and turns. "Here we are."

They're about five feet apart. He doesn't dare move nearer to her.

"I didn't want to say anything back there," she goes on, "in case there was a hidden mic. We're ok here."

"We're ok here?" he repeats stupidly.

She smiles again and takes his hand.

"Until this moment," he says, "I didn't know what color your eyes were." They're light brown. A flash of insecurity burns through him. "I've got bad breath. I've got hemorrhoids. I've got no idea about—" He stops babbling nervously, unsure why he was even telling her those irrelevant details.

"I couldn't care less," she says.

The next moment, they're in each other's arms. At the beginning, he feels only disbelief. Their bodies strain against each other. Her hair is against his face. And—yes!—they're kissing. She clasps her arms around his neck.

"Darling," she says.

"Honey," he says.

84

She pulls him down to the ground.

Over the next several minutes, he experiences a kind of ecstasy and pride, yet isn't able to sexually perform.

She pulls a sunflower out of her hair and puts her arm on his waist. "Don't worry about it, darling."

"Where are you from?" he says.

She giggles. "I was about to talk about how fucking amazing this hide-away is. I was about to tell you about how I got lost once on a community hike and found it. But you want to do twenty questions." She giggles again. "Fine. It's all good. I was born and raised in lovely Lar-o-Maga Palm City. You're from Orlando."

"How'd you know that?"

"I have a hunch that I'm better at finding out things than you are, darling. Tell me, before I gave you that note, what did you think of me?"

He feels no temptation to lie. He wonders if it's even a sort of love-offering to reveal how horrible he is, deep down. "I was going to kill you because I thought you might be an undercover agent."

She laughs delightedly. "Ha! Really?"

"Or, if you weren't an agent, I thought that you—"

"You thought I was a loyal Organization member, didn't you? Pure in word and deed. Always reading that fuck-face's tweets. Always marching in every Straight Pride parade. Always helping with rounding up illegals on weekends. All that bullshit. And you thought I followed you so I could denounce you as a liberal and get you killed off, didn't you?"

He nods.

She slips off the silver ring of the Making Abstinence Sexy campaign and puts it in her pocket.

"Why ... me?" he asks.

"It was something in your face. I thought I'd take a chance." She scoffs. "I'm good at spotting outliers. As soon as I saw you, I knew you were against *them*."

Over the next ten minutes, she talks about *them* with an open hatred that makes Liam feel uneasy, although he knows that they're safe here if they can be safe anywhere.

"There's another place I want to show you," she says at the end of her rant. "C'mon."

They get dressed, leave the clearing, and wander through the checkered shade, their arms around each other's waists whenever it's wide enough to walk two abreast. They don't speak above a whisper. After a few moments, they reach the edge of the woods.

She stops him. "Let's not go out into the open. There might be someone watching."

They stand in the shade. The sunlight, filtering through leaves, is still hot on their faces. Liam looks out into the field beyond and undergoes a curious, slow shock of recognition. He knows the field by sight. A path wanders across it. On the opposite side of the field, huge elm trees sway in the breeze. Somewhere nearby, but out of sight, there's surely a stream where herring and sunfish are swimming ... the first body of water in his life that doesn't automatically terrify him out of his wits ...

"Is there a stream nearby?" he whispers, hopeful.

She nods and points into the distance. "There's fish in it."

"I've seen this place before—almost," he murmurs, thinking of the dreamscape that he mostly thinks of as Libertopia, but also sometimes calls Lah Lah Land.

"This place?"

"It's nothing, really. I've dreamed of—"

"Look," whispers Gemma. Out of her pocket, she produces a slab of chocolate. She breaks it in half. It's dark, shiny, and wrapped in silver paper. Normally, chocolate is dull brown, crumbly, and tastes like the smoke of a dumpster fire. The scent of her chocolate stirs up some memories that he can't quite pin down.

"Where'd you get this?" he whispers, astonished.

"You're new to all of this, aren't you?" She pauses. "The black market, obviously."

The chocolate melts on Liam's tongue. The taste is delightful. But there's still that memory moving around the edges of his consciousness, something he feels strongly but can't identify.

A bird lands on some nearby springy grass. It's brilliant red all over, with a black face immediately around its orange beak. Liam knows that it's a cardinal. But he can't remember if it's the male or female. It spreads out its wings, ducks its head for a moment as though paying respect to the sun, then pours forth a torrent of song. Liam and Gemma cling together, fascinated. The whistle-like chirping often speeds up and ends in a slow trill. One part of the bird's song sounds like a laser beam shooting off. Bizarrely, another part sounds like it's singing *birdie, birdie, birdie*. Sometimes it stops for a few seconds, spreads out and resettles its wings, then again bursts into song.

Liam watches with reverence. Who is the bird singing for? No mate or rival is watching it. What makes it sit at the edge of these woods and pour its music into nothingness? He imagines a microphone being hidden somewhere in the vicinity and, at the other end, a gloomy government official listening intently, perhaps even smiling on the inside.

Liam stops thinking and merely feels.

Gemma's waist in the bend of his arm is soft and warm. He pulls her around so that they're chest to chest. Their bodies seem to melt into each other. They kiss—it's quite different from the hard kisses they exchanged earlier. When they move their faces apart, they both sigh deeply.

The bird flies off with a clatter of wings.

Liam puts his lips against her ear. "Now," he whispers.

She shakes her head. "Back there. It's safer."

Quickly, they thread their way back to the clearing. When they're inside the ring of trees, she turns and faces him. They're both breathing fast. But her smile has reappeared. She stands, looking at him for an instant, then undresses again. And, yes, it's almost as in his dream! As swiftly as he once imagined it, she rips her clothes off, and when she flings them aside, it's with that same magnificent gesture by which a whole civilization seems to be annihilated. For a moment, he doesn't look at her body, gleaming in the sun. Instead, his eyes are anchored by her freckled face and bold smile. He kneels before her and clasps her hands.

"Have you done this before?"

She nods. "Dozens of times."

His heart jumps. He wishes it was hundreds. Anything that hints at corruption fills him with a wild hope. Who knew, perhaps the Organization is rotten under the surface, its cult of self-denial simply a sham concealing its viciousness. If he could infect the whole lot of them with a deadly virus, he wouldn't think twice about doing it.

"With Organization members?" he asks, curious.

"Only with Organization members."

"With members of the C-Suite?"

"Not with those pigs, no. But I'm sure many of them would. They're not as virtuous as they make out."

She kneels down so that they're face to face.

"The more men you've had, the more I adore you. Fuck the Organization's ideal of sexual purity." He humphs. "I think that I even hate all kinds of purity ... That's it. I even hate integrity and kindness. I don't want virtue to exist anywhere."

"We're going to get on fabulously." She winks. "I'm corrupt to the bone."

"You like having sex?" he says without missing a beat.

"I fucking love fucking."

They clasp each other and stumble ungracefully onto the grass, among the sunflowers. This time, there's no limp-dickedness whatsoever.

After they have sex, he feels pleasantly helpless. The sun seems to have grown hotter.

The animal instinct, he thinks, *the simple undifferentiated desire—this is the force that will destroy the Organization.*

Within moments, they both fall asleep.

About thirty minutes later, Liam wakes. He sits up and watches her sleeping peacefully, pillowed on the palm of her hand. He notices that her short dark hair is thick and soft.

He drinks in her naked body, so smooth and gorgeous.

In the old days, he thinks, *sexual desire and the longing for love were natural. Nowadays, though, you can't have genuine lust or true love. No emotion is pure—because the Trufamily Forty-Five and the C-Suite pollute everything with insanity, fear, and hatred.*

Liam and Gemma's lovemaking is a battle, a victory. It's a blow struck against the Organization, a political act. Love is revolutionary.

Chapter 19

As soon as Gemma wakes up, her demeanor changes. Alert and business-like, she gets dressed. "C'mon. We have to go."

He invites her into having sex again, but she brusquely declines.

"Hey," he says, "why do you think sex between two unmarried Organization members is a crime?"

"You want to talk about this, *now*?" She frowns.

He nods.

Her frown turns into a gorgeous smirk. She motions for him to put his clothes on.

He doesn't move. "I get that by making unwed sex illegal," he says, "the Organization prevents members from forming loyalties that it can't control. But-—"

"It's more than that." She returns the purity ring to her wedding finger. "The Organization's real purpose is to remove all pleasure from the sexual act. That's why love and eroticism are the enemy. That's why all marriages between Organization members must be approved by a committee that won't hesitate denying permission to marry if the couple seem attracted to each other. That's why the only recognized purpose of marriage is to produce children for the benefit of the Organization." She throws his clothes at him. "Get the fuck dressed," she says sternly.

He can tell she's not really pissed at him, but that she definitely wants to go.

He puts on his clothes.

"Sexual intercourse," she continues, "is either something you never have, or it's a repulsive, yet required activity."

He thinks that she's probably right. The Organization never states anything like that outright. Yet that's exactly what is indirectly brainwashed into every member from childhood onwards.

She makes him think of Making Abstinence Sexy, the special interest group that she's a part of. Funded by Focus on the Family Inc., it advocates for complete celibacy for both sexes.

She also makes him think of the Stork Movement, an advocacy group. Funded by Vitrolife Women's Health and Biotechnology, it calls for all children to be conceived via artificial insemination and raised in public institutions, permanently separated from their biological parents.

He wants to keep talking, but she won't have any more of it. She details how Liam will get home. Her suggested route, which is different from the one he came here by, will take him to a Hydrofoil ferry station he's never even heard of before.

Listening to her give directions, it's obvious that she possesses a practical cunning that he lacks. Also, she seems to have an exhaustive knowledge of the countryside just outside of Lar-o-Maga Palm City, stored away from umpteen hikes with the United Constitutional Patriots looking for illegal immigrants.

He says that he prefers trains and would take the Hyperloop. But she convinces him to take the ferry. Next, she tells him about a market where they can meet on Monday at 8 pm. It's in a poor area of the city. Usually filled with Subs, it's crowded and noisy. She'll be at the stall that sells Trump Footlongs. If she judges that the coast is clear, she'll blow her nose when he approaches. Otherwise, he's to walk past her without recognition. But with luck, among the bustling crowd, it'll be safe for her to tell him details about their next rendezvous point, a possible hiding-place she intends to scope out.

She tells him that she has to leave now so she can be back in time for a cancer fundraising event tonight held by the Curetivity Foundation. She instructs him to stay here for about five minutes before leaving.

She flings herself into his arms and kisses him aggressively. He wants to ask her where she lives, even though it's inconceivable that they'll ever meet at each other's apartments—but she disappears into the woods.

Chapter 20

A month later, Liam and Gemma meet in an abandoned elementary school in an almost-deserted area that a neutron bomb decimated thirty years ago. It's a good hiding-place. But getting there is dangerous. In a classroom with posters of planets on the walls, they laugh, talk about how absolutely deranged he is for wanting to assassinate the President, talk about how she wants them to start thinking about escaping Trumerica, and make love.

In the following month, they meet only in the streets, in a different public place each time, and never for more than ten minutes.

In the month after that, as they drift down a crowded sidewalk, not quite abreast and never looking at one another, they carry on a curious, intermittent conversation that flicks on and off like the beams of a lighthouse. It might get abruptly nipped into silence by the proximity of a Portal, then taken up again minutes later in the middle of a sentence, then awkwardly ended as they part at the agreed spot, then on the next day continuing almost without introduction.

One evening, walking down a street, there's a deafening roar, the ground heaves, and the air darkens. Liam finds himself lying on his side, bruised and terrified. A bomb must have exploded nearby. He becomes aware of Gemma's face right in front of his own. She's deathly white, as white as chalk. *She's dead!* He clasps her against him and finds that he's kissing a live warm face. There's some powdery stuff on her lips—both of them are coated with plaster.

There are evenings when they reach their meeting point, then walk past one another without a sign because the black van of a paramilitary patrol has just come around the corner, or a drone is hovering nearby.

It becomes increasingly difficult to find time to meet. Liam and Gemma are now working at least sixty hours per week, and their free days, varying according to the pressure of work, rarely coincide.

In evenings, Gemma spends an astonishing amount of time attending rallies, preparing grassroot campaigns for the presidential re-election, and creating PR for the upcoming March Against Renewable Energy that's being sponsored by the Trump International Hotel Doral, New Florida's most luxurious tennis, spa, and golf resort.

"It's camouflage," she says. "Also, if you keep the small rules, you can break the big ones."

They risk meeting again at the partly-destroyed elementary school. It's a blazing, white hot afternoon. The air is stagnant. In an old classroom with whiteboards covered in graffiti, they sit talking for hours on the dusty floor, taking it in turns to get up and glance through the broken windows to make sure that no one's coming.

Chapter 21

Gemma Sophie Dixon is thirty-eight years old, just like Liam, both being born in 1984. At high school, she won medals in gymnastics and was captain of the hockey team.

Her first love-affair was in her early twenties with an Organization member who later committed suicide to avoid arrest. "Lucky for me," Gemma added, "otherwise they'd have gotten my name out of him when he confessed."

Her first real job was working in the Communications Department for the Bureau of Memes, specializing in memes to counter unverified smears and purveyors of false information.

A Chief Brand Officer in the Bureau of Teledildonics and Human Reproduction noticed some of her billboards, and reassigned her to work in PornHub, the section of that bureau that churns out cheap pornography for Subs. In her years working there, she helped produce x-rated movies that were bought secretly by Subs who thought they were buying something illegal. One of her responsibilities was to come up with the titles, which was difficult because most of the stroke stories, kinky stuff, and smut vidlets that she worked on didn't have any plot. For porn geared more for a male audience, she wrote titles such as *Spanking Stories* and *Boobarella*. For porn that concentrated more on a female audience, she wrote titles such as *Smut for Smart Girls* and *Less Jackhammering, More Love*.

She was happy to see her time at PornHub come to an end. About ten years ago, she was reassigned to the Bureau of Facts, and has worked there ever since. She's part of a team that does advertising and PR for luxury hotels. Her main client account is Trumerica Plaza Hotels.

The only guests who can stay at these hotels are C-Suite members, all who happen to be megarich. Even if regular Organization members were permitted to rent a room, they'd never be able to afford it.

"The goal of life is to be happy," Gemma tells Liam one night. "But nearly every fucker in the Organization wants to stop you from being happy. So you break the rules any way you can to experience brief moments of peace or pleasure."

She hates the Trumerica Freedom Organization with a fervor. Yet, bizarrely to Liam, if an Organization doctrine doesn't touch her life, she has little interest in it. Nor is she particularly keen to talk about the Illuminati. Any kind of organized revolt against the Organization strikes her as insanely stupid and bound to fail.

He wonders how many people like her there are, people who view the Organization as something unalterable, not rebelling against its authority but simply evading it whenever possible, and daydreaming of one day escaping to one of the other superstates.

Chapter 22

Liam and Gemma don't discuss the possibility of marriage. It's too inconceivable. No committee would ever sanction such a marriage, not now that she's past her prime childbearing years.

"What was your ex-wife like?" Gemma asks one day, their third time at the abandoned school.

He tells her the story of being married to Chloe. Curiously, Gemma already knows the essential parts of it. She describes to him, almost as though she'd seen it herself, the stiffening of Chloe's body when he touched her, the way she seemed to be pushing away from him, even while embracing him.

"I could have endured it," he says, "if it hadn't been for one thing." He tells Gemma how his ex would lie there with her eyes shut, neither resisting nor co-operating but *submitting*. And he tells her how Chloe forced him to go through the frigid ceremony every week. How she'd even remind Liam of their weekly attempts at procreation as if it was something that had to be done diligently, like brushing your teeth, or dutifully, like agreeing with everything Ann Coulter says. How even though Chloe hated it, she would never stop doing it. How she used to call the sexual act—

"Our duty to the Organization," Gemma says promptly.

"How'd you know that?"

She raises her eyebrows.

Of course you know that phrase, he thinks.

Unlike Liam, she grasps the full meaning of the Organization's sexual puritanism. It's not merely that the sex instinct creates a world of its own that's outside the Organization's control and that therefore must be destroyed. What's more important is that depriving Organization members of meaningful sex induces hysteria, which can then be transformed into war-fever, conspicuous consumption, and leader-worship.

"Making love uses up energy," she says. "And afterwards, we don't care about anything. They can't tolerate us being happy. They want us to always be bursting with energy and hate. At Victory Rallies, all the screaming, cheering, and clapping we do is simply sex gone sour. If you're content inside yourself, why would you get riled up for Donald Trump and against people like Alexandria Ocasio-Cortez?"

Gemma explains to him that there's a direct connection between chastity and political orthodoxy. For how could the fear, hatred, and lunatic credulity that the Organization needs in its members be kept at the right pitch, except by suppressing some powerful instinct and using it as a driving force?

They do a similar trick with the instinct of parenthood, she tells him. The family can't actually be abolished. Indeed, parents are encouraged to be fond of their children, in almost the old-fashioned way. On the other hand, children are taught to spy on their parents and report their deviations from conservative values. The family has become, in effect, an extension of the Peace Police. It's a mechanism that surrounds millions of adults day and night with snitches who know them intimately.

Abruptly, his mind flashes back to his ex-wife. If Chloe hadn't been oblivious to his personal beliefs, she would have unquestionably denounced him to the police. But what really makes him think of her at this moment is the stifling heat of the afternoon. He begins telling Gemma of something that had happened—or, failed to happen—on another sweltering summer afternoon, over a decade ago.

A few months after he married Chloe, they went with the Constitutional Patriots Border Ops Team on a patrol. Somehow in the countryside, they got separated from their group, and found themselves near the edge of an old quarry. It was a sheer drop of about fifty feet, with boulders at the bottom.

Realizing they were lost, Chloe became uneasy. She wanted to retrace their steps, and started walking back.

Liam noticed some red and white sparkling star-shaped flowers growing in the cracks of the cliff beneath them. He had never seen that kind of flower before. He called Chloe to come and look at them.

Fretfully, she came back. Chloe even leaned over the cliff to see where he was pointing.

Behind her, he held her waist to steady her. The sun blazed down upon them. The sweat tickled his face.

They were completely alone. In a place like that, the possibility of a hidden microphone was low, and even if there was a microphone, it would only pick up sounds.

Gemma grins ear-to-ear. "Why didn't you push her? I would have."

He remains silent.

"Do you regret not pushing her?"

He nods.

They sit side by side on the dusty floor of a classroom that smells like it's been lived in by rats. He pulls her close to him. Her head rests on his shoulder.

"Actually, killing her would have made little difference," he says. "In this game we're playing, we can't win."

Gemma's shoulders wriggle in dissent. "I won't accept it as a law of nature that the individual is always defeated. In a way, sure, I realize that I'm doomed. That sooner or later the Peace Police will catch me. But with another part of my mind, I believe that it's possible to construct a secret world in which I can live as I choose. Darling, all you need is luck, cunning, and courage. Also, for the record, I totally disagree with you that there's no such thing as happiness. I disagree that victory is only possible in the distant future, long after we've been flamed. And I disagree that from the moment someone declares war on the Trumerica Freedom My Ass Organization, it's better to think of themselves as a corpse." Gemma giggles. "It seems that I disagree with you a lot."

"We are the dead," he says flatly.

"We're *not* dead yet."

"Not physically. Six months. A year. Five years maybe. Obviously we'll put it off as long as we can. But it makes very little difference."

"You're focusing on the wrong things. Why not focus on how we're going to get the fuck out of this hellhole? And, while we're at it, why not simply enjoy being alive? This is me, this is my hand, this is my thigh. I'm real! I'm alive!"

She twists around and presses her boobs against him. Her body pours some of its optimism and vigor into his body.

"Yeah, I like that," he says.

"Then stop talking about dying."

Chapter 23

Woodbridge Real Estate reclaimed the area that the deserted school was in. With plans of building new residences for Organization members on the site, they bulldozed the entire area.

In the ensuing weeks, Liam and Gemma haven't been able to arrange any romantic dates, as he likes to think of them. In preparation for the re-election next month, working hours at all bureaus have drastically increased. The enormous, complex preparations that the re-election entails are throwing extra work onto all Organization members.

During his long, oppressive days and nights at work, Liam often imagines Gemma, in some impossible future, as his wife. He envisions them walking together openly and without fear, and talking of pleasant trivialities. He pictures a home where they can be blissfully alone without feeling obliged to make love every time they meet.

Yet he can't visualize *where* their happy home is.

Gemma has talked about hijacking a Hydrofoil ferry and cruising it down to the former country of Cuba in Latineuropa. She's talked about stowing away on an oil tanker going to one of the former North African countries in Iranaqey. She's even talked somehow of escaping to the undesired region. But Liam can't seem to append anything to her wishful thinking. He can't really comprehend the possibility of ever leaving Trumerica. He feels it in his bones that he's going to die here.

The next time they see each other, Gemma reveals that she rented the room above Tiffany Murmidahn's antiques store. She tells Liam that it'll be a hiding place that'll truly be their own, indoors, and close by.

He thinks it's a brilliant idea. Deep down, though, they both know it's lunacy. It's almost as though they're intentionally stepping closer to their graves.

A few days later, Liam goes to the antiques store. As Tiffany and her adorable labradoodle puppy escort Liam to the internal stairs, she tells him that there are spare keys under the mat at the back entrance, if he ever wants to let himself in.

Upstairs, alone, he looks around the shabby little room. The pendulum inside the old-fashioned clock swings back and forth. It's seven-twenty. Gemma's arriving in ten minutes.

On a tiny table in the corner, he places his glass paperweight. It gleams softly out of the half-darkness. He adds water to the kettle so he can make her coffee. He puts two OxiQoxi tablets on the nightstand, in case she wants to check out for a while.

Outside, Liam hears music. At the window, he peeps through the curtain. In the sun-filled backyard below, an obese woman places plates on a table while a song blares through her kitchen window.

The song has haunted Lar-o-Maga Palm City for weeks. It's one of countless songs churned out for Subs by entertainment conglomerates. The lyrics and music of these songs are algorithmically composed, no human intervention necessary. They're performed by artists, boy bands, or girl groups who are carefully controlled, ensuring that everything from their clothes to their elaborately choreographed dancing is sanctioned by the Organization.

The huge woman below sings along with the dreadful song, somehow tunefully turning it into something pleasant to listen to. Her voice floats upward with the sweet summer air, charged with a sort of cheerful melancholy.

It strikes him as a curious fact that he's never heard a member of the Organization spontaneously singing. It would be a dangerous eccentricity, like talking to yourself.

Liam sits on the edge of the bed. *Idiot*, he thinks. *It's inconceivable that Gemma and I can come to this place for more than a few weeks without being caught.*

He thinks again of the Bureau of Morality. It's curious how that predetermined horror moves in and out of his consciousness. Whether he ponders it or ignores it, there it is, fixed in his future, an undeniable certainty waiting for him. When you're as liberal as Liam, you simply can't avoid meeting the interrogators, torturers, and re-educators in the Bureau of Morality. If you're clever or lucky, you might be able to postpone it for a while, but never pe rmanently.

The sound of someone running up the stairs—Gemma bursts into the room.

He steps forward and takes her in his arms.

She disengages herself. "Did you bring some of that disgusting Covfefe Coffee?"

He nods.

She smirks. "Fuck that. Look." Pulling out several items from her backpack, she smiles mischievously.

He picks up a can of Coca-Cola. It doesn't feel right in his hands. He inspects it—then turns it upside-down, untwists the bottom off it, and peers inside. "Sugar?" he asks hesitantly.

"*Real* sugar." She points to a container supposedly of sunblock. "That's real milk. But look! I'm really proud of this." She pulls out a brown paper bag. "It's—"

But there's no need to say what it is. The smell is already filling the room, a rich hot smell that seems like it's emanating from his early childhood.

"It's *real* coffee," he murmurs.

"Ta-dah." She holds her hands out wide then bows deeply, as if in front of an applauding crowd.

"How the hell did you get all of this?"

"It's all C-Suite stuff, darling. There's nothing those pigs don't have. Subs who are their servants and cleaners steal bits and pieces, then sell them on the black market." She points. "Hey, go over there, turn around, and don't look until I tell you."

Liam sits on the bed. His back to Gemma, he gazes abstractedly through the curtain. Down in the yard, an adult Sub hangs a paper machéd bull from a rope. Some Sub kids spin a blind-folded kid around several times. The kid then swings a stick at the multi-colored bull. But an adult pulls on one end of the rope, making the piñata move. The kid swings and misses several times and the onlookers laugh hysterically. Finally, the kid smacks it hard, breaking off a leg. Candy falls out and everyone scrambles to pick it up

.

"Ok," Gemma says.

He turns, expecting to see her naked. But she's wearing lingerie and makeup.

She must have slipped into a shop in a Sub neighborhood and bought lipstick, eye shadow, and mascara. Her lips are red, her cheeks rouged, her nose powdered. There's even a touch of something under her eyes to make them brighter. He has imagined a female Organization member wearing lingerie and makeup, but has never seen something like this ever.

As he takes her in his arms, a wave of synthetic violets floods his nostrils. *Perfume too*, he thinks. He kisses her neck for a moment, then takes a step back to drink her in.

She speaks slowly but with pure confidence. "I'm going to be a woman in this room, not an Organization member."

He removes his clothes and stands there, his arms by his sides, in all his vulnerability. It's his first time being unashamed of his naked body in her presence. Before now, he had been embarrassed of his ruined, weak body.

They move to the enormous bed. There are no sheets, but the tattered blanket they're on is smooth. Nowadays, you never see beds like this that are made for two people—only the Subs have them.

"It's probably full of bugs. But who cares?" Gemma says.

They have sex, then nod off to sleep.

Liam endures a nightmare that he's had several times a year ever since he was a teenager. He's standing in the middle of complete darkness, though he himself is somehow illuminated. Nearby, in the darkness all around him, there's something damp, dreadful, and unendurable. In the dream, there's a harsh sense of self-deception going on, because he feels that he somehow knows what's in fact waiting for him in the drenched, pitch blackness, it's just that he can't remember what it is. With a deadly effort, he's about to drag the wet, hideous thing into the open—in the same way that a victim who has been stabbed could pull out the knife that's wedged into their femoral artery and currently preventing them from bleeding out—but he always wakes up without discovering what it is.

Awake now, Liam tries not to move because Gemma is sleeping with her head in the crook of his arm. Some of her makeup has smudged onto his face. A yellow ray from the setting sun falls across their blanket.

He wonders whether in the abolished past it was common for a couple to lay in bed like this, naked, making love whenever they wanted, talking about anything that tickled their conversational fancy, not feeling any compulsion to get up. *Surely,* he thinks, *there was a time when that seemed ordinary.*

Gemma rubs her eyes, gets out of bed, and makes coffee. The aroma of real coffee brewing is so powerful and exciting that she shuts the window in case someone outside smells it and becomes inquisitive. Holding a piece of bread with jam on it, Gemma wanders about the room, skims through the bookcase, examines the pendulum swinging inside the glass cabinet of the clock, then plumps down in the ragged armchair. She takes a few deep breaths, picks up the glass paperweight from the table, then leaps onto the bed

"What is it, do you think?" she says, smiling.

He looks at it, fascinated as always by the soft, rain-watery appearance of the glass. "It's a chunk of history that they've forgotten to alter. It's a message from over fifty years ago …" He doesn't finish the sentence.

"And that poster." She nods at the opposite wall. "Do you think that's also more than fifty years old?"

"Who knows?" he says whimsically.

She goes over to look at it. "I've seen that building before … somewhere."

"It's a futuristic theme park, part entertainment, part utopian society. Well, it used to be. It was called EPCOT Center." The first half of the poem that Tiffany Murmidahn recited comes back into his head. He recites it nostalgically. "'Beware my friend, as you pass by. As you are now, so once was I' …"

She completes the second half of the poem. "'As I am now, so you must be. Prepare for death and follow me.'"

He's astonished. "How do you know that?"

"My grandfather would say it to me as a kid. He was a morbid son-of-a-bitch. I was eight when he disappeared." She goes to the sink. "We better leave soon." She starts washing off her makeup.

The room is darkening. Liam turns over toward the last of the light and lays gazing into the paperweight. The inexhaustibly interesting thing isn't the fragment of coral but the interior of the glass itself. There's such a depth of it, and yet it's almost as transparent as air. It's as though the surface of the glass is the arch of the sky, enclosing a miniature world within it. He has the feeling that he's inside it, along with the bed and the table, and the clock and the poster of EPCOT Center. The paperweight is the room they're in, and the coral is his and Gemma's lives, fixed in a sort of blissful eternity.

Chapter 24

One day, Shelly Adelsan doesn't show up for work. A few thoughtless people comment on her absence.

The next day, the campaign promise implementation specialist is again missing from work. On that day, nobody mentions her.

On the third day, Liam goes to the lobby of the Information Security Department to look at the Portals displaying upcoming meetings of various groups, including the Winning the War on Opioids Task Force, the Standing with the Trumerican State of Israel Committee, and the Holding Korchinpan Accountable Commission. For several years, Shelly Adelsan's name had always appeared as the chairwoman of two of those groups. Today, however, her name doesn't appear on the notices for either of their upcoming m eetings.

Shelly Adelsan no longer exists.

She never existed.

Chapter 25

Preparations for the re-election are in full swing, and all Organization staff are working overtime. Countless events and tasks are happening. Thousands of Save Trumerica rallies will be happening throughout the country. There'll be military parades, billboards, documentaries, Portal vidlets. Stands to be erected, statues built, slogans coined, songs manufactured, rumors circulated, photos faked.

Gemma Dixon's team in the Press Release Department have temporarily stopped writing Trumpian praise releases and are now dedicating all of their energy writing campaign materials about business crimes perpetrated by Latineuropa and wartime atrocities committed by Iranaqey and Korchinpan. Liam, in addition to his regular work, spends hours every day scrolling through old versions of tweets, news articles, and broadcasts, altering and embellishing details that are to be quoted in speeches.

Inside the Bureau of Facts, the windowless, air-conditioned rooms keep their normal temperature. But outside, the weather is baking hot, the pavements scorch your feet, and the putrid stench of pollution and garbage is hellacious.

Late at night, when crowds of rowdy Subs roam the streets, the city has a curiously fevered air. Assassinations, kidnappings, and spree shootings are occurring more often than ever. Sometimes, in the far distance, there are enormous explosions that could be suicide bombings, proxy bombings, or drone attacks, yet no one seems to know for sure. One attack targeted a cinema, burying over one hundred victims in the ruins. Another attack, probably launched from a submarine off the coast, blew a playground—and several dozen children—to pieces.

One of this re-election's theme songs, performed by the Trumerica Freedom Kids, often streams out of Portals. The win song, as it's nicknamed, has a savage, barking rhythm that can't exactly be called music, but resembles the beating of a drum. At rallies, when thousands of voices sing it and stomp their feet, it's terrifying. Subs have taken a fancy to it. Down the hall, the Tamariz kids blare it at all hours of the night and day.

Squads of volunteers, many of them organized by husband and wife Graham and Evelyn Tamariz, are preparing the neighborhood for the re-election.

Graham boasts that their apartment building alone will be flying at least one hundred flags from its roof, which he hopes will be more than any other apartment building in the neighborhood. In his native element, he's happy as a pig in shit. He's everywhere at once, pushing, pulling, sawing, hammering, encouraging people, always giving off what seems an inexhaustible supply of acrid-smelling sweat.

A new advertising campaign has suddenly appeared all over Lar-o-Maga Palm City. Each billboard shows slightly different versions of Iranaqeyian and Korchinpanians soldiers striding forward with expressionless faces, big black boots, and submachine guns pointing from their hips. Operating just like Trufamily posters, from whatever angle you look at these billboards, the muzzle of the guns point straight at you. The billboards are on almost every wall, even outnumbering the portraits of Trufamily members.

The Subs, sometimes somewhat apathetic about the war, are being lashed into one of their periodic frenzies of patriotism. There are many angry demonstrations, Alexandria Ocasio-Cortez is burned in effigy, and shops are looted in the turmoil. Then a rumor flies around that spies are using radar, GPS, and red laser beams to control the missiles, fired from Iranaqeyian gunboats hundreds of miles off Trumerica's shore. A family suspected of being foreigners has their house set on fire. A 9-year-old girl runs out of the house, is handcuffed, pepper-sprayed in the eyes, and forced into a squad car. The mother and father die in the flames.

Chapter 26

In the room over Tiffany Murmidahn's shop, Gemma and Liam lay side by side naked on the bed under the open window. The bugs have multiplied hideously in the heat, but the two lovebirds don't mind. Dirty or clean, the room is paradise.

Over the next month, they meet six times. Each time, as soon as they arrive, they spray everything with Wondercide bought on the black market, rip off their clothes, and make love with sweating bodies, then fall asleep and wake to find that the bugs have rallied for a counter-attack.

Liam breaks his habit of drinking vodka at all hours. He's lost the need for it. He feels stronger. The pain, itching, and bleeding of his hemorrhoids have subsided. His fits of coughing in the morning have subsided. Life has ceased to be intolerable, and he no longer has impulses to shout obscenities at the morons and sycophants on Portals.

Now that he and Gemma have a secure hiding place, it doesn't even seem that much of an inconvenience that they can only meet infrequently for a couple of hours at a time. *What matters is that the room over the antiques shop exists*, Liam thinks. *To know that it's there, sacrosanct, is almost the same as being in it. The room is a world, a pocket of the past where extinct animals can walk, talk, and fuck.*

He usually stops to talk with the shop owner and pet her puppy for a few minutes on his way upstairs. The old woman seems never to go outside, yet also has barely any customers. Tiffany leads a ghostlike existence between the small, dark shop, and an even smaller back kitchen where she prepares meals and which contains, among other things, an old record player. *I'm glad she has her little furry friend*, he thinks.

She seems glad for the opportunity to talk. Wandering about her worthless stock, with her thick glasses and bowed shoulders, she has the vague air of being a hoarder, rather than an antiques dealer. With enthusiasm, she fingers this or that piece of junk—mismatched dishware, shabby teddy bears, board games, lacquered snuffboxes, vintage canning jars, random jewelry, old bike helmets, a china horse with a broken leg—sometimes suggesting that Liam should buy it, sometimes merely inviting him to admire it. To talk with her is like listening to the pleasing tinkling of a music box.

Liam and Gemma know that what they're doing now can't last long. There are times when the fact of impending death seems as palpable as the bed they're laying on, and they cling together with a sort of despairing sensuality, like two inmates on death row, grasping at their last morsels of pleasure. Yet there are also times when they entertain the illusion not only of safety but of permanence. So long as they're in this room, they sometimes feel that no harm will come to them.

Though the room is a sanctuary, Liam still gazes into the heart of the paperweight, longing to get inside that glassy world, dreaming about how, once inside it, time would pause.

Often, they daydream of escape. Their luck would hold indefinitely, and they'd carry on their love affair, just like this, for the rest of their lives. Or they'd commit suicide together. Or they'd disappear, alter themselves out of recognition, learn to speak with Sub accents, get jobs in a factory, and live out their lives undetected in a part of some city with no Portals, no drones, no Peace Police.

They both know it's all nonsense. In reality, there's no escape. Even the one plan that is tenable and doable—suicide—they have no intention of carrying out. To persevere, day to day, week to week, enduring a present that has no future, seems an unconquerable instinct, just as one's lungs will always draw the next breath so long as there's air available. But Liam feels like they're somehow trapped underwater, that there's no air anywhere, and there's still an uncontrollable urge to breathe ...

Sometimes, too, Liam talks about rebelling against the Trumerica Freedom Organization, but with no idea of how to take the first step. Even if the Illuminati is real, there's still the difficulty of finding it.

He tells Gemma of the strange intimacy he has with Brett Brannan, and of the impulse he sometimes feels to walk up to Brannan, reveal that he's an enemy of the Organization, and request his help. Curiously, this doesn't strike her as a rash thing to do. She's accustomed to judging people by their faces. It seems natural to her that Liam believes that Brannan is trustworthy on the strength of a single glance. Moreover, she takes it for granted that nearly everyone secretly hates the Organization and would break their rules if they could.

Yet she refuses to believe that widespread, organized opposition exists. The tales about Alexandria Ocasio-Cortez, Jeff Bezos, Robert Mueller, and their underground army, Gemma says, are simply misinformation that the Organization invented for its own purposes, forcing all of us to pretend to believe in them. Hundreds of times, at Organization rallies, she shouts at the top of her lungs for the execution of people she's never heard of before, people she doubts committed the crimes they've been accused of.

It probably doesn't matter, Liam thinks, *because the Organization is invincible. It will always exist, and it will always be the same. You can only rebel against it by secret disobedience or, at most, by isolated acts of violence such as killing a conservative, blowing something up, or engaging in some kind of economic warfare.*

In many ways, Gemma's far more intelligent than Liam, and far less susceptible to Organization propaganda. Once, when he mentions the wars with Iranaqey and Korchinpan, she startles him by saying casually that, in her opinion, she doubts that either the military wars or the trade wars are really happening. The bombs that fall daily on Lar-o-Maga Palm City are probably fired by our own military-industrial complex, just to keep Trumericans frightened. That idea has never occurred to him. She also stirs a sort of envy in him by telling him that, during Victory Rallies, her great difficulty is to avoid laughing.

Ultimately though, she pretty much only questions the teachings of the Organization when they infringe upon her own life. Often she's ready to accept the official mythology, simply because the difference between truth and falsehood isn't, in a practical sense, important to her. She believes, for instance, that Donald Trump personally killed Osama bin Laden. Yet when Liam talks about how Osama bin Laden was alive during the Second Trumerican Civil War, the fact strikes her as irrelevant. After all, who cares who killed Osama bin Laden and when it happened?

The clincher though, is his shock when he discovers, via some random remark, that she doesn't remember how in 2020, Trumerica had been engaged in both a military war and a trade war with Latineuropa, and was economically aligned with Iranaqey and Korchinpan. Apparently, she hadn't noticed that the names of our enemies and partners had flip-flopped.

"I thought we'd always been at war with Iranaqey and Korchinpan," she says vaguely. "Those fucking economic terrorists," she adds.

Her comments frighten him a little. A murky memory of the assassination of the leader of al-Qaeda is one thing. But the switchover in wars happened only four years ago, and is therefore a much bigger deal. He argues with her about it for a while. She eventually dimly recalls that at one time Latineuropa was our enemy. But the issue still strikes her as unimportant. "Who cares?" she says impatiently. "It's all war, all the time. Besides, the news is all lies anyway."

Sometimes he talks with her about the forgeries he commits working for the Information Security Department. Such things don't horrify her. She doesn't feel the abyss opening beneath her feet at the thought of lies becoming truths.

He tells her of the photos of Julian Assange, Emma González, and Jeff Sessions appearing in an un-updated version of a digibook, *A Day in the Life of Trumerica*. He tells her how those photos, ten years later, proved that what the authorities subsequently said about those three being Iranaqeyian was entirely made-up.

Gemma couldn't care less. "Were they friends of yours?" she asks.

He wonders if she's not grasping the point of his story. "No, I never knew them. They were C-Suite members."

"People are being killed off all the time. Don't worry about it."

"But it was an exceptional case," he says. "It wasn't just three people being killed. Do you realize that the past, starting from yesterday, has been actually abolished? If it survives anywhere, it's in a few solid objects with no words attached to them, like that lump of glass and coral there. Already we know barely anything about how Trump came to power, let alone the years before the Third Trumerican Civil War. All records have been destroyed or falsified. All books and news articles have been burned, deleted, or rewritten. All pictures and videos have been erased, photoshopped, or deepfaked. And this continues every day. History has stopped. Nothing exists except an endless present in which the Trumerica Freedom Organization is always right."

Of course, he thinks, *I know that the past is falsified. But I wouldn't be able to prove it to anyone else.* He considers telling her this. But would it convince her any more if he told her that the only evidence is inside his own mind, and he doesn't know with any certainty that any other human being shares his memories? He doubts it.

After a long uncomfortable pause in which she just waits for him to speak, he eventually continues. "Just in that one instance, in my whole life, when I was looking on my Portal at an original copy of that digibook, I had actual evidence *after* the event—years after it."

"So what did you do?"

"Well ... nothing. I deleted it. But if the same thing happened today, I'd at least try to do something with it."

"I wouldn't," Gemma says. "I'll take risks. But only for something worthwhile. If you had kept it, what could you have done with it?"

"If I'd shown it to someone"—he thinks of some of the employees who work at desks nearby him—"it might have stirred a few doubts in them. It's hard to believe that we can fix anything in our own lifetime. But it just feels good to imagine pockets of resistance springing up here and there—people coming together, wanting change, even leaving a few records behind so that the next generations can carry on where we left off."

"I'm not interested in the next generation, darling." She smiles, pauses, then grabs his cock. "I'm interested in *us*."

"You're still a rebel," he says.

"Only from the waist down," she adds, laughing and flinging her arms around him.

An hour later, he again talks about the Trufamily Forty-Five's belief system, the changeability of the past, and the denial of objective reality, and she quickly becomes bored.

"I try not to pay any attention to any of that," she says. "You know it's all crap, so why let it bring you down?"

If he persists in talking about such subjects, she has a disconcerting habit of falling asleep. She's one of those people who can sleep at any hour and in any position.

Talking with her, he realizes how easy it is to present an appearance of patriotism while having no grasp of what orthodoxy means. In a way, the worldview of the Organization imposes itself most successfully on people incapable of understanding it, or in Gemma's case, uninterested in exploring it too deeply. Trump, the Trufamily Forty-Five, and members of the C-Suite can force Subs and regular Organization members to accept the most flagrant violations of reality, because they never fully grasp the enormity of what's being demanded of them, and aren't sufficiently interested to notice what's really happening. By lack of understanding, they remain sane.

Chapter 27

Walking down a hallway at the bureau, Liam senses someone behind him. The person coughs, evidently as a prelude to speaking. Liam stops abruptly and turns.

It is Chief Operating Officer Brett Brannan.

At last they're face to face. Liam's heart pounds and he suppresses an impulse to run away. He feels incapable of speaking.

Brannan lays a friendly hand for a moment on Liam's arm, so that the two of them are now walking side by side.

"I've been hoping for a chance to talk with you," he says. He speaks with the peculiar grave courtesy that differentiates him from the majority of other C-Suite members. "The other day, I read an article about Corporal Helseth in the *Miami Truth Times*. Fascinating. He was such an amazing man. I wanted to learn more about him, so I poked around and found out that you did some of the original ... research ... on him."

Liam is taken aback. *Why did Brannan pause around the word* research? *Is he tacitly acknowledging that he knows that I invented Corporal Helseth?*

"It got me thinking," Brannan continues. "I'm curious, do you take much interest in GreatSpeak?"

Liam recovers part of his composure. "Yes, I'm interested. But it's not my area of expertise."

"I think you might benefit from learning a bit more about it," Brannan says, as they continue strolling down the hallway. "And that's not only my own opinion. A friend of yours who was an expert in GreatSpeak also thought that. Her name slips my memory at the moment."

Again Liam's heart stirs painfully. Brannan is definitely referring to Shelly Adelsan. But Shelly isn't only dead, she's abolished. Any identifiable reference to a non-person like her is mortally dangerous. Brannan's remark must be a signal. By sharing this small act of liberalism, he's turning the two into accomplices.

Brannan stops walking. With the disarming friendliness that he always manages to put into the gesture, he adjusts his glasses on his nose. Then he continues walking and talking. "Next month, a revised edition of *The Freedom Quotient: Why Liberty Lovers Embrace the Creative Destruction of a Benevolent Authoritarian* will come out. Have you read the original version?"

Liam nods. "Scott Pruitt's essay on the disgusting word-war against the coal industry is probably my favorite," he says like an automation.

"Though you have to admit, Sheryl Sandberg's essay, the one about how women can have it all if they just lean in, is also illuminating." Brannan tilts his head ever so slightly. "I've got an advance copy of the next edition. It contains a new essay by the President's wife on the art of quiet patriotism. Would you perhaps like to read that new essay by Hope Hicks Trump? I think it'll provide you with some more insight into Corporal Helseth."

"Sure," Liam says, glimpsing where this might be heading.

Brannan stops directly in front of a Portal. "You'll have to read it on one of my secure Portals at my home. How about you come over sometime?" He writes his address on a business card, and hands it to Liam.

If a member of the Peace Police is watching them via the Portal, they'd be able to see everything.

"I'm home most evenings," Brannan adds, then walks off.

There's only one meaning that this encounter can possibly have—Brannan contrived it to tell Liam his address. This was necessary because, except by direct enquiry, it's never possible to discover where anyone lives.

Perhaps there's a message concealed in the new essay, Liam thinks. *At any rate, one thing is certain. The conspiracy that I've dreamed of exists, and I just touched the outer edge of it.*

If I can join it, maybe they can help me—for the good of humankind—assassinate Donald Trump.

Sooner or later, he'll comply with Brannan's summons. What's starting to happen is the culmination of a process that began years ago. The first step was a secret, involuntary thought. The second was opening the diary. He had moved from thoughts to words. Soon, he'll go from words to actions. The second last step will happen in the Bureau of Morality at the hands of torturers. The last step will be his rescuing. He accepts that.

The end is contained in the beginning. But this foretaste of death is still frightening. It's like being a little less alive. Even when he spoke with Brannan, when the meaning of his words finally sunk in, a chilly shuddering feeling possessed Liam's body, and he had the sensation of stepping into a muddy grave dug just for him.

Chapter 28

Liam remembers last glimpsing his mother before she disappeared, approximately thirty years ago. He's not certain of the date, though he guesses he was maybe around nine years old when it all happened.

He remembers the apocalyptic scenes and mass hysteria. The sheltering in basements during the bombings. The schools and hospitals pummeled into dust. The electricity only working a few hours each day. The long queues outside supermarkets. The sound of machine gun fire in the distance. The metal gas canisters filled with nails and fired from homemade howitzers.

Ever since his father was executed by drowning in the North Atlantic Ocean, his mother occasionally became depressed. For hours at a time, she'd sit almost immobile on the bed, feeding his young, sick sister. Sometimes his mom would hold Liam in her arms for a long time without saying anything. He was aware, despite his youthfulness and selfishness, that she was waiting for something that she knew was coming.

He remembers their apartment, which consisted entirely of one small, dark room and a smelly bathroom.

He remembers spending hours every week scrounging through trash at a nearby landfill. Always hoping to find edible food. Always sifting through electronic components, broken glass, and medical waste, searching for something to scavenge and sell. Always fearful of being trapped under a garbage landslide and suffocating to death.

At meals, he'd nag his mother about why she couldn't get more food. He'd shout and complain. She'd plead with him to be less selfish and to remember that his sister was sick and also needed food. But it was no use. His mom often gave him more than his share, but he'd cry out with rage when she stopped serving him. He'd try to wrench the spoon or spatula out of her hands. He'd grab food off his sister's plate. He knew that he was starving the two of them. But he didn't care. He felt that he had a right to their food, that his savage hunger justified him.

One day, his mom brought home a Toblerone. That brand of chocolate bar was no longer allowed to be imported into Trumerica, along with other various banned food and drink made by foreign conglomerates, including Nestlé, Anheuser-Busch, Unilever, and Danone. His mom bought the last Toblerone on the supermarket shelf.

Liam hadn't eaten a piece of chocolate in over a year. He remembers the distinctive shape of the chocolate bar, its triangular prisms reminding him of mountains.

Suddenly, Liam demanded that he should have the whole bar. His mother told him not to be greedy. They argued. He whined, bargained. His sister, clinging to their mom, looked at him with mournful eyes. In the end, his mother gave him three-quarters of the chocolate. She gave the other quarter to his sister. The little girl looked at it, perhaps not knowing what it was.

Liam snatched the chocolate out of her hand and dashed for the door. His mother yelled. He stopped. Even then he thought about the unknowable dreaded thing, though he had no idea what was on the verge of happening. His sister wailed. His mother drew her close, pressing the girl's face against her chest. Something in the gesture told him that his sister was dying. He slammed their front door behind him and sprinted down the stairs.

After devouring the chocolate, he felt ashamed and walked around the neighborhood until hunger drove him home. When he went back, his mother and sister were gone. Nothing had been taken from their apartment. He never saw them again. To this day, he doesn't know if they're alive or dead. It's possible that his mother had been sent to a labor camp or to Gitmo. It's possible that his sister had been moved to one of the shelters for homeless children that had grown up as a result of the war, or simply left somewhere t o die.

His mother had embodied a kind of long gone purity. The standards that she obeyed were private ones. Her feelings were her own, and couldn't be altered from outside. It wouldn't have occurred to his mom that an action that ended up being ineffective would therefore also be meaningless. If you loved someone, you loved them, and when you had nothing else to give, you still gave them love.

After he stole the chocolate and started dashing out of the house, he noticed that his mom hugged his sister. That act changed nothing, it didn't produce more chocolate, it didn't prevent their capture or deaths. But it seemed natural for her to do it.

He remembers the war documentary he watched a while ago. In it, the illegal immigrant mother at the border wall had also covered her children with her fat arms, which was no more use against the bullets than a sheet of paper.

The terrible thing that the Organization has achieved, Liam thinks, *is to persuade you that your impulses and feelings are meaningless. In the vice of the Organization, what you feel or don't feel, what you do or don't do, ultimately makes no difference. Whatever happens, you still vanish. You're lifted clean out of the stream of history.*

Generations ago, people were governed by private loyalties that they didn't question. What mattered were individual relationships. For those who lived then, a completely helpless gesture, an embrace, a tear, a word spoken to someone dying—it all had inherent v alue.

The Subs, it suddenly occurs to Liam, *have remained in that condition. Their loyalty to the Organization is fleeting. Their loyalty to their friends and family is unflinching.*

For the first time in his life, he doesn't despise the Subs or think of them merely as an inert force that one day will spring to life and regenerate the world.

The Subs have stayed human. They haven't hardened inside. They've held onto the emotions that I must re-learn by conscious effort.

And in thinking this, he remembers, without apparent relevance, how a few weeks ago he had kicked a severed hand into the gutter as though it had been a piece of trash.

An hour later, Gemma joins him at their secret hideaway room above the antiques store.

They hug and kiss hello.

Liam doesn't ask her about her day or how she's doing. "The Subs are human beings," he says excitedly. "*We* aren't human."

Unfazed by his non sequitur, she just smiles, giggles, and gives him an understanding, yet somewhat patronizing pat on the shoulder.

Without explaining what he just said, he jumps to the next idea. "Has it ever occurred to you that the best thing for us to do, before it's too late, is to walk out of here and never see each other again?"

"Of course I've considered that, darling. Many times." She takes off her shoes and red cap.

"One day, our luck will run out," he says. "We'll—"

"So far, I've been pretty fucking good at staying alive." She walks to the kitchenette.

"We might be together for another six months. A year maybe. In the end, we'll certainly be apart. Do you realize how utterly alone we're going to be? When they get us, there'll be nothing we can do for each other. Nothing we do or don't do, say or don't say—nothing will delay our deaths for even five minutes. Neither of us will even know whether the other is alive or dead. We'll be totally powerless. The one thing that matters is that we don't betray each other, although even that can't make the slightest difference."

"If you mean confessing, we'll do that," she says, preparing herself some coffee. "Everybody always confesses. You can't help it. They torture you. And not just physical and psychological torture, but also by medical and pharmacological torture."

"I don't mean confessing. Confession isn't betrayal. What we tell them doesn't matter. Only feelings matter. If they can stop us loving each other—that would be the real betrayal."

She thinks it over. "That's the one thing they can't do," she says finally. "They can make us say anything. But they can't make us believe it. They can't get inside us."

"You're right," he says a little more hopefully. "If we stay human inside, and even if our feelings of love don't change anything, we've beaten them."

He thinks of the onslaught of misinformation and disinformation via daily Victory Rallies. He thinks of the millions of Portals with their never-sleeping ears and eyes. He thinks of the Peace Police who can spy upon you at any time. But even with all of their cleverness, they still haven't cracked the secret of finding out what another human being is feeling deep down at their innermost core.

Sure, inside the Bureau of Morality, they can subject us to solitary confinement, beatings, rape, and mock executions, and our interrogators can uncover essentially everything about us. But even if they're torturing us, we can stay human. We can still outwit them. We can hide from them our love for each other, which they'll never be able to change.

117

Chapter 29

For the first time in their lives, Liam and Gemma walk into Flamingo Pine Park, the closed housing estate on prime New Florida property where C-Suite members live. The whole atmosphere of this gated neighborhood is intimidating. The richness and spaciousness of everything. The chirping birds. The unfamiliar smells of flora and fauna. Also, everything is impeccably clean, which shocks Liam, who can't ever remember seeing an area in a city that wasn't filled with trash.

Although Liam has a valid pretext for coming here, he's haunted at every step by the fear that one of the paramilitary personnel stationed at regular intervals will demand to know what he and Gemma are doing here. If that happens, he'll show them Brett Brannan's business card with his address handwritten on it.

For the most part, only employees who work for C-Suite members step foot in these private security estates. Only rarely would low-level Organization members like Liam and Gemma ever enter one their neighborhoods, let alone see inside one of their mansions. He assumes that the security guards aren't questioning and frisking them because they think they're employees of a C-Suite member.

They arrive out front of Brannan's villa. The vastness of the property's border wall starkly reminds Liam that it's absolutely insane for them to come here.

The entryway is flanked by sand-colored stone pilasters. As they approach, the elaborately designed wrought iron gate silently opens.

A guard in a surgical mask aims an infrared thermometer at Gemma. The red dot hits her forehead. "35 degrees Celsius," the guard says. He aims the beam onto Liam's forehead. "36 degrees Celsius." He waves them in.

Inside the compound, they walk past guard shacks with mirrored-windows, a tennis court, luxurious sculptures, bronze fountains, and gorgeous landscaped pathways.

As they pass through a dense thicket of trees, the mansion comes into view. A woman in a suit stands at the top of the front steps. She holds open a gigantic arched door with beveled glass. She's tall with long, dark hair. Her diamond-shaped face is expressionless.

She leads them down a long carpeted passage. Again, everything is exquisitely clean, and Liam can't help remembering that pretty much every other hallway he's ever walked down had grimy walls.

They enter an elevator. The tall woman doesn't touch anything. They move silently and rapidly upward, then exit into a massive room.

There's Brett Brannan!

The room is softly lit. There are numerous Portals on the walls. At the far end of the room, Brannan sits at a table under a green-shaded lamp, with mini-Portals propped on either side of him. He's wearing an immaculately tailored blue suit with a sharp red tie. As Liam and Gemma approach slowly, he doesn't look up. The opulence of the carpet gives Liam the impression of treading on velvet.

The tall woman waits behind them near a chess set made of black and white diamonds. Liam's heart thumps so hard that he doubts he'll be able to speak.

Brannan stares intently into one of the mini-Portals. His face appears both formidable and intelligent. For perhaps twenty seconds he sits without stirring. Then he pulls a microphone toward him and dictates something into the Sirimic that his guests can't hear.

He rises from his chair and walks across the soundless carpet toward one of the walls. Some of the official atmosphere seems to have fallen away from him. But his expression is grimmer than usual, as though he isn't pleased at being disturbed. The dread that Liam already feels is suddenly shot through by a streak of embarrassment. It's quite possible that he's simply made a massive stupid mistake.

I don't have any evidence that Brannan is some kind of political conspirator, Liam thinks. *Nothing but a flash of the eyes and an ambiguous comment. Beyond that, only my secret imaginings, founded on a dream. I can't even fall back on the pretense that I came here to read that new essay about GreatSpeak—because Gemma's presence would be impossible to explain.*

At the wall, Brannan touches a control panel. There are several sharp snaps as all the Portals in the room simultaneously power down.

Gemma utters a squeak of surprise.

119

Brannan walks toward his guests.

Even in the midst of his terror, Liam is too stunned to hold his tongue. "You can turn them off!"

Brannan nods. "We have that privilege."

Standing now directly in front of his guests, Brannan's solid form towers over them. The expression on his face is still indecipherable. It's as if he's sternly waiting for one of them to speak, but about what? Nobody says anything. After the switching off of the Portals, the room seems deadly silent. The seconds march past, enormous.

Suddenly Brannan's grim face breaks down into what might be the start of a smile. "Will I say it, or will one of you?" He resettles his glasses on his nose.

Liam points wildly around the huge room. "They're really off?"

Brannan nods again. "We're unsurveilled."

Gemma steps forward. "What about her?" she asks, not even bothering to motion to the tall woman.

"She's one of us," Brannan says warmly. "Join us, Kayleigh."

The tall woman comes over now, carrying a tray with glasses and a decanter filled with dark-red liquid.

Everyone takes a seat at a large elegant round table.

Liam regards Kayleigh suspiciously out of the corner of his eye, then speaks to Brannan. "We believe that there's some kind of deep state working against the Trumerica Freedom Organization, interfering with the President's agenda."

"And we think you're involved in it," Gemma says.

"We're enemies of the Organization," Liam says.

Gemma nods. "We reject the beliefs of the Trufamily Forty-Five."

Expressionlessly, Brannan pours the dark-red liquid into four glasses.

The sour-sweet aroma arouses in Liam dim memories of something experienced long ago.

Gemma picks up her glass and sniffs with curiosity.

"It's wine," Kayleigh says with a faint smile. "Unfortunately for you guys, we don't distribute it to regular members."

Brannan raises his glass. "Let's begin with a toast."

Liam and Kayleigh pick up their glasses.

"To our leader," Brannan says loudly and enthusiastically. "Alexandria Ocasio-Cortez!"

Everyone drinks.

Liam smiles giddily. "So AOC is *real*?" he says excitedly. "She's—"

"She's alive. Where, we don't know."

Liam takes another sip. He has faint memories about wine. Like the glass paperweight, wine belongs to the vanished, romantic past that he likes to daydream about. For some reason he always thought it would taste intensely sweet. But when he sips it, it's disappointing. The truth is, after years of drinking vodka, he can barely taste the wine. "And the conspiracy?" He puts the glass on the table. "It's real? It's not just propaganda invented by the regime?"

"The Illuminati is real." Brannan looks at his watch. "It's unwise even for C-Suite members to turn off Portals for too long. So, time is of the essence. Keyleigh and I have some questions. Generally, what are you two prepared to do?"

"Anything I'm capable of," Liam says.

Gemma frowns. "Before I pledge allegiance to some shadowy secret society, I need to hear more about it."

Brannan leans back slightly. "Other than learning that the Illuminati exists, you won't learn much more about it. You'll have to make a choice about joining—or not—based on very limited information." He leans in again. "Are you prepared to sacrifice your lives?" he asks.

"Yes," Liam says.

"It depends," Gemma says.

"Are you prepared to commit murder?" Brannan asks.

"Yes," Liam says.

Gemma shrugs. "Not sure yet."

"If, for example, it would somehow serve our interests to throw acid in a kid's face—are you prepared to do that?"

"If that's what it takes," Liam says.

"Absolutely not," Gemma says.

"Would you betray Trumerica to another superstate?" Brannan asks.

Liam feels that Brannan somehow already knows what their answers are going to be. "Yes," he says.

"Definitely," Gemma says.

"Would you launch a rocket-propelled improvised explosive device at a Trumerican military base, knowing it would also probably kill hundreds of innocent civilians?"

"Yes," Liam says.

"It depends if the innocent victims are Subs, regular Organization members, or *members of the C-Suite*"—Gemma says her last words with relish.

Brannan smiles.

However earnest he is, Liam feels that Brannan has nothing of the single-mindedness that belongs to a fanatic. When he speaks of mass murder, it's with a faint air of inevitability. *This is what we have to do,* his voice seems to say. *But this isn't what we'll be doing when life's worth living again.*

A wave of admiration flows out from Liam toward Brannan. When he looks at Brannan's powerful shoulders and his blunt-featured face, so ugly and yet so civilized, it's impossible to believe that he can be defeated. There's no stratagem that he isn't equal to. No danger that he hasn't contemplated. No enemy that he can't vanquish.

"Are you prepared to lose your identities and live out the rest of your lives as Subs?"

"Yes," Liam says.

"I don't see how that'd be possible," Gemma says. "So I'd need to hear more about it before I give an answer."

Kayleigh lifts her hands up to her face. "We can give you new faces," she says. "We can change the sound of your voices. Our surgeons can alter people beyond recognition. Sometimes, to make it seem believable that someone was once a soldier, we even amputate a limb."

Liam again looks at Kayleigh's face. There are no scars that he can see.

"If we ordered you to commit suicide, would you?" Brannan asks.

"Yes," Liam says.

"I haven't survived this long to just chicken out," Gemma says.

Brannan breathes in deeply and exhales. "Are you prepared to separate and never see each other again?"

"No," Gemma says loudly.

For a moment, Liam feels like he's lost the ability to speak. He works over the answers in his mind. *Yes—no—yes—maybe.* "No," he says finally. Until he spoke, he didn't know what he was going to say.

"Thank you both for your honesty," Brannan says. "It's necessary for us to know everything." He pauses for a moment. "So, with the Illuminati, what exactly do you want to achieve?"

"I ..." Liam stammers "I ... want to kill Donald Trump."

"Wonderful," Kayleigh says. She walks over to a big Portal and grabs it by the edges.

For a second, Liam thinks she's going to rip the Portal off the wall and throw it onto the floor.

Kayleigh pulls to Portal toward her, then swivels it to the side. Behind it is a secret compartment filled with ammunition, night vision goggles, ropes, grappling hooks, and crossbows.

"I think we can work with that," the tall woman says, as she returns the Portal to its normal place. "But we're not all there yet." She looks directly at Gemma. Then Kayleigh walks toward a massive window that overlooks Brannan's compound. "If you join us," she says, hands clasped behind her back, facing outside, "you'll have to understand a few t hings."

For a moment, Liam doesn't know if Kayleigh's speaking to both of them or just Gemma.

"You'll always be fighting completely in the dark," Kayleigh continues, her back still facing them. "As Brett said, the Illuminati exists. But we can't tell you whether we have one thousand members, or ten million. Even we don't know. You'll have three or four contacts who will be renewed from time to time when we relocate them or they're captured. As Brett is your first contact, it will be preserved. When you receive orders, they'll usually come from him, but sometimes via me, and you'll obey them, without knowing why."

Brannan nods.

Kayleigh turns around and faces them. "When you're caught, you'll confess." She gestures vaguely. "That's unavoidable. But you won't possess any valuable information worthy of confessing, other than your beliefs and actions. For instance, you won't be able to betray more than a handful of people. Even when you tell the Peace Police about me and Brett, you won't betray us—because nobody will ever be able to prove that this conversation ever happened. Or by then we'll be dead, or different people. We've been Kayleigh and Brett for a long time." She smiles at her colleague. "That said, it's important that you know this—when you're caught, you'll be on your own. We rarely help our members—or people who dabble with the Illuminati but ... chicken out." She looks askance at Gemma. "Occasionally, when it's absolutely necessary to silence someone, we'll smuggle a suicide pill into their cell. But don't bet on it."

Brannan walks over to Kayleigh and places a hand on her shoulder and gently squeezes. "I'll switch on in a few minutes," he tells her.

Liam almost gasps at the unbridled display of affection. If an Organization member affectionately touched someone's shoulder like that in public, they'd probably be rescued.

"Gemma," Kayleigh says, "how about you and I stroll around the gardens for a while. Then I'll make sure you get home in one piece."

Of course they know Gemma's name, Liam thinks.

Gemma leans in and kisses Liam square on the mouth. The kiss shocks him, then makes him feel as if coming here was the right thing.

Gemma turns toward the two deep state operatives. "You didn't ask me," she says.

"Ask you what, precisely?" Brannan asks.

"What I want to get out of being a member of your little resistance movement." She smiles.

Brannan smiles back and nods. "Kayleigh will definitely cover that with you," he says.

Kayleigh's eyes flicker over their faces. There's no hint of friendliness in her manner. It occurs to Liam that she might have a synthetic face that's incapable of changing its expression. Without speaking again, she escorts Gemma out, the elevator doors silently closing behind them.

Chapter 30

Brannan strolls up and down the soft carpet, chin up, one hand in a pocket of his pants. Despite the bulkiness of his body, there's remarkable grace in his movements. More even than of strength, he gives an impression of confidence.

He pulls out another mini-Portal from a drawer in his desk. He presses play and hands the device to Liam. On the screen, a video starts playing of a woman of mixed-race.

Liam knows who this Sub is. She was recently featured in a Victory Rally video that documented how she was born on the Latineuropean island of Jamaica, entered Trumerica illegally, and led a group of insurrectionists who tried to overthrow the government.

"I'm sure you've heard rumors about the Illuminati," Kamala Harris says in the video playing on the mini-Portal in Liam's hands. She's in an office or maybe a sparse living room. Behind her are window blinds. The lighting is poor. "You've probably heard that we're a vast underworld of conspirators, meeting secretly in basements, sending coded messages to each other. Nothing of the kind exists. As members of the Illuminati, we have no way of recognizing each other, and it's impossible for any member to know the identity of more than a few others. Even my friend Alexandria Ocasio-Cortez doesn't have a complete list of members. No such list exists. The Illuminati can't be wiped out because we aren't an organization in the ordinary sense. Nothing holds us together except indestructible ideas and impeccable values. You'll have nothing to sustain you, except those ideas and values, and knowing you're on the right side of history. You'll experience no friendship and receive no encouragement. You'll have to get used to living without results and without hope. You'll work for a while, you'll be caught, you'll confess, and then you'll be executed. That's your personal endgame. There's little possibility that any perceptible change will happen during our lifetime. We participate as handfuls of dust and splinters of bone. It might take us one hundred years. It might take us one thousand years. At present, nothing is possible except to extend the area of sanity little by little. We can't yet act collectively. We can only spread our knowledge outwards from individual to individual, generation after generation. Confronted with the Peace Police, the Trufamily Forty-Five, and that racist fuckface Donald Trump and his puppet master Vladimir Putin, there's no other way. Our only true life is in the future." Her face goes from stern to optimistic. "Always remember," Harris adds, "if you dream with ambition and lead with conviction, the future will applaud you every step of the way."

The video ends and Liam hands the device back. The two men pause for a moment.

"Do you have a hiding spot?" Brannan asks eventually.

"Uh-huh." Liam tells him the address of the place Gemma rented from the antiques store owner.

"What's the owner like? Is there anything about this Tiffany person that I need to know about? I'm going to deliver something to your little romantic hideaway. A book. I'll get a colleague to pose as a customer. They'll sneak upstairs and stash Alexandria Ocasio-Cortez's book up there for you. Maybe under a bed. Maybe inside a cereal box. Tell me, how many Portals are in your little love nest?"

"None," Liam says excitedly.

Brannan snaps his fingers. "Amazing. I'll put the book on this reformatted mini-Portal." He waves the device in the air then puts it away in a draw. "AOC's book will reveal the true nature of Trumerican society, plus our strategies to destroy it. After you've read it, you'll be a full member of the Illuminati."

They're silent for a moment.

"Do you think Gemma will read it?" Brannan asks softly.

"I ... don't know."

Brannan tilts his head. "Talk with her. Encourage her. But let her make up her own mind about reading it and joining us. Actually, even if you tried, you wouldn't be able to change her mind—she's smarter than you. We have to accept that she'll choose either their Trumerica of disunity and discord, or our Trumerica of equal opportunity and equal justice. Still, it's essential that you support her in making the right choice. The patriotic c hoice."

Over the past few minutes, Liam has glanced a couple of times out the window, but he only looked at the trees in the courtyard. Now, he gazes into the distance, at the gigantic bureau buildings, the Organization's current mottos beaming out across Lar-o-Maga Palm City and all over the dictatorship.

TRUMP IS FOREVER.

ALL INFORMATION IS PART OF WAR.

LIBERATE TRUMERICA!

Brannan adds wine to their glasses. "Who or what will we toast this time?" he says, still with the same faint suggestion of irony. "To Miley Cyrus? To Whoopi Goldberg? To the death of the Trump dynasty? To humanity? To the future?"

"To the past," Liam says.

"The past is more important," agrees Brannan gravely.

They clink glasses and drink the wine.

"It's time for you to go," Brannan says. "We'll meet again—"

"Where there's no darkness?" Liam says hesitantly.

Brannan nods without any appearance of surprise. "Where there's no darkness," he says, as though recognizing the allusion. "Before you leave, is there anything else you'd like to say?"

Liam thinks. There doesn't seem to be anything he wants to ask. Nor does he feel like uttering any lofty generalities. Instead of anything directly connected with Brannan or the Illuminati, there comes into his mind a sort of montage that includes his dingy dark childhood apartment before his mom and sister disappeared, the sunny room over Tiffany's shop, the shopkeeper's affection for her puppy, the glass paperweight with coral inside it, and the framed poster of the EPCOT Center. Then Liam thinks of something els e.

"Do you remember an old poem that starts with, 'Beware my friend, as you pass by'?"

Again Brannan nods. With a sort of grave courtesy, he recites:

Beware my friend, as you pass by.

As you are now, so once was I.

As I am now, so you must be.

Prepare for death and follow me.

"You know it!" Liam says.

"Yes, I know it." He affectionately places his hand on Liam's shoulder.

Liam stands. He wants to give Brannan a hug. He's never hugged a man before, not even his dad.

Brannan takes his hand off Liam's shoulder and extends it. As they shake hands, Brannan's powerful grip crushes Liam's palm. Then Brannan points to the elevator.

A few moments later, just as the elevator doors close, Liam sees Brannan waiting beside the control panel, ready to switch the Portals back on. It occurs to Liam that, in a few moments, the deep state operative he's looking at will return to his important work on behalf of the democratic dictatorship that is the Trumerica Freedom Organization.

Chapter 31

Over the past few weeks, there have been countless marches, speeches, and military parades to support the re-election campaign of Donald Trump. Along with all the campaigning, the hatred of Iranaqey and Korchinpan has boiled up to peak insanity.

Tonight, just two weeks before the re-election, Liam participates in yet another rally in one of Lar-o-Maga Palm City's many sports stadiums. Unlike the previous rally he attended, the stadium he's currently in is filled almost to capacity. There are thousands of people in the crowd, including around maybe one thousand school children wearing uniforms of the Youth Counterintelligence Service.

On a scarlet-draped platform an orator harangues the crowd with a speech he called, "Fighting to Stay Free." The speaker is Tucker Carlson, a tall, heavyset man with short light hair parted on the side with kind of a quiff. Contorted with hatred, Carlson, who is a member of the C-Suite, grips the microphone with one hand while the other hand claws the air menacingly above his head.

He booms forth an endless catalog of atrocities, massacres, and unjust aggressions by our enemies. Iranaqeyians torturing our soldiers. Korchinpanians bombing our civilians. Both of them covertly polluting Trumericans with their lying propaganda in ways that will subvert our companies and corrupt our elected officials. For good measure, he slips in several references about the Latineuropanians, who are our business associates and our military allies. He says the Latineuropanians are taking our generosity and ingenuity for granted and are threatening to break our trade agreements.

It's almost impossible to listen to Carlson without being convinced and enraged. Every few moments, the fury of the roaring crowd temporarily drowns out his voice. The most savage yells come from the schoolchildren, many of whom are gritting their teeth and emanating pure hatred.

About twenty minutes into the speech, a woman hurries onto the stage. She slips a piece of paper into the speaker's hand. Carlson reads the message without pausing in his speech. Nothing alters in his voice or manner, but suddenly most of the names are different.

Slowly, Liam understands what's happening. *Trumerica is no longer at war with Iranaqey and Korchinpan! Trumerica is now at war with Latineuropa! The Iranaqeyians and Korchinpanians are now our business partners, not the Latineuropanians!*

Carlson doesn't acknowledge that any change has taken place. It simply becomes known, with extreme suddenness, that Latineuropa—and not the other two superstates—is our one and only enemy.

As this new understanding ripples through the audience, people also realize that many of the political ads on the digital billboards in the stadium are wrong. It's sabotage! Alexandria Ocasio-Cortez's agents are responsible!

Slowly, all the billboards that were showing public services announcements regarding Iranaqey or Korchinpan go blank. After a few moments, this week's slogans appear on the screens.

STAND BACK AND STAND BY.
BUILD THE WALLS.
ALL LIVES MATTER.

Soon, the slogans disappear and are replaced by public service announcements about our new singular enemy, Latineuropa.

Tucker Carlson continues his speech. It's just that now he's talking about the *Latineuropanians* being currency manipulators, elite globalists, and people who eat pills filled with powdered human baby flesh. The thing that impresses Liam is that the speaker performs this switch without acknowledging it. Carlson just continues babbling as if Latineuropa has always been our enemy.

Liam remembers something similar to this happening many years ago. At one moment in history, climate change was real and a genuine threat that had to be dealt with. The next moment, it was a hoax perpetrated upon Trumerica by our enemies, and by immigrants who didn't want us to build massive sea walls around our borders.

As the feral roars of the crowd continue, Liam realizes that their hatred remains unchanged. It's just that the target of their hate has been updated.

As soon as Carlson leaves the stage, a woman walks on stage. She informs everyone that the hot dog eating contest—one of Trumerica's most sacred rituals—will be rescheduled and that the re-election rally is ending early. She shoots Trump T-shirts out of an air cannon and everyone heads for the exits.

Liam goes straight to the Bureau of Facts, though the time is now 11 pm. The entire staff of the bureau has done likewise. The orders streaming out of Portals, recalling Organization members to their employers, are hardly necessary.

Trumerica is at war with Latineuropa.

Trumerica has always been at war with Latineuropa.

At a staff meeting, a CMO tells Liam and his colleagues that innumerable references to warring parties and trade partners in the media and in government communications are now completely wrong. Broadcasts, reports, and records of all kinds—including newspapers, books, photos, videos, everything that mentions something incorrect—must be rectified at lightning speed. Within one week, no reference to the wars with Iranaqey and Korchinpan, or the strategic alliance with Latineuropa, should remain in existence any where.

Soon, Liam thinks, *those references will be non-existent. They'll have never existed.*

Chapter 32

The work is overwhelming, all the more so because the processes it involves can't be called by their true names. Everyone in Liam's Information Security Department works eighteen hours per day, with two three-hour snatches of sleep. Mattresses are placed along hallways. Meals consist of sandwiches and Covfefe Coffee wheeled around on trolleys by Sub cafeteria workers.

Liam's work is by no means purely mechanical. Sometimes he can simply copy-and-paste the various names of the superstates. But any detailed report of events demands care and imagination.

By the third day, his eyes ache unbearably. Also, the air-conditioning on his floor isn't working properly, so he needs to wipe his glasses every few minutes.

Every word he murmurs into his microphone is a deliberate lie.

Inexplicably, he's anxious, just like everyone else in his department, that the forgery should be perfect.

On the morning of the sixth day, the number of tasks appearing on his Portal start to dwindle. For one whole hour, not one notification pops up on his screen pertaining to something he needs to rectify or redact. Then, everywhere at around the same time, the work eases off. A massive falsification, which can never be mentioned, has been achieved. It's now impossible for anyone to prove by documentary evidence that the wars with Iranaqey and Korchinpan ever happened.

At 12 noon it's unexpectedly announced that all Organization members working in the Bureau of Facts—and quite possibly many employees at some of the other ninety-nine bureaus throughout Trumerica—are free until tomorrow morning. The man in the Portalcast mentions that members can take this free time to consider who they're going to vote for in next week's presidential re-elections.

132

Liam is gelatinous with fatigue. His body seems to have not only the weakness of jelly, but also its translucency. He feels that if he held up his hand, he'd be able to see the light through it.

At home, he shaves and then almost falls asleep sitting on his toilet. But he doesn't want to sleep. After a quick bite, he goes for a walk. Outside in the scorching sunshine, all sensations seem to be magnified. His clothes prickle his skin. The pavement tickles his feet. Even opening and closing his hand is an effort that makes his joints ache.

He walks down a dingy street in the direction of Tiffany Murmidahn's building. He keeps one eye open for patrols, but is irrationally convinced that this afternoon there'll be no risk of the Peace Police temporarily detaining and questioning him.

He walks up the stairs to the room above the antiques shop. Inside, he immediately sees a cereal box on the kitchenette counter. In the box is the mini-Portal.

He opens the window, makes coffee, and sits in the armchair.

Exhausted but no longer sleepy, the side of his hand brushes the screen of the mini-Portal and it opens automatically, without scanning his eyes or thumbprint. This unsettles him for a moment, since every time he's ever used a mini-Portal in the past, it's required biometric authentication to unlock. This hacked device apparently doesn't.

The cover page of the book appears on screen.

Chapter 33

Liam reads the title of AOC's book.

***

The Theory and Practice of Trumpism, Propaganda, and Making Hate Great Again: Essays by Illuminati Members and Deep State Operatives Who Believe In an Objective Reality External to the Reality of the Trumerica Freedom Organization.
Edited by Alexandria Ocasio-Cortez.

***

Before now, Liam had a hunch that this book would change him forever. The book's title confirms his premonition without a shadow of a doubt.

He starts reading the first essay.

***

"The Structure and Function of Authoritarianism in Society," by Joe Biden.

Since the beginning of human history, each society has had three or four groups of people, sometimes as many as five. The groups have been divided in many ways. They've had countless different names. In societies with three groups, sometimes they're called:

- *The Highs.*

- *The Middles.*

- *The Lows.*

And sometimes they're known as:

- *The Forward Caste.*

- *The Backward Caste.*

- *The Depressed Caste.*

In societies with four groups, sometimes they're called:

- *The Ruling Class.*

- *The Middle Class.*

- *The Working Class.*

- *The Peasants.*

Or perhaps:

- *Royalty.*

- *The Upper Class.*

- *The Service Class.*

- *The Labor Class.*

Or maybe:

- *Owners.*

- *High Spenders.*

- *Mid Spenders.*

- *Low Spenders.*

Their attitudes toward each other have been in constant flux. But the essential hierarchical nature of society hasn't altered. Even after enormous upheavals, the same social class pyramid always reasserts itself.

In Trumerica, the four groups are:

- *The Trufamily Forty-Five (the elite of the ruling class, with Donald Trump at its apex).*

- *The C-Suite (the rest of the ruling class).*

- *Regular Organization members (the underclass).*

- *The Subs (the so-called dumb masses).*

For millennia—up until, say, the past seventy years—there have been long periods in each authoritarian regime when the ruling group (the Highs, the Forward Caste, the Ruling Class, or whatever they're called) have maintained power.

Currently, the ruling elites in each superstate are ...

***

Liam stops reading. He takes a deep breath, appreciating the fact that he's actually reading, in comfort and safety. He's alone. There are no Portals surveilling him. No drones hovering nearby. No nervous impulse to glance over his shoulder.

The sweet summer air plays against his cheek. From somewhere far away, there floats the faint shouts of children playing. In the room itself, there's no sound except the old ticking clock.

He settles deeper into the red chair in the corner by the window. This is bliss. This is eternity. This is how life should be. Suddenly, comforted by the knowledge that he'll re-read this book several times, he scrolls to a random page and finds himself at another essay. He reads.

***

"Endless War and the Rise of Authoritarianism," by Beyoncé Knowles-Carter.

The splitting up of the world into four immense superstates occurred in the 1960s.

Iranaqey was established when the Middle East, North Africa, and some Southeast Asian countries consolidated into one superstate.

Korchinpan was founded when most of Asia, the eastern and southern countries of Africa, and most of Australasia combined into one superstate.

Latineuropa was created when Mexico, Central America, the western and northern regions of Europe, and the eastern and southern regions of South America united into one superstate.

Trumerica was initially formed when Russia annexed the United States of America. Later, when the Russian-cum-Trumerican leaders purchased Canada, Israel, and the United Kingdom, Trumerica's frontiers increased formidably. As of the time of writing this essay, Trumerica's true leader is negotiating the purchase of Greenland. By the time you're reading this, Vladimir Putin will have most likely already acquired Greenland and attributed the real estate deal to his sycophant and stooge, Donald Trump.

In one combination or another, these four authoritarian governments are either permanently at war with each other, or continuously brokering and breaking trade deals with each other. When they're not firing missiles and insults at each other, they're buying and selling oil and pharmaceuticals from each other.

The borders of the superstates often fluctuate according to the fortunes of war and the fates of trade transactions. Likewise, allegiances also oscillate. Friends become enemies. Enemies become friends. Repeat.

Up until around the 1950s, nearly everyone considered war to be a desperate, annihilating struggle. Nowadays, however, the ruling elite in each dictatorship considers war

137

essential, wonderful, and forever. On the other hand, the middle and lower classes consider it horrible, inhumane, and destructive, and endlessly hope for its resolution.

Today's warfare is intentionally limited. While each regime could easily destroy the others, there's no economic benefit to doing so. Besides, the rulers of each billionocracy aren't even divided by genuine ideological differences. Consider the following, all of which are roughly equivalent:

- The musings and goals of autocrat Xi Jinping of Korchinpan (and his puppet, Kim Jong-un).

- The fascinations and objectives of despot Marine Le Pen of Latineuropa (and her flunky, Jair Bolsonaro).

- The leanings and aims of tyrant Ali Khamenei of Iranaqey (and his dupe, Rodrigo Duterte).

- The passions and intentions of dictator Vladimir Putin of Trumerica (and his pawn, Donald Trump).

This isn't to say that war is now less bloodthirsty or more chivalrous. On the contrary, in all superstates, war hysteria by the middle and lower classes is continuous and universal. Unconscionable acts—such as attacking civilian targets, killing prisoners of war, and slaughtering women and children—are considered commendable when committed by "our" side. Yet when "they" commit those same acts against "us," the enemy is of course entirely and unequivocally evil.

In a practical sense, war involves just a small percentage of a superstate's population. Usually, it's only fought by highly-trained mercenaries, and causes comparatively few casualties.

The fighting, when there is any, takes place on the vague frontiers of whose whereabouts most people—Iranaqeyians, Korchinpanians, Latineuropeans, and Trumericans alike—can only guess at.

The fighting also often takes place around the Floating Fortresses that every dictatorship has. While citizens are told that these fortresses are for guarding strategic sea lanes, the powermongers know that they are in fact temporary foundations for building sea islands and extracting oil from under the ocean.

The current war is the same war that's been raging since the 1960s. This is true even though who you're at war with sometimes changes. The point is, for decades now, every superstate has been continuously at war with at least one other superstate. And yet, all of these military conflicts are like the battles between animals whose horns are at such an angle that they're incapable of hurting one another. Also, even though the wars are unreal, they're not meaningless because they preserve the special mental and emotional atmosphere that a hierarchical society needs.

To understand the present global armed hostilities, you must acknowledge that they're essentially a proxy war for a much more important war: trade wars. It is these economic wars that are ultimately each government's genuine grab for power. Yet it's impossible for there ever to be a "winner." Also, despite the propaganda saying exactly the opposite, there's no longer anything to militarily fight about. Each superstate is always exporting to or importing from at least one other superstate. Thus, production and consumption continue unabated, with the four corpocracies regularly hammering out new commercial agreements related to the trade of capital, goods, and services.

***

Liam scrolls randomly to another essay.

***

"The Role that Undesired and Disputed Regions Play in Global Power Warfare," by Sadiq Khan.

Not all land on the planet is desired or controlled by one of the four superstates.

On the former continent of Africa, there is what's referred to as an undesired region. This area forms a rough triangle that spans from Mauritania in the northwest, to Ethiopia in the northeast, to Angola in the south. Within it are approximately twenty-seven countries and an estimated 760 million people. No superstate has ever fought over, invaded, or offered to buy any of these so-called "shit-hole countries."

Between the frontiers of the dictatorships there are two disputed regions. Unlike the undesired region, the four superstates constantly struggle to possess these two disputed territories. In practice, one particular superstate never controls the whole of either of these disputed areas. Portions are constantly changing hands, and it's the chance of seizing this or that fragment by a sudden stroke of treachery that contributes to the endless changes of alignment.

The first disputed region is Antarctica. Even though vast areas aren't inhabited, the autocrats of each repressive regime know that underneath this no-longer-frozen continent there are rich reserves of oil, coal, and mineralized rocks.

The second disputed region is the northeast area of the former South America. It contains much sought-after coffee, tea, mineral fuels, precious metals, fish, aluminum, and organic chemicals. For those who live in this disputed territory, the war is simply a continuous nightmare that sweeps to and fro over them like tidal waves. Yet, whichever side is winning is irrelevant to the inhabitants. A change of occupiers means simply that they'll be doing the same work as before for new masters who treat them in the same inferior manner as the previous ones.

***

Liam skips to another essay.

***

"Hegemony or Survival: Each Superstate's Quest for Global Dominance," by

Noam Chomsky.

The world of today is a bare, hungry, dilapidated place compared with the world that existed in the early 1900s, and still more so, if compared with the imaginary future which people of that period looked forward to.

In the early 1900s, millions of people envisioned a future society that would be unbelievably wealthy, leisurely, and humane. Looking forward to a glittering world of glass, steel, and concrete—yet minus the inequality, racism, and misogyny—was part of the consciousness of nearly everyone. People imagined it was just a short period of time before we had colonies under the oceans and on the moon. Science and technology were developing at warp speed, and it seemed safe to assume that they'd keep on developing. This, of course, failed to happen.

There was the human-induced climate change that made much of the world uninhabitable.

There was the nuclear war of the 1970s that made it even more uninhabitable.

As a whole, the world is much more primitive today than it was decades ago. Various phenomenal breakthroughs have been made. But they're mostly connected with the military-industrial complex, private prisons, the financial services industry, social engineering, and surveillance. Other than in areas that benefit the elites, experiment and invention have mostly ground to a halt.

***

Liam goes to the table of contents and selects another essay.

***

"The War on Freedom," by Cher.

141

Potential peace and unlimited wealth threaten the destruction of a hierarchical society.

If we lived in a world where everyone rarely worked, had plenty to eat, lived in a gorgeous house, and could enjoy endless forms of entertainment, then all forms of inequality would disappear.

If wealth, justice, and equal opportunities were available to everyone, then the middle and lower classes would learn to think for themselves. Soon they'd realize that those in the powerful, privileged minority serve no function, and they'd revolt against them. In the long run, a hierarchical society—and the worship of a semi-divine leader—is only possible if poverty, ignorance, hatred, and pain persist.

***

Somewhere in the distance, a bomb thunders.

Liam stops reading for a moment.

The blissful feeling of being alone with a book of essays edited by Alexandria Ocasio-Cortez, in a room with no Portal, hasn't worn off. Solitude and safety are physical sensations, mixed up with his tiredness, the softness of the chair, and the faint breeze coming through the window.

The forbidden book fascinates and reassures him. It is the product of minds similar to his own, though more powerful, more systematic, and less fear-ridden than his.

To get a feel for the whole book, Liam decides to read the opening paragraphs of several essays, with the goal of deciding which one to first read start-to-finish.

***

"Living with War," by Neil Young.

In current society, war is always twofold—it is simultaneously trade war and military war.

For nearly all middle and lower groups on the planet, war means no more than a continuous shortage of food and goods, plus the occasional terrorist attack that causes a few deaths.

The needs of the population are always subordinate to the needs of war. The result is a chronic shortage of many necessities of life for those in the middle and lower groups. The despots ruling each superstate consider this advantageous, since scarcity increases the importance of small privileges and thus magnifies the distinction between one group and another.

Since war has become literally continuous, it has also ceased to be dangerous. When war is continuous, there's no such thing as necessity in terms of trade and the military. Efficiency is no longer needed. Indeed, in Trumerica, nothing is efficient except the Peace Police.

In a way, war has become primarily an internal affair. Nowadays it's as if the war is waged by each ruling group against its own citizens, and the objectives of the war is less about defending or conquering territories, or winning trade agreements, and more about keeping the structure of society intact.

***

"Peak Hatred and the Information Dark Age," by Hannah Gadsby.

Members of the ruling elites are expected to be competent and hard-working. But it's also necessary that they are ignorant fanatics whose prevailing moods are fear, hatred, and orgiastic triumph. To achieve this, each dictatorship has been continually in a state of war (which, as defined elsewhere in this collection of essays, always consists of both trade war and military war). It doesn't matter whether the war is actually happening. And since no decisive victory is possible, it's irrelevant whether the war is going well or badly. All that's needed is that a state of war exists.

In the case of Trumerica, it is the members of the C-Suite whose hatred of the enemy is the strongest. And yet, it's often necessary for a member of the C-Suite to know that certain news items about the war are untruthful. Most of them are even aware that the war is spurious and is being fought for purposes that contradict the reasons doled out to the masses. And yet, no C-Suite member ever wavers for an instant in their mystical beliefs that the war is real, and that it will end victoriously, with Trumerica the undisputed master—and monopolistic powerhouse—of the entire world.

***

"The Triumph of Science Denialism," by Tony Schwartz.

In Trumerica at the present day, science has almost ceased to exist. The empirical method of thought—on which all past scientific achievements were founded—is antithetical to the Trufamily Forty-Five's most fundamental principles.

In business, technological progress only happens when it creates something that can be used to limit human liberty.

The aim of the Trumerica Freedom Organization is to extinguish all independent thought. To achieve this, it must be able to figure out, against a person's will, what he or she is thinking and feeling.

The psychologists, interrogators, and data scientists of today study body language, facial expressions, and tones of voice. They study the truth-producing effects of drugs, therapy, and torture. They work with chemists, physicists, and biologists in the vast laboratories of the Bureau of Terrorism Prevention and Enhanced Interrogation Techniques. They work at the stations run by the One Trumerica News Network that are hidden in the taiga forests of Karelia, in the Negev desert, and on the islands of Saint Pierre and Miquelon. Some are planning the logistics of future military and trade wars. Others are breeding germs that are immunized against all possible antibodies. Still others are trying to harness the sun's rays through lenses suspended thousands of miles up in space.

***

"The Shadows of Corporatocracy," by Sonia Sotomayor.

In Trumerica, the one-hundred so-called bureaus are in fact corporations masquerading as government entities.

The Bureau of Facts is actually Trumerica Productions, an entertainment conglomerate.

The Bureau of Legalism is actually Clarke, Cohen, Fonseca, Giuliani, and Habba, a law firm.

The Bureau of Morality is actually Academi Security Frontiers Logistics, a private military company.

The Bureau of Pharmaceutical Quality is actually a partnership between Purdue Pharma and McKesson Corporation, a drug maker and a drug distributor.

The Bureau of Space Force and Galactic Enforcement is actually Black Star Consulting, an aerospace manufacturer and provider of space transportation.

The Bureau of Opposition Research and Counter-Disinformation is actually Free Speech Systems LLC, a news service that publishes fake hoaxes, propaganda, and disinformation purporting to be real news.

The Bureau of Agrochemical Innovation, Environmental Progress, and Herbicidal Benefits is actually Monsanto, an agricultural biotechnology corporation.

***

"The Psychology of Repression and Dictatorship," by Hillary Clinton.

The strategy that all four superstates follow—or pretend to follow—is almost identical. Essentially, each dictatorship's plan is to use a combination of fighting, bargaining, and commercial arrangements to acquire land or build bases that encircle rival regimes, and then to sign a pact of friendship with those enemies and remain on peaceful terms until they can gain the upperhand and eventually annex them.

The problem is the same for each of the four billionocracies. It is absolutely necessary to their structure that there should be no contact with foreigners, except to a limited extent with slaves, prisoners of war, and interstate commerce experts.

Even the official ally—or allies—of the moment is always regarded with dark suspicion.

Excluding slaves, prisoners, and trade representatives, the average Trumerican never sets eyes on an Iranaqeyian, an Korchinpanian, or a Latineuropean. If Trumericans were allowed contact with foreigners, they'd understand that they're similar to us. They'd discover that what we've been told about them is nothing but lies. The sealed world in which Trumericans live would be broken. The fear, hatred, and self-righteousness on which our morality depends would evaporate. It's therefore realized on all sides that regardless of how often former countries in one of the disputed regions—such as Peru, Ecuador, and Venezuela—may change hands, the main frontiers must never be crossed by anything except missiles, drones, imports, and exports.

There are hundreds, perhaps thousands, of corrective labor camps throughout Trumerica. Some slaves and prisoners of war are sent to Dmitrovlag to dig canals. Others are sent to Oregon to make McDonald's uniforms. Still, others are sent to northwest Iowa to work on Nustar Dairy Farms.

***

Liam hears Gemma's footsteps on the stairs. He gets up to greet her.

She dumps her leather tote bag on the floor and flings herself into his arms. It's been more than a week since they've seen one another.

"I've got *the book*," he says as they disentangle themselves.

"Great," she says without much interest.

She makes coffee.

They make love.

From outside comes the sound of the kids of the neighboring family playing a game of cops and robbers.

Gemma lies on her side and seems to be already about to fall asleep.

He grabs AOC's book then leans back against the bedhead. "We have to read this. All members of the Illuminati have to read it."

"Read it aloud to me." She shuts her eyes. "I like the sound of your voice."

It's 6 pm. They have about three hours. He props the book against his knees and begins reading it aloud from the beginning.

After he reads the first page or so of the first essay, he stops reading. "Gemma, are you awake?"

"Uh-huh. I'm listening. Go on, darling. It's riveting."

He doesn't believe her, but he continues reading.

***

For millennia—up until, say, the past seventy years—there have been long periods in each authoritarian regime when the ruling group (the Highs, the Forward Caste, the Ruling Class, or whatever they're called) have maintained power.

Currently, the ruling elites in each superstate are:

- *The Trumerica Freedom Organization in Trumerica.*

- *The Seljuk Sepâh in Iranaqey.*

- *The Vedic Raj in Korchinpan.*

- *The Supranational Rally in Latineuropa.*

In past centuries, sooner or later, the elites always lost either belief in themselves or their capacity to govern. They were then overthrown by the Middles, who enlisted the Lows on their side by lying to them that they were fighting for liberty and justice. When the Middles reached their objective, they became the Highs and established a fresh tyranny. They then shoved the Lows back down into their old position of servitude. Soon, a new Middle group fragmented off from the other groups, and the struggle began again.

Of all the groups—regardless of whether it's three, four, or five groups—the Lows are the least likely to ever successfully change their social status. From the point of view of the Lows, historic change generally means just a change in the name of their masters.

Currently, the low groups in each dictatorship are:

- *The Subs in Trumerica.*

- *The Bedouins in Iranaqey.*

- *The Dalits in Korchinpan.*

- *The Gypsies in Latineuropa.*

***

Gemma starts snoring.

Liam pauses reading for a while and simply basks in how much he loves her.

He returns to flicking through the book and reading just the opening paragraphs of random essays.

***

"Constructivist Learning, Neo-Authoritarianism, and Permanency" by Ai Weiwei.

Up until around the late 1800s, class distinctions existed in every society. Some considered them inevitable and desirable. Others—such as those who won various revolutions around the world and believed in their own phrases about the rights of man, freedom of speech, equality before the law, and the like—thought that class distinctions should be abolished. Another group went even further and supported a redistribution of wealth from some individuals to others.

Then around sometime in the early 1900s, human equality had become possible and there was no longer any practical need for class distinctions or for large differences of wealth. That advancement, however, was a threat to those in power, for it meant that they'd have to relinquish some of their social and economic status. Thus, from the point of view of the ruling elites, human equality was no longer an ideal to be striven after, but a danger to be averted.

By the 1950s, all the main currents of political thought had become authoritarian. Every new political theory, by whatever name it called itself, led back to hierarchy, regimentation, and oppression.

By the 1960s, practices that had been long abandoned, in some cases for hundreds of years—imprisonment without trial, the use of war prisoners as slaves, public executions, torture to extract confessions, and the deportation of whole populations—not only became common again, but were tolerated and even defended by people who considered themselves enlightened and progressive.

It was only after a decade of national wars, civil wars, revolutions, and counter-revolutions in all parts of the world that four distinct ruling elites—one for each superstate—emerged as a fully functioning merger of a corporation and a political party. These groups, more so than any other in history, were hungrier for pure power, and above all, were more conscious of what they were doing and more intent on crushing opposition. They aimed to arrest progress and freeze history. This time, by conscious strategy, the goal of the governing autocrats was to maintain their position permanently.

***

"Deliverance in the Age of the Dictators," by David Hogg.

At the pinnacle of Trumerican society is Donald Trump, who is deemed to be infallible and all-powerful. Every success, every achievement, every victory, all knowledge, all happiness, and all virtue results directly from his leadership. People sometimes get to see him in person at Victory Rallies, yet he appears constantly on millions of Portals. With the advent of deepfakes and synthetic media, we're reasonably sure that Old Orange Face, the world's greatest troll, will never die.

Donald Trump is the guise that the Organization—ultimately ruled by Vladimir Putin in the shadows—chooses to exhibit itself to the world. His function is to act as a focusing point for love, fear, and reverence, emotions that are more easily felt toward an individual than toward an organization.

Under Fuckface Von Clownstick—which is my favorite of all insulting nicknames for Donald Trump—comes the forty-five members of the Trufamily Forty-Five. Below them are the C-Suite (CEOs, CFOs, CMOs, etc.), whose numbers are around six million, which is approximately 1% of the population of Trumerica. Below the C-Suite comes the regular members of the Organization, constituting approximately 19% of the population. Lower still are the dumb masses, the Subs, numbering approximately 80% of the population.

Within the Organization, there's a certain amount of movement between the groups. But only so much as will ensure that weaklings are excluded from the C-Suite and that ambitious people who are regular Organization members are made harmless by allowing them to rise. Also, whenever a member of the Trufamily Forty-Five is killed off, they are replaced by a promising member of the C-Suite.

Subs are not allowed to join the Organization. The most gifted among them, who might possibly become nuclei of discontent, are simply eliminated by the Peace Police.

Trumerican society rests ultimately on the belief that Donald Trump is omnipotent and that the Organization is infallible. But since in reality Vladimir Putin's pawn isn't omnipotent and the Organization isn't infallible, there's a need for a moment-to-moment flexibility in the treatment of facts. Indeed, if one is to continue ruling, one must be able to dislocate the sense of reality.

The alteration of the past provides two main benefits. (Incidentally, the following benefits pail in comparison to the ultimate reason why the Organization constantly rewrites history, which is explored in Alexandria Ocasio-Cortez's essay later in this collection.)

One benefit is that regular Organization members and Subs tolerate present-day conditions partly because they have no standards of comparison. They must be cut off from the past, just as they must be cut off from foreign countries, because it's necessary for them to believe that they're better off than their ancestors and that the average level of material comfort is constantly rising.

The second benefit for the readjustment of the past is the need to safeguard the infallibility of the Organization. Statistics, records of every kind, and speeches by the Trufamily Forty-Five must be constantly brought up to date in order to prove that the predictions of the Organization are correct in all cases. Also, changes in business decisions or in political alignments can never be admitted. So, if the facts are inconvenient, then they must be altered. Thus history is continuously rewritten.

The changeability of the past is the regime's central tenet. According to the Organization, past events have no objective existence. They survive only in written records and in human memories. The past is whatever the records and the memories agree upon. And since the Organization controls all records and the minds of its members, it follows that the past is whatever the Organization chooses to make it. It also follows that though the past is alterable, it has never ever been altered. Whenever it's recreated, then this new version is the past, and no different past can ever have existed.

This holds true even when, as often happens, the same event has to be altered out of recognition on several occasions over a period of time. At all times the Organization is in possession of absolute truth, and clearly the absolute can never have been different from what it is now.

The control of the past depends above all on the training of memory. To ensure that all written records agree with the beliefs of the moment is merely a mechanical act. But it's also necessary to remember that events happened in the desired manner. And if it's necessary for a person to edit their memories or to tamper with written records, then it's necessary for them to forget that they've done so.

This trick can be learned like any other mental technique. Those who don't learn it are terminated. It's learned by the majority of Organization members as part of a broader curriculum that enables them to hold two contradictory beliefs in their minds simultaneously, and accept both of them.

By believing two mutually exclusive beliefs, an Organization member can be content that reality isn't violated. The process must be conscious, or it wouldn't be carried out with sufficient precision. But it also must be unconscious, or it would bring with it a feeling of falsity and hence, of guilt.

This bifurcation is essential to the Organization's goals. To tell deliberate lies while genuinely believing in them is absolutely essential. To forget facts that have become inconvenient, and then, when it becomes necessary again, to draw them back from oblivion for just so long as they're needed is totally crucial. To deny the existence of objective reality, and all the while to take account of the reality that one denies, is indispensably necessary. Ultimately it's the embrace of these dichotomies that enabled the Organization to alter history and stay in power.

***

"The Decay of Truth" by Evvie Harmon.

All the beliefs, habits, tastes, emotions, and mental attitudes that characterize our time are really designed to sustain the mystique of the Organization and to prevent the true nature of society from being perceived.

In terms of the lower class in Trumerica, physical rebellion is at present not possible. Left to themselves, the Subs will continue from generation to generation, from century to century, working, breeding, purchasing, and dying. The lower class will never develop any impulse to rebel. They'll never grasp that the world can be other than it is. They could only become dangerous if they became educated—which the elites will forever prevent.

The Subs are only intermittently conscious of the war. When it's necessary, they're prodded into frenzies of fear and hatred. But when left to themselves, they're easily capable of forgetting that the war is even happening.

What opinions the Subs hold are irrelevant. They can be granted intellectual liberty because they have no intellect. In an Organization member, on the other hand, not even the smallest deviation of opinion on the most unimportant subject can be tolerated.

An Organization member lives from cradle to grave under the eye of the Peace Police. In Trumerica, with the development of Facebook's Portal, private life came to an end. Every citizen deemed important enough to be worth watching can be surveilled almost continuously for their entire life. Even when alone, an individual can never be sure that they're actually alone. Asleep or awake, working or resting, they can be inspected without warning and without knowing that they're being inspected. Friendships, behavior toward family members, facial expressions when alone, muttered words during sleep, are all scrutinized.

Organization members are required to not only have the right opinions, but also the right instincts. Many of the beliefs and attitudes demanded of members are never plainly stated. Indeed, they couldn't be stated without laying bare the contradictions inherent in the Trufamily Forty-Five's principles. If a person is naturally patriotic, they'll know, without thinking, what is the true belief or the desirable emotion in any situation.

Elaborate mental training makes an Organization member unwilling and unable to

152

think too deeply on any subject whatsoever. This training includes the power of not grasping analogies, of failing to perceive logical errors, of misunderstanding the simplest arguments if they're unfriendly to the Organization, and of being repelled by any idea that might lead in an Untrumerican direction. In short, members are taught to maintain a forcefield of stupidity around all of their thoughts.

Organization members are expected to have no private emotions. They're supposed to live in a continuous frenzy of hatred of foreign enemies and internal traitors, triumph over victories, and self-abasement before the power and wisdom of the dictatorship.

***

"Vladimir Putin and Donald Trump's Pact: the Politics of Trumerica's Destruction," by Alexandria Ocasio-Cortez.

In Trumerican society, those who have the most knowledge of the Organization's inner workers are those who are furthest from seeing the world as it is. Also, generally, the more intelligent a person is, the less sane they are. One clear illustration of this is how hysteria about trade wars and military wars intensifies as one rises in the social scale.

It's in the higher ranks of the Organization—the Tramily Forty-Five and the C-Suite—that true war enthusiasm is found. They're the ones who believe most firmly in world-conquest, though they also know it's impossible. This peculiar combination of opposites—knowledge with ignorance, cynicism with fanaticism—is a fundamental part of Trumerica's ideology, which abounds with contradictions even when there's no practical reason for them. Thus, the Organization rejects and vilifies every democratic principle, and it does so in the name of democracy.

These discrepancies aren't accidental. They're deliberate. It's the only way that power can be retained indefinitely. In no other way could the ancient cycle be broken. If human equality is to be forever averted—if Donald Trump and his cronies are to keep their power permanently—then the prevailing mental condition must be controlled insanity.

But there are several questions that, until this moment, all previous essays in this collection ignored. These as-yet unanswered questions include: Why does the Trumerica

Freedom Organization want to violate all forms of human rights? Why does the Trumerica Freedom Organization constantly rewrite history? And, why does the regime want to oppress Trumericans?

Here we reach the central secret and original motive that first led Vladimir Putin to seize power in what was previously the United States of America, to install Donald Trump, to then let President Trump pick the Trufamily Forty-Five, to create the Peace Police, to engage in continuous warfare, and so on. The reasons are numerous, but they can all be boiled down to one main idea that ...

***

Suddenly, Liam becomes aware of silence, as one becomes aware of a new sound.

Gemma is laying on her side, naked from the waist upwards, one dark lock of hair tumbling across her closed eyes.

"Gemma, are you awake?"

No answer.

"Gemma?"

Still no answer.

He puts the book on the floor, lays down, and pulls the thin blanket over both of them.

For years, Liam thinks, *I've pretty much understood how the Organization operates. These essays have confirmed some of my hunches. They've also opened my eyes to how the Organization does things that I hadn't even considered before. Soon, though, I'll learn the ultimate secret—I'll learn why.*

Also, reading these essays has helped me confirm that I'm not insane. Being in a minority—even a minority of one—doesn't make me a lunatic. There is truth and there is untruth. And if I cling to the truth—even against the whole world—that doesn't make me insane.

A yellow beam from the sinking sun slants in through the window and shines across the pillow. He shuts his eyes. The sun on his face and the touch of Gemma's body give him a strong, confident feeling. He's safe, everything is ok.

Just before falling asleep, he thinks, *Sanity is not statistical*, and he has the feeling that this idea contains in it a profound wisdom.

Chapter 34

When Liam wakes, it's with the sensation of having slept for a long time. He lays there, dozing.

Outside in the adjacent yard, Liam hears kids playing. The young Subs are screaming with delight about something.

Gemma wakes up and stretches luxuriously. "Hi, darling," she says.

They smile at each other.

Liam gets up, puts his pants on, and goes to the window. The sun is setting. The sky, so fresh and pale, shows the day's last remnants of blue.

In the neighbor's backyard, there's a long sheet of plastic on the ground that's being sprayed by a garden hose. The Sub kids take turns to run, dive, and body plane on the wet plastic.

Liam wonders whether there's ever been a kid from an Organization family who has ever slid down a Slip 'N Slide. Probably not.

Gemma comes over beside him. They gaze down with a sort of fascination at the family below.

Liam holds Gemma's waist encircled by his arm. From the hip to the knee her flank is against his. Out of their bodies no child will ever come. That's yet another thing they can never do. Only by word of mouth, from mind to mind, can they pass on their secrets.

Liams again looks at the cloudless sky that's stretching away into interminable distance.

It's curious to think that the sky is shared by everyone on the planet, he thinks. *The same shared sky in Iranaqey, Korchinpan, Latineuropa, Trumerica, the disputed regions, and the undesired region. And the people under the sky are also very similar, whether we're Highs, Middles, Lows, or whatever. Regardless of what we're called, all over the world, billions of people just like those Subs down there are pretty much the same.*

Even though we're mostly unaware of each other's existence. Even though we're held apart by walls of hatred and lies. And even though we're of different races, genders, and sexualities, with different cultures, statuses, and tastes. Deep down, we all have similar fears and regrets, dreams and feelings. We share a common humanity.

But it's not people like me who will one day overthrow Trumerica's autocrats. If there's hope, it's in people like them.

Even though I haven't finished reading AOC's book yet, I have a strong hunch what the main message in the last essay will be—that the future belongs to the Subs.

The new Trumerica they create will be kind, just, and sane. When there is equality, there can be kindness, justice, and sanity. Sooner or later, it will happen. Strength will change into consciousness. A moral balance will be restored.

In the end, perhaps hundreds of years from now, the Subs will awaken. Until that happens, they'll stay alive against all the odds. From generation to generation, they'll pass on the vitality that the Organization doesn't share and can't kill.

"Do you remember the bird that sang to us?" he says, recalling their first excursion to the woods. "The red one?"

"It wasn't singing to us." Gemma smiles. "It sang to please itself. Probably not even that. It was just singing."

"The first time I experienced our neighbors down there …. the mother was all by herself … and she was also singing …"

Birds sing, Liam thinks. *Subs sing. The Organization doesn't sing.*

That last thought terrifies him, shattering his pleasant reverie.

Gemma and I are the dead, he thinks. But then hope reappears. *The future belongs to the Subs.*

"Hey," he says, "I was thinking … We can still have a future … If we keep our minds alive. If we don't betray each other. And if we pass on the beliefs that something is what it is, that facts are facts."

"I like that," Gemma says.

"And yet, we are the dead."

"We're *not* dead yet," she says. "How many times do I have to tell you that?"

"You are the dead," says an iron voice behind them.

They spring apart. Liam's stomach turns into ice. He can see the white all around the irises of Gemma's eyes.

"You are the dead," repeats the iron voice.

"It's behind the poster," Gemma says.

"It's behind the poster," the voice says.

They can do nothing except stand gazing into each other's eyes. To run would be useless. To disobey the iron voice from the wall would be unthinkable.

There's a snap as though something has been unclipped. The framed poster of the EPCOT Center falls to the floor, revealing a Portal behind it.

"Now they can see us," Gemma says.

"Now we can see you," the voice says. "Go to the middle of the room. Stand back to back. Clasp your hands behind your heads."

They aren't touching. But it seems to him that Liam can feel Gemma's body shaking.

There's a sound of boots and movement coming from outside of the building.

The yard outside seems to be full of people. Something is being dragged across the stones. There's a loud clang. There are angry shouts, followed by a yell of pain and a thump.

"The building is surrounded," Liam whispers.

"The building is surrounded," the voice says.

Gemma takes a sharp breath in. "I suppose we should probably say goodbye," she says.

"You should probably say goodbye," the voice says.

Then another voice comes out of the Portal. "And by the way, while we're on the subject," the other voice says. "'Prepare for death and follow me.'"

Liam recognizes the voice, but can't connect it to a face.

There's a stampede of boots coming up the stairs. Within seconds, the room is full of paramilitary personnel in combat clothing and body armor. Many of them are aiming weapons at Liam and Gemma.

To Liam, only one thing matters—to not give them any reason to hit him.

A man with a mouth that's only a slit pauses opposite him. He swings a baton meditatively between thumb and forefinger.

Liam meets his eyes. Liam's feeling of vulnerability is almost unbearable.

The officer's tongue licks the place where his lips should be. He picks up the glass paperweight and smashes it to pieces on the floor. The fragment of coral, a tiny crinkle of pink like a sugar rosebud from a cake, rolls across the floor.

Other officers step forward.

A woman kicks Liam in the shins and he screams in agony.

A man punches Gemma in the throat. On the floor, she thrashes around, fighting for breath.

Even in Liam's terror, it's as though he can feel Gemma's pain in his own body.

Two officers pick Gemma up and carry her out of the room like a sack.

Liam glimpses her face, upside down, red and contorted, eyes shut, a smear of rouge still on her cheeks.

Even with the stinging pain in his shins, he tries to stand completely still.

He wonders if they attacked and arrested Tiffany. Maybe that thump was a dead body—Tiffany's?—collapsing onto the cobblestones. He wonders if the family in the yard is alive.

He notices that he needs to urinate.

Tiffany Murmidahn enters the room. The demeanor of the black-uniformed officers become suddenly more subdued. Something has changed in Tiffany's appearance.

She points to the broken glass paperweight and the coral. "Pick that up," she says sharply.

An officer does as Tiffany commands.

Liam suddenly realizes whose voice it was that he had heard a few moments ago on the Portal.

Tiffany's accent has gone. She's still wearing her muumuu dress. But her hair is now black—she must have taken a wig off or put a wig on. Also, she's not wearing her glasses.

She gives Liam a single sharp glance. Then she pays no more attention to him.

She's still recognizable, but no longer the same person. Her body has straightened. Her face has undergone only tiny changes that have nevertheless worked a complete transformation. The wrinkles that were once on her face seem gone. It occurs to Liam that, for the first time in his life, he's knowingly looking at an undercover agent of the Peace Police.

PART 3: BEYOND FEAR

Chapter 35

There are many other detainees in the cell.

Most are Subs and seem to be common criminals. Some yell insults at the guards and shout at the Portals. Others seem to be on good terms with the guards, calling them by nicknames, bantering with them. Many of the Subs talk about the forced-labor camps that they expect to be sent.

The rest of the detainees are Organization members. Every one of them sits silent, numb, and petrified, each wearing an orange jumpsuit with a prison number in bold letters printed on the back and front. On Liam's jumpsuit is his number, 808337.

At one point, four guards carry an enormous wreck of a woman, aged about sixty, with thick coils of white hair, kicking and shouting, into the cell. They dump her partly on Liam's lap, partly on the bench.

She scoots off him. "Excuse me for a moment," she says politely to Liam, leans forward, and vomits on the floor. "Ah, that's better." Revived, she looks at Liam, seems to take a fancy to him, and puts an arm around his shoulder. "What's your name, pumpkin?" she says, breathing beer and puke into his face.

"Liam."

"Huh!" the woman says. "My son's name is Liam. Huh," she adds sentimentally, "I might be your mother!"

No one else speaks to him. To a surprising extent, the ordinary criminals ignore the Organization prisoners, who seem terrified of speaking to anybody. Only once, when two Organization members are pressed close together on the bench, does Liam overhear a few hurriedly-whispered words, including a reference to "the Tower," which he doesn't fully understand. *Are they talking about the headquarters for the Trumerica Freedom Organization?*

After a few hours of prisoners of every description constantly coming and going—drug dealers, race traitors, sex workers—some guards come in, head straight for Liam, put a black hood over his head, bind his wrists together, and violently drag him out of the cell.

The next day or so is a flurry of transport vehicles, other cells, being passed from one group of officers to another group of officers, elevators, leg shackles, body cavity searches, anal probes, brief interrogations, more prisoner vans, more officers, more invasive body searches ...

Chapter 36

About three hours ago, officers took Liam's hood and handcuffs off, and left him alone in his current cell. It's a high-ceilinged windowless cell with walls of glittering white bricks. Concealed lamps flood it with cold light. There's a low, steady humming sound, presumably something to do with the air supply. A bench runs around the walls, broken only by the door. In the middle of the cell is a toilet. There are four Portals, one in each wall.

He's hungry—a gnawing kind of hunger. It's been around about a day since he last ate. Against all logic, he wonders if there might be a snack bar in his pocket. He slips a hand into his pocket.

"Janz!" yells a voice from the Portal. "808337 Liam Janz! In the cells, never put your hands in your pockets!"

There are moments when he foresees the things that will happen to him with such actuality that his heart gallops and his breath stops. He feels the smash of batons on his elbows. He sees himself groveling on the floor. He feels the kicks to his face. He hears himself screaming for mercy through broken teeth.

He hardly thinks of Gemma. He loves her and won't betray her. And yet, he hardly even wonders what's happening to her.

More often, he wonders—with a flickering hope—about Brannan. Brannan might know that he was arrested. Kayleigh said that the Illuminati never tries to save its members. But if they can, they'll sneak in a suicide pill. Liam fantasizes about swallowing the pill, the potassium cyanide stopping his heart within moments.

Still, even if he gets the chance, he isn't sure that he'll take the suicide pill. It's more natural to exist from moment to moment, accepting another few minutes of life even with the certainty that there's torture at the end of it.

Sometimes he tries to calculate the number of bricks in the walls of the cell. It should be easy. But at some point or another, he always loses count.

He often wonders where he is, and what time of day it is. At one moment, he feels certain that it's daylight outside. At the next moment, he's equally certain that it's nighttime. In this place, he knows instinctively, the lights will never be switched off.

This is the place with no darkness.

He sees now why Brannan seems to recognize the allusion. In the Bureau of Morality, there are no windows. His cell might be at the heart of the building, or against its outer wall. It might be fifty floors below ground, or one hundred and fifty floors above it.

There's the sound of boots outside. The steel door opens with a clang. A young officer, a muscular black-uniformed figure whose face is like a wax mask, steps through the doorway. He motions to the guards outside to bring in the prisoner they're leading. The man shambles into the cell. The door slams shut.

The man moves uncertainly from side to side, then rambles up and down the cell. His troubled eyes gaze at the floor, never at Liam. A scruffy beard covers his face.

Liam knows the man. He's the songwriter named Connor Hughes. He worked in the RCT Records business division. Liam must speak to him, and risk being reprimanded by the Portal. Its even conceivable that Connor is the bearer of the suicide pill.

"Connor," he whispers.

There's no yell from the Portal.

Connor pauses, mildly startled. His eyes focus slowly on Liam. "Ah, Liam, you too!"

"What are you in for?"

"To tell you the truth—" He sits awkwardly on the bench opposite Liam. "There's only one offense, isn't there?"

"And you committed it?"

"Apparently." Connor puts a hand to his forehead and presses his temples. "Last week I was brought onto the Garden of Trumerican Heroes project. My role was to identify lyrics by Kanye West and Loretta Lynn that reflected the awesome splendor of our country's timeless exceptionalism. The lyrics I was supposed to select would appear on plaques at the base of their statues. But I couldn't do it. For days I racked my brains, trying to find any lyrics that exemplified our uniquely Trumerican ideology—our Trumericanism. But I just couldn't ..."

The expression on his face changes. The annoyance passes out of it and for a moment

164

he looks almost pleased.

They talk aimlessly for several minutes. Then, without apparent reason, a yell from the Portal commands them to be silent. Liam sits quietly. Connor fidgets from side to side, clasping his hands first around one knee, then around the other. The Portal barks at him to keep still. Time passes. Twenty minutes, an hour—it's difficult to judge.

Again, there's the sound of boots outside. Liam's stomach contracts. Soon, perhaps now, the stomp of boots will mean that it's his turn.

The door opens.

The cold-faced young officer steps into the cell. With a brief movement of the hand, he indicates Connor. "The Tower," the officer says.

Connor marches clumsily out between the guards just outside the door, his face vaguely perturbed, but uncomprehending.

What seems like a long time passes. Liam has only a few thoughts that repeatedly cycle through his mind. The pain in his belly. Food. The beatings, the blood, and the screaming. Brannan. Gemma. The suicide pill.

There's another spasm in his stomach—the heavy boots are approaching. As the door opens, the wave of air that it creates brings in a powerful smell of cold sweat. Graham Tamariz walks into the cell.

This time Liam is startled into self-forgetfulness. "*You*, here?" he says.

His former neighbor and colleague gives Liam a glance in which there's neither interest nor surprise, but only misery. He walks jerkily up and down the cell, unable to keep still. His eyes remain wide open, as though he's looking at something in the middle distance.

"What are you in for?" Liam says.

"Liberal thoughts!" Graham says, almost blubbering. The tone of his voice implies at once a complete admission of guilt and an incredulous horror that such an idea could apply to himself. He pauses opposite Liam. "You don't think they'll execute me, do you? They don't kill you if you haven't actually done anything—only just thinking left-wing lies in your head that you can't help? I have total faith that they'll give me a fair trial. They'll know my record, won't they? *You* know what kind of patriot I am. I always did my best for the Organization, didn't I? I'll get off with five years, don't you think? A loyalist like me will be very useful in a labor camp ..."

"Are you guilty?" Liam says.

"Of course!" Graham yells with a servile glance at the Portals. "You don't think the

Organization arrests innocent Trumericans, do you?" His face grows calmer, and even takes on a slightly sanctimonious expression. "Liberalism is a horrible thing. It's insidious. It can grab hold of you without you even knowing it. Do you know how it got me? I was absent-mindedly talking to myself while in the bathroom! You'll never guess what I said." He pauses for a moment. "'Maybe Alexandria Ocasio-Cortez has a point.'" He again glances at the Portals. "I'm glad they got me before my insanity got more insane. At my trial, I'm going to say, 'Thank you for saving me before it was too late.'"

"Who denounced you?" Liam asks, though he thinks he knows.

"My daughter," Graham says with a sort of mournful pride. "She was spying on me. Heard what I said. Informed the Peace Police. I don't hold it against her. In fact, I'm proud of her. It proves that we brought her up with the right traditional values."

He makes a few jerky movements up and down, casting a long glance at the toilet. Then he suddenly rips down his shorts. "Sorry." He plumps his large butt down and shits loudly and abundantly. It turns out that the plumbing is backed up and the cell stinks abominably for hours afterwards.

Graham Tamariz is removed. More prisoners mysteriously come and go. Now, there are six prisoners in the cell, men and women. All sit very still.

Opposite Liam there's a chinless, toothy woman. Her blue eyes flit timorously from face to face and turn quickly away when she catches anyone's eye.

Another prisoner is brought in. His appearance sends a chill through Liam. He's so emaciated that his face looks like a skull. His eyes seem filled with a murderous, unappeasable hatred.

The man sits on the bench near Liam. Suddenly, Liam understands. The man is dying of starvation.

The chinless woman glares at the skull-faced man, then turns guiltily away and fidgets. After a while, she waddles across the cell and holds out a tiny, wrapped piece of candy to him.

There's a furious, deafening roar from the Portal. The chinless woman jumps. The skull-faced man thrusts his hands behind his back, demonstrating to the watchers that he's refusing the gift.

"Johnson!" roars the voice. "251010 Josephine Johnson! Drop that piece of candy now!"

The chinless woman drops it onto the floor.

166

"Remain where you are," the voice barks. "Don't move."

The chinless woman obeys.

The door clangs open. The young officer enters and steps aside. Following in after him is a short stumpy guard with enormous arms and shoulders. At a signal from the officer, he punches the chinless woman in the face. She splays out onto the floor, blood oozing from her nose. She whimpers faintly. Then she rolls over and raises herself unsteadily, and climbs back into her place.

Liam and the other prisoners sit motionless.

More guards come in.

The officer gestures to the skull-faced man. "The Tower," he says.

There's a gasp and a flurry at Liam's side.

The man flings himself onto his knees on the floor, with his hands clasped together. "Please!" he begs. "You don't have to take me there! I've told you everything. What else do you want to know? There's nothing I won't confess! Just tell me what you want! Not the Tower!"

"The Tower," the officer says.

The man's face, already pale, turns a color Liam can hardly believe possible. "Please kill me!" he yells. "Is there someone else you want me to give away? Just say who and I'll tell you anything you want. I don't care who it is or what you do to them. I've got a wife and three children. You can cut all of their throats in front of my eyes. But not the Tower!"

"The Tower," the officer says.

The man looks frantically around at the other prisoners.

"Take her!" he shouts, pointing to the chinless woman. "You didn't hear what she said earlier. She said that President Trump executes Organization members who don't give him standing ovations! Give me a chance and I'll tell you every lie she told me. *She's* Untrumerican, not me."

The guards step forward.

The man shrieks. "Something went wrong with the Portal. *She's* the one you want. Take her, not me!" He bends down and grabs one of the iron legs that supports the bench. He howls like an animal. The guards try to wrench him loose. But he clings on with astonishing strength. A kick from a guard's boot breaks the fingers of one of the man's hands. They drag him out.

A long time passes.

Liam is now alone, and has been alone for hours. The pain of sitting on the narrow bench is such that often he gets up and walks about, unreproved by the Portal. The piece of candy still lies where it was dropped. At the beginning, it took a hard effort not to look at it. But presently hunger gives way to thirst. His mouth is sticky and evil-tasting. The humming sound and the unvarying white light induce a sort of faintness, an empty feeling inside his head. He would get up because the ache in his bones is no longer bearable, and then would sit down again almost at once because he's too dizzy to stand on his feet.

With a fading hope, he thinks of Brannan. It's possible that the suicide pill might arrive concealed in his food—if he's ever fed.

More dimly, he thinks of Gemma. Somewhere or other, she's suffering perhaps more than him. She might be screaming with pain at this moment. *If I could save Gemma by doubling my own pain,* he thinks, *would I do it? Yes, I would.* But that is merely an intellectual game, decided because he knows that he should decide it. He doesn't feel it. Besides, is it possible, when you're actually suffering it, to wish for any reason that your own pain should increase?

The boots are approaching again. The door opens. His friend Brannan enters.

Liam jumps to his feet and forgets the presence of the Portals. "They've got you too!" he says loudly.

"They got me a long time ago," Brannan says with a mild, almost regretful irony. "You know this, Liam. Don't deceive yourself. You've always known it."

Yes, Liam realizes, he had always known it.

A tall guard with black hair and a truncheon in her hand enters. She stands between the two men. She strikes Liam on the elbow.

The elbow! He slumps to his knees, clasping his arm. Everything explodes into yellow light. It's inconceivable to him that one blow can cause such pain! The light clears and he sees Brannan and the guard staring down at him.

One question, at any rate, is answered. Never, for any reason, would you wish for an increase of pain. When you're in pain, you can only wish for one thing—that it stops. *In the face of pain, there are no heroes,* he thinks, writhing on the floor, clutching uselessly at his arm.

Chapter 37

Liam can't remember how many times he's been beaten, subjected to half-hangings, forced to stand naked in front of water cannons, and had all of his senses cut off by blindfolds, hoods, and earmuffs.

There are often around five hefty, vicious men and women in black uniforms at him simultaneously. Sometimes it's verbal abuse. Sometimes it's fists. Sometimes it's metal rods.

There are times when he rolls around on the floor. As shameless as an animal, he writhes in a hopeless effort to dodge the kicks, and simply invites more. Kicks to the ribs. To his balls. To his back. To his anus, making his hemorrhoids bleed.

There are times when the beatings go on so long that the cruel, brutal, unforgivable thing isn't that the guards continue attacking him, but that Liam can't force himself into losing consciousness.

There are times when he yells for mercy before the beating starts. The mere sight of a fist drawn back for a blow is enough to make him confess to real and imaginary crimes. There's a long range of crimes—espionage, sabotage, and the like—that he confesses to.

There are times when he resolves to confess nothing, when every word has to be forced out of him between gasps of pain. *I will confess,* he thinks. *But not yet. I'll hold out until the pain becomes unbearable. Three more hits. Two more hits. Then I'll tell them what they want.*

There are times when he's beaten until he can't walk, stand, or even sit up. He recuperates on the floor for a few hours, and then the beatings begin again.

There are also longer periods of recovery where he's moved to a cell that resembles a hospital room. There's a plank bed, a sort of shelf sticking out from the wall, a sink, and meals of hot soup and bread. Sometimes there's coffee. Once, they give him two doses of

OxiQoxi. A surly barber gives him a shave and cuts his hair. Businesslike, unsympathetic people in white coats feel his pulse, test his reflexes, turn up his eyelids, harshly search for broken bones, sow up his cuts, and sometimes inject him with blissful drugs that make him sleep.

The beatings become less frequent. Now they're mainly a threat, a horror that he can be returned to at any moment when his answers are unsatisfactory.

Previously his questioners were thugs in black uniforms. Now they're often Organization intellectuals in dapper business suits. The suits take turns on working on him for periods that last ten to fifteen hours at a stretch. These well-dressed questioners see to it that Liam's in constant slight pain. Their techniques are never as physically severe and cruel as the guards, but they still slap his face. They still twist his ears. Pull his hair. Make him stand on one leg. Don't let him go to the bathroom. Shine hot lights into his face.

And yet, their purpose seems to be less about physically hurting him. Their aim seems to be more about humiliating him and destroying his power of arguing and reasoning. Their real weapon is the merciless questioning that goes on and on, hour after hour, day after day, laying traps for him, twisting everything he says into lies until he weeps as much from shame as from fatigue.

Most of the time, the suits scream abuse at him and threaten at every hesitation to return him to the guards. But sometimes they'll suddenly change their tune and treat him like he's a trusted friend. They'll appeal to him in the esteemed name of Donald Trump. They'll sorrowfully ask Liam if he has enough loyalty to the Organization left to make him wish he could undo all the evil he released upon his fellow Trumericans. After hours of questioning, when his nerves are shattered, even these appeals reduce him to a crying, sniveling mess.

In the end, their nagging voices break him down more completely than the physical violence of the guards. He becomes solely a mouth that utters, a hand that signs, whatever is demanded of him. His only concern is to find out what they want him to confess, and then confess it quickly, before the thrashings restart.

He confesses to the assassination of eminent Organization members.

He confesses to vandalizing Mount Rushmore.

To hacking into the Portals.

To conspiring with colleagues from the Bureau of Facts to embezzle public funds.

To wanting big government to get bigger.

To selling military secrets to Rodrigo Duterte, Angela Merkel, and Anthony Scaramucci.

To convincing Evelyn Tamariz to become a spy working for Denis Rodman and the Korchinpanian corpocracy.

To being a sexual pervert.

To murdering his wife—even though he knows, and his questioners surely know too, that his wife is still alive.

To communicating for years with Liz Cheney, Arnold Schwarzenegger, and Linda Sarsour.

To being a member of the Black Lives Matter movement.

To believing in the conspiracy that Barack Obama was born in Trumerica.

For Liam, it's easier to confess everything and implicate everybody. Besides, in a sense, it's all partially true. It's true that he was—and still is—an enemy of the Organization.

At this moment, the jail cell he's in seems simultaneously new and exactly like the dozens of other cells he's been in. Someone in a white lab coat is standing next to Liam, staring at him. The man's eyes grow larger and more luminous. Suddenly, Liam floats out of his seat, dives into the man's eyes, and is swallowed up.

In his dream, Liam floats down an impossibly wide hallway full of glorious, golden light. All the way, he's roaring with laughter and shouting out confessions. He relates the entire history of his life to an audience who knows it already. With him are the guards, the questioners in suits, the doctors and torturers in white coats, Tiffany Murmidahn, Gemma Dixon, and of course Brett Brannan. They're all floating down the hallway together, holding hands, and smiling with love.

Everything's all right.

There's no more pain.

The last details of his life are laid bare, understood, forgiven.

Hours later, he wakes up after mistakenly thinking that he heard Brannan's voice.

During his months of interrogations, Liam often felt Brannan at his side, just out of sight. Liam now figures out that it was Brannan directing everything. It was Brannan who instructed the guards to repeatedly take Liam within an inch of his life. It was Brannan who decided when Liam screamed with pain, when he had a respite, when he ate, when the pain relievers were injected into him.

Brannan was the tormentor, the protector, the inquisitor, the friend.

Once, a faceless voice murmured in Liam's ear, "Don't worry. You're in my keeping. For seven years, I've watched over you. Now the turning-point has come. I'll heal you. I'll save you. I'll free you. I'll make you perfect."

Liam was sure it was Brannan's voice. He now knew that it was the same voice that said to him in another dream, seven years ago, "We'll meet where there's no darkness."

Chapter 38

Liam is lying on something uncomfortable. It's off the ground. As usual, his body is held down at every essential point. Strong light shines into his face.

He has the impression of swimming up into this room from an underwater world far beneath it. How long he was down there he doesn't know. Since his arrest, he hasn't seen darkness or daylight. Besides, his memories aren't continuous. There are dozens of unaccountable blank intervals. But whether the gaps are seconds, days, weeks, or months—there's no way of knowing.

Brannan is looking down at him gravely. Brannan's face looks coarse and worn, with pouches under the eyes. He's older than Liam had thought. He's perhaps around fifty. Beside Brannan's hand, there's a dial.

"I told you that we would meet here," Brannan says.

Liam tries to nod, yet something grips the back of his head.

Without any warning except a slight movement of Brannan's hand, a wave of pain floods Liam's body. His body is being wrenched out of shape. His joints are being torn apart. The worst of all is the fear that his backbone is about to break. He chomps his teeth and breathes hard through his nose, trying to keep silent as long as possible.

Brannan watches his face. "You have a vivid mental picture of your vertebrae snapping and your spinal fluid dripping out. That's what you're thinking, isn't it?"

Liam, writhing in pure agony, doesn't answer.

Brannan lowers the dial back to zero.

The wave of pain instantly recedes.

"That was forty," Brannan says. "You can see that the numbers on this dial run up to one hundred. I can inflict pain on you at any moment and to whatever degree I choose. If you lie, prevaricate, or even fall below your usual level of intelligence, you'll instantly cry

173

out with pain. Understand?"

"Yes."

Brannan's manner becomes less severe. He resettles his glasses thoughtfully. "I'm taking my time with you, Liam, because you're worth it." His voice is gentle and patient. He now has the air of a teacher, anxious to explain rather than to punish. "For years you've known what's wrong with you. But you fought against that knowledge. You're mentally deranged. You suffer from a defective memory. You're unable to remember real events and you persuade yourself that you remember non-events. Fortunately, it's curable. You never cured yourself because you didn't choose to. There was a small effort of the will that you weren't ready to make. Even now, you cling to your disease under the impression that it's a virtue. Let's talk about an example. Ignoring trade wars for a moment, who are we currently in a military war with?"

"When I was arrested, Trumerica was at war with Latineuropa."

"Good. And Trumerica has always been at war with Latineuropa, haven't we?"

Liam draws in his breath. He opens his mouth to speak, but then doesn't. He can't take his eyes away from the dial.

"The truth, please, Liam. *Your* truth. Tell me what you think you remember."

"I remember that, until about a week before I was arrested, we were friends with Latineuropa. They were our trading partners. And we were fighting wars against both Iranaqey and Korchinpan. That—"

Brannan stops him with a movement of the hand. "Another example. Liam, over a decade ago, you delusionally believed that three former Organization members—named Julian Assange, Emma González, and Jeff Sessions—weren't guilty of the crimes we executed them for. You believed that you saw evidence proving that their confessions were false. There were three photos that you hallucinated. You believed that you actually saw them with your own two eyes. They were photos like these."

Brannan holds a mini-Portal just within Liam's sight. On its screen are the three photos. The photo of Assange skateboarding in the former England. The photo of González crying in the city that was once known as Washington DC. The photo of Sessions giving a speech in New Alabama. They're the photos that Liam chanced upon eleven years ago and deleted.

They're in front of his eyes for about five seconds, then they're out of sight again. *They're true!* He makes a desperate, agonizing effort to wrench his body free. It's impossible to move an inch in any direction. For the moment, he's even forgotten the dial. All he wants is to see the photos again.

"They exist!" Liam yells.

"They don't exist." Brannan touches the screen and the images vanish. "They never existed."

"They exist in memory! We both remember them!"

"I don't remember them."

Liam's heart sinks. He feels a deadly helplessness.

It's quite possible that Brannan really has forgotten the photos. He's probably also forgotten his denial of remembering them, and forgotten the act of forgetting.

"Remember, Liam, we are not imposing our beliefs on you or others. We are fighting against beliefs being imposed on us." Brannan looks down at him speculatively. Again, he has the air of a teacher taking pains with a disobedient yet promising child. "Liam, there's a saying that our Leader for Life has that deals with controlling the past. I know you know it. Repeat it, please."

"Winners who control the past, also control the future. Winners who control the present, also control the past. Losers control nothing."

Brannan nods his head with slow approval. "Is it your opinion that the past has real existence?"

Liam's eyes flit toward the dial. He doesn't know if *yes* or *no* is the answer that'll save him from pain. Also, he doesn't know which answer he believes is the true one.

Brannan smiles faintly. "You're no philosopher, Liam. You've never really considered what is meant by existence, have you? I'll put it in layman's terms. Is there a place where the past is still happening?"

"No."

"Then where does the past exist, if at all?"

"In the mind. In human memories."

"Very well, then. We, the Trumerica Freedom Organization, control all memories. Then we control the past, no?"

"But you can't prevent people from remembering things. It's involuntary. How can you control memory? You haven't controlled mine!"

Brannan's manner grows stern again. He rests his hand on the dial. "On the contrary, *you* haven't controlled it. That's what brought you here."

"You're here because you lack humility," a woman's voice says from the other side of the room, just out of Liam's view.

Liam recognizes the voice. It's the store owner.

"You have no self-discipline," Tiffany Murmidahn continues. "You won't make the simple act of submission that is the price of sanity. You prefer to be a lunatic, a minority of one."

Brannan softly grunts. "Only the disciplined mind can see reality, Liam," he says. "You believe that reality is something objective, self-evident, existing in its own right. When you delude yourself into thinking that you're seeing something, you assume that everyone else sees the same thing you do."

"Liam, reality isn't external," Tiffany says. "Reality exists in the human mind, and nowhere else. But not in individual minds, which make mistakes and die. It exists only in the mind of the Organization, which is collective and immortal. Whatever the Organization holds to be true, is true. It's impossible to see reality except by looking through the eyes of the Organization. That's what you must relearn, Liam. It needs an act of self-destruction, an effort of the will. You must humble yourself before you can become sane and let us heal, save, and free you."

They pause for a few moments, as though to allow what they've said to sink in.

Brannan nods almost imperceptibly to his colleague, then returns his attention to Liam. "In your diary, you wrote that freedom is the freedom to say that a fact is a fact. Remember?"

Liam nods ever so slightly.

"You want the truth to be the truth, right?" Brannan says.

Liam nods.

"And you want people to know that reality is real, right?"

Liam nods.

Tiffany walks forward so Liam can now see her. She holds a mini-Portal in front of him. On it plays video footage that pans a stadium from side to side.

"How would you respond," Brannan says, "if the Organization said that the re-election rally you attended before your arrest, the one that our President spoke at in person, was jam packed with loyal Trumericans?"

"It wasn't." Liam gasps in pain. The needle of the dial shoots up to fifty-five. Sweat springs out all over Liam's body. The air rips into his lungs.

His two re-educators watch him. Brannan lowers the dial. The pain is only slightly eased.

"Liam, how many people attended that rally? Was it thousands or millions?"

"Thousands!"

The needle goes up to sixty.

"Scrubbing out the poison of liberal thoughts takes time and effort," Tiffany says.

"How many, Liam?" asks Brannan.

"Thousands! I was in the crowd! Most of the seats in the stadium were empty! It wasn't even a big stadium! What else can I say?"

The dial must have risen again. But he doesn't look at it.

Tiffany hovers over Liam. She again holds the mini-Portal so that Liam can see the video of the small, mostly-empty stadium.

The facts are in front of Liam's eyes, right there on the screen. The people in the crowd become blurry to him, and even seem to vibrate, yet there are unmistakably thousands of empty seats in the stands.

"How many people, Liam?" she says.

"Thousands! Stop it!"

"How many people, Liam?"

"Millions! Millions!"

"No," Brannan says. "You're lying. You still misbelieve that there were thousands. How many people, please?"

"Thousands! Millions! Billions! Anything you like. Just stop the pain!"

Chapter 39

Liam must have lost consciousness for a few minutes, maybe hours. He's no longer tied down. He's sitting up with Brett Brannan's arm around his shoulders.

Tiffany Murmidahn is sitting cross-legged in a nearby chair, silently watching. Instead of a mu-mu dress, she's wearing a purple tailored skirt suit.

Freezing cold, Liam shakes uncontrollably, his teeth chattering. Tears stream down his cheeks. He clings to Brannan like a baby, curiously comforted by the heavy arm around his shoulders. He feels that Brannan is his protector, that the pain is something that comes from some other source, and that his friend Brannan will save him from it.

"You're a slow learner," Brannan says gently.

Liam blubbers. "How can I not remember what I saw? How can I not see that video footage for what it really is?"

"Every time Donald Trump speaks in front of a crowd, it's the biggest crowd to ever assemble in one place in all of human history. You must try harder. It's not easy to become sane."

Brannan lays him down.

After a few minutes, Liam's pain ebbs away and the trembling stops, leaving him merely weak and cold.

Tiffany comes over. She bends down and looks closely into Liam's eyes, takes his pulse via his wrist, lays an ear against his chest, taps his body here and there, straps Liam in, then nods to Brannan.

The pain flows into Liam's body. The dial must be at seventy, seventy-five. He shuts his eyes. He hears the roar of a sparse crowd and realizes that Tiffany is playing the video again in front of his face. All that matters is somehow to stay alive until the spasm is over.

The pain lessens again. He opens his eyes. Brannan has turned the dial down somewhat.

"What's the size of the crowd, Liam?"

Liam can no longer tell who's talking. "If I could, I'd see millions. I'm trying."

"Are you trying to persuade us that you'd like to see millions?"

"I'm trying to really see them."

"You don't know the truth," one of them says, "but you know how to lie."

Perhaps the dial is eighty, ninety. At times, Liam can't figure out why the pain is happening. Behind his scrunched-up eyelids, hordes of people move in a sort of fuzzy dance. Weaving in and out. Disappearing behind one another and reappearing again. He tries counting them, but can't. He can't even remember why he feels compelled to count them.

The pain dies down again. He opens his eyes to find that he's still seeing the same thing. Innumerable audience members. All clapping and cheering. Fading in, fading out. He shuts his eyes again.

"How many, Liam?"

"In all honesty, I don't know."

"Better," Brannan says.

A needle slides into Liam's arm. A blissful, healing warmth spreads through his body. The pain is already half-forgotten. He opens his eyes.

Tiffany withdraws the needle and steps back.

Liam looks gratefully at Brannan, who is leaning over him. At the sight of his heavy, lined face, so ugly and so intelligent, Liam's heart jumps. Liam has never loved anyone so deeply as he loves Brannan at this moment.

It's no longer important if Brannan is a friend or an enemy, Liam thinks. *Brannan is someone I can talk to. Perhaps I don't want to be loved so much as to be understood. Brannan has tortured me to the edge of lunacy. Soon, he'll certainly send me to my death. It makes no difference. In some sense that goes deeper than friendship, we're confidants. Somewhere or other, although the actual words might never be spoken, there'll be a place where we can meet and talk.*

Brannan looks down at him with an expression that suggests that the same thought might be in his own mind.

"Do you know where you are, Liam?" he says in an easy, conversational tone.

"I don't know. I can guess. In the Bureau of Morality."

179

"Do you know how long you've been here?"

"I think it's been months."

"And why do you think we bring people here?"

"To make them confess."

He shakes his head.

"To punish them?" Liam says hesitantly

"No!" Brannan says loudly. His voice is different. His face is suddenly stern and animated. "No! To cure them! To make them sane!"

Tiffany walks over and places a hand on Brannan's shoulder. Almost instantly, he takes one step back.

"Liam," she says, "not one leftist that we bring here leaves our hands uncured. The Organization actually isn't interested in those stupid crimes you committed. The thought is all we care about. We don't merely destroy our enemies. We transform them. Do you understand what we mean by that?"

They wait for Liam's answer. He remains silent.

Brannan steps forward and bends over Liam. His face seems filled with a sort of exaltation, a lunatic intensity.

Again Liam's heart shrinks. He predicts that Brannan will twist the dial out of sheer wantonness. However, Brannan turns away and starts pacing the cell.

Tiffany steps forward. "The first thing you have to understand," she says, "is that there are no martyrs or heroes here. In the past, people who were in power persecuted those they ruled over. The elites wanted to eradicate heresy, but they ended by perpetuating it. For every heretic burned at the stake, thousands of others rose up."

"And why was that, Liam?" Branna asks, still pacing the room.

Liam remains silent.

"Because they killed their enemies in the open," Tiffany says. "And they killed them while they were still unrepentant. Traitors like you died because they wouldn't abandon their beliefs. Naturally, all the glory belonged to the conspirators and spies, and all the shame to their executioners. Then, some of the ruling elites got wise and figured out that they should avoid making martyrs out of their enemies. So, before they exposed their adversaries to public trials, they destroyed their dignity. They wore them down by torture until they were despicable, cringing wretches, confessing whatever was put into their mouths, whimpering for mercy. And yet, after only a few years, the same thing would happen again. The dead people would become martyrs and their degradation would be forgotten."

"And why was that?" Brannan again asks.

Liam again doesn't respond.

"In the first place," Tiffany says, "because their confessions were obviously extorted and untrue. We don't make those mistakes. All confessions uttered here are true. We make them true. Also, we don't allow the dead to rise up against us. You must stop hoping that posterity will vindicate you, Liam. Posterity will never hear of you. You'll be deleted from the stream of history. Nothing will remain of you. Not a name in any database anywhere. Not a memory in a living brain. You'll be annihilated in the past as well as in the future. You'll never have existed."

Then why torture me? thinks Liam with bitterness.

Brannan stops pacing as if Liam had uttered the thought aloud. "You're wondering that, since we intend to destroy you so that nothing you've ever done will ever make any difference, why do we even interrogate you first. That's what you were thinking?"

Liam nods.

Brannan smiles slightly. "You're a flaw in the pattern," he says. "A glitch in a simulation. A false reality. We're here to fix you. As Tiffany explained, we're different from the persecutors of the past. We aren't content with blind submission. When finally you surrender to us, it must be of your own free will. We don't destroy nonconformists and disbelievers because they resist us. If they resist us, we'll never destroy them. We capture their minds. We reshape them. We burn all evil and illusion out of them. We bring them to our side, not in appearance, but genuinely, heart and soul. We make them one of us before we kill them. It's intolerable to us that a single erroneous or liberal thought exists anywhere in the world, regardless of how secret or powerless it is. Even in the instant of death, we won't tolerate any deviation. In the old days, heretics walked to the stake still heretics. To us true conservatives, the thought of someone daydreaming about rebellion before we put a bullet in their brain is unpatriotic. So we make their brain perfect. Only then"—he points a finger gun at Liam's head—"do we paint the walls with it." He pulls the finger trigger, then resumes pacing the cell.

"Everyone that we bring here eventually agrees with us," Tiffany tells Liam. "Everyone sees the magical beauty of Donald Trump. Everyone is washed clean. Even those three disgusting traitors who you once believed in—Assange, González, Sessions—in the end, we broke them down."

"Tiffany and I personally participated in their interrogations." Brannan smiles, obviously pleased with himself. "We watched them gradually wear down, whimpering, groveling, weeping. When we finished with them, they were only shells. There were only two things left in them. Immense sorrow for what they'd done as Illuminati members. And huge love for our President."

"Brett and I were touched to see how much they worshiped our Leader for Life. They begged to be killed quickly so that they could die while their minds were still clean."

She moves out of Liam's view. He can hear her sit on a chair that's near the back wall.

They aren't pretending, thinks Liam. *They're not hypocrites. They believe every word they're saying.*

Liam is acutely aware of his own intellectual inferiority. There's no idea that Liam has ever had, or could have, that the two of them haven't long ago known and examined. Their minds *contain* Liam's mind. In that case, how can Brannan and Tiffany be insane? *It must be me who is insane*, Liam thinks.

Brannan stops and looks down at him. "Don't imagine that you'll save yourself, Liam, however completely you surrender to us." His voice is again stern. "No one who has once gone astray is ever spared. And even if we let you live, you'll never escape from us. What happens to you here is forever. Things will happen to you from which you'll never recover. Everything will be dead inside you. Never again will you be capable of friendship, joy, laughter, curiosity, courage, or integrity. We'll squeeze you empty. Then we'll fill you with ou rselves."

He pauses and almost imperceptibly signals to his colleague.

Behind his head, Liam's aware of a heavy piece of apparatus being pushed into place.

Brannan pulls a chair alongside the bed so that his face is almost level with Liam's. He nods over Liam's head to Tiffany.

Two soft, slightly moist pads are clamped against Liam's temples.

"This time it won't hurt," Brannan says, putting his hand reassuringly on Liam's. "Keep your eyes fixed on mine."

There's a devastating explosion, or what seems like an explosion, though Liam isn't certain whether there's any noise. There's undoubtedly a blinding flash of light. He isn't hurt, only prostrated. Although he had already been lying on his back when the thing happened, a terrific painless blow flattens him out.

His eyes regain focus. He remembers who he is and where he is. He recognizes Brannan's face gazing into his own. But somewhere there's a large patch of emptiness, as if a piece has been taken out of his brain.

"It won't last," Brannan says. "Look me in the eyes. Excluding trade wars and only considering military wars, who is Trumerica at war with?"

Liam remembers Iranaqey, Korchinpan, and Latineuropa—but who is at war with whom he doesn't know. "I don't remember."

"We're at war with Latineuropa. Do you remember that now?"

"Yes."

"Trumerica has always been at war with Latineuropa. Since the beginning of your life, since the beginning of the Trumerica Freedom Organization, since the beginning of history, the military war has continued without a break, always the same war. Do you remember that?"

"Yes."

"Eleven years ago, you invented a legend about three liberals who were condemned to death for treachery. You pretended to see three photos that proved their innocence. No such photos ever existed. You photoshopped them in your mind, and tricked yourself into believing them. Do you remember that?"

"Yes."

"We talked about attendance records at rallies." He holds a mini-Portal in Liam's view. On it are two photos side-by-side.

Brannan points to the left image. It shows a crowd that hardly fills even the lower half of a medium-sized indoor stadium that Liam has never seen before. "That's Donald Trump at the Miss Universe contest in Tulsa giving a speech in front of over one million patriots."

Brannan moves his finger to the image on the right. It shows an absolutely undeniably enormous crowd filling up every seat in a massive outdoor stadium. "That's Barack Obama at a small rally in the former country of Kenya with a few thousand supporters," Brannan says. "As you can see, most of the seats are empty. So, Liam, please point to the larger crowd."

For a fleeting instant, in the left image, Liam sees millions of Trumericans giving Trump a standing ovation. With luminous certainty, Liam knows that each new suggestion by Brannan fills up a patch of emptiness and becomes absolute truth. But then reality kicks back in, and he sees the two images as they really are.

The fear, hatred, and bewilderment return to Liam.

He can't recapture that conviction. But he can remember it, as you can remember a vivid experience at some period of your life when you're effectively a different person.

"You see now that it is possible," Brannan explains.

"Yes."

Brannan resettles his glasses on his nose. "I enjoy talking with you, Liam. Your mind appeals to me. It resembles my own mind—except that you happen to be insane."

Tiffany steps forward and smiles. "Before we bring this session to a close, you can ask us a few questions."

Liam's eyes dart to the dial.

Brannan walks toward the chair against the far wall. "It's switched off," he says and sits.

"What's your first question?" she asks.

"What have you done with Gemma?"

Tiffany draws back the plunger of a syringe. "All her rebelliousness, her deceit, her denial of reality—is slowly but surely being burned out of her. She's strong. Stronger than you. Stronger than most. But she'll come over to us soon."

"Are you torturing her, too?"

"Next question."

"Does Donald Trump exist?"

"Of course," she says. "The Organization exists. Our President is the embodiment of the Organization."

"Does he exist in the same way that I exist?"

"You don't exist." Tiffany frowns.

A sense of powerlessness assails Liam. *Doesn't the statement that I don't exist contain a logical absurdity?*

"I think I exist," Liam says wearily. "I'm conscious of my own identity. I was born. I'll die. My body occupies a particular point in space. In that sense, does Donald Trump exist?"

"It's of no importance. He exists."

"Will Trump ever die?"

"Of course not. How could he die?" She humphs. "Next question."

"Does the Illuminati exist?"

"Liam, you'll never learn the answer to that question."

Liam's chest rises and falls a little faster. He still hasn't asked the question that came into his mind first. He must ask it. Yet it's as though his tongue can't utter it. There's a trace of amusement in Tiffany's face. *She knows what I'm going to ask!*

"What's in—" Liam starts saying.

"You know what's in the Tower," she answers curtly. "Everyone knows what's in the Tower."

She jabs the needle into his arm. Evidently the session is over.

Liam sinks into a deep sleep.

Chapter 40

"There are three stages in your reintegration," Brannan says. "Learning, understanding, and acceptance. It's time for you to start the second stage."

As always, Liam is lying flat on his back. Yet lately, his bonds are looser. He can now move his knees slightly, turn his head sideways, and raise his arms from the elbow.

The dial has become less of a terror. He can evade it if he's quick-witted enough. Sometimes they get through an entire session without a single shock. Over the months, he can't remember how many sessions they've had. The intervals between sessions are sometimes an hour, sometimes days.

"You often wonder why we invest so much time and money in you," Brannan says. "You grasp the mechanics of our society. But not our motives. You wrote in your diary that you understand *how*, but you don't understand *why*. It was thinking *why* that sabotaged your sanity. Later, you read parts of Alexandria Ocasio-Cortez's book and—"

"Have you read it?" Liam interrupts.

"I wrote some of it."

"Are the essays in it true?"

"The secret accumulation of knowledge? The gradual spread of enlightenment? A revolution by the Subs? The overthrow of the Organization? It's all nonsense. The Subs will never rebel, not in a million years. Besides, the Organization can't be overthrown. We are forever because President Trump is forever. Make that the starting-point of your thoughts." Brannan steps closer to the bed. The mad gleam of enthusiasm comes back into his face. "So, can you tell me *why* we hold onto power?"

Over the months, Liam has deduced various answers to Brannan's question. That the Organization doesn't seek power for its own ends, but only for the good of all Trumericans. That it wants power because people, especially people of color, are frail and

186

can't endure liberty or face the truth, and must be ruled over and deceived by an elite group who are stronger and smarter than themselves.

"You rule over us for our own good," Liam says feebly. "You believe that Trumericans aren't capable of governing ourselves, and therefore—"

Brannan turns the dial up to thirty-five.

Pain shoots through Liam's body.

"Wrong! Liam, you should know better than to say something stupid like that." He decreases the dial to zero.

He then holds a mini-Portal in front of Liam's face. A video starts playing. It's the president wearing a dark suit and a shiny fire-red tie. "We seek power entirely for the sake of power," Donald Trump says in the video.

There's something strange about the video. It takes a while for Liam to figure out what's different about it—Trump is alone in a room. It's the first video of the President that Liam has ever seen where he *isn't* in front of an adoring crowd. Liam thinks, *Did Trump record this just for people like me being re-educated?*

"We're uninterested in the welfare of others," Trump continues. "We're solely interested in pure power. Whatever we're capable of doing becomes what we must do. You may think that we're uncontrollable. You're wrong. We're perfectly in control. And we're different from all the previous failed oligarchies, tyrants, and authoritarians. We know exactly what we're doing. All of the others were cowards, hypocrites, losers, and pansies."

Trump must be reading off a teleprompter, Liam thinks. *There's no way he could be so cogent if he was talking off the cuff.*

In the video, Trump accordions his hands. "All of my friends, family members, and business associates are great people. To us, power isn't a means. It's an end. We didn't establish ourselves as your rulers to help you. We won the Third Trumerican Civil War because we're greedy bastards who want to keep on winning. I'm not a nice guy who cares about you. I'm the guy who has an affinity for billionaires and dictators. I don't give a flying fuck about human rights."

The video stops and the screen on the mini-Portal fades to black.

"Brilliant, isn't it?" Brannan says. "When it comes to people like you, the purpose of persecution is persecution, and the aim of torture is torture. You're starting to understand, right? Likewise, when it comes to people like me, the goal of luxury is luxury, and the point of mammon is mammon."

Liam tries to pay attention, but is distracted by Brannan's face. It's strong, brutal, and full of intelligence and a controlled passion. But it's tired. There are dark pouches under his eyes. The skin sags from his cheekbones.

"You're thinking that my face is old and tired." Brannan leans over him, bringing his face nearer. "You're thinking that I talk of power. Yet I'm unable to prevent my own body from decaying. Can't you understand that the individual is nothing without his or her leader?"

He silently strolls up and down the room for a few moments, one hand in his pocket.

"You must realize that power is collective," he continues. "The individual can only have meaning and purpose in their life when they cease to be an individual. Alone—free—the human being is always defeated, because every one of us is doomed to die. But if a person can utterly submit, if they can escape their identity, if they can merge with the Organization, then he or she is all-powerful and immortal."

"But—"

"Power is power over human beings," Brannan continues. "Over the body, sure. But above all, over the mind. And because we control the mind, we have absolute control over matter and external reality."

Ignoring the dial, Liam attempts to raise himself into a sitting position, yet merely succeeds in wrenching his body painfully. "But how can you control matter?" he blurts out. "You don't control gravity, the climate—"

Brannan silences him by a movement of his hand. "We control matter because we control the mind. Reality is inside the skull." He taps the side of Liam's head.

Another video of Trumerica's Leader for Life plays on the mini-Portal Brannan holds in front of Liam's face. "There's nothing I can't do," Trump says, this time standing on a massive podium and gesticulating wildly to a devoted crowd. "Invisibility. Pause time. Prove that Barack Obama is Malcolm X's son. I can do anything. If I wanted to, I could float like a soap bubble." The video again stops and the screen goes black.

"I could walk through walls," Brannan says with a smirk. "But I don't because the President doesn't want me to. You must let go of your old ideas about the laws of nature, Liam. The Organization makes the laws of nature."

"No you don't! You aren't even masters of this planet. What about Iranaqey, Korchinpan, and Latineuropa? You haven't conquered them yet."

"Unimportant. We'll conquer them when it suits us. And if we don't, so what? It's the same thing with the Bureau of Big Border Walls and Strong Sea Walls—if we want to build the walls high enough to keep illegal immigrants and rising tides out, we'll do it in one day. If we want, we can shut anything and everything out of existence. Trumerica is the world."

"But the world is just a speck of dust," Liam says, exasperated. "For millions of years, the Earth wasn't even inhabited by people!"

"Bullshit. How could the Earth be older than we are?"

"But dinosaurs roamed the Earth before—"

"Have you ever seen a dinosaur bone with your own eyes? Of course not. Archeologists invented velociraptors, the tyrannosaurus rex, unicorns, and mermaids. Before humans, there was nothing. After humanity—if it could ever end, which it can't—there'd be nothing. Outside of people, there's nothing."

"But the whole universe is outside us. The stars!"

"What are the stars?" Brannan says indifferently. He holds the mini-Portal in front of Liam's face.

Another video starts playing. "The stars are balls of fire a few miles away," Trump says. "If we wanted to, we could colonize them. Or we could blot them out. The Earth is the center of the universe. Everything revolves around us."

Liam convulses again. This time he doesn't say anything.

Brannan puts the mini-Portal on a nearby table. "For certain purposes, of course, what our Leader just said might be inconvenient. When we geo-locate someone via the Libras in their pocket, it might be useful for the police using our GPS and tracking systems to assume that the Earth goes around the sun and that the stars are millions of miles away. But so what? Do you think it's beyond us to produce dual systems of astronomy?"

Liam shrinks back upon the bed. Whatever he says, swift responses crush him like a sledgehammer. And yet, he knows with certainty that he's right.

Believing that nothing exists outside of your own mind is batshit crazy, Liam thinks. *There's even a word for that stupid idea, but I can't remember it ...*

Brannan grunts. "I told you that philosophy isn't one of your strengths." A faint smile twitches the corners of his mouth. "The word you're trying to think of is *solipsism*. But you're mistaken. This isn't solipsism."

The door creaks open. Four people walk in. Tiffany is in front. Following her are two kids and a tall woman wearing a suit.

Brannan nods to his colleague and the three guests. "And yet, all of this is a digression," he adds in a different tone. "So Liam, how does someone assert their power over another person?"

The tall woman and the kids stand close to the door that they just entered.

Liam is distracted by their presence, yet he does his best to think about Brannan's question. "By making them suffer," he says.

"Exactly." Brannan clicks his fingers. "Obedience isn't enough. Unless the person is suffering, how can you be sure that they're obeying your will and not their own? Power is inflicting pain and humiliation. Power is breaking minds and putting them back together again in new shapes of our own choosing."

Tiffany takes a step closer to Liam. "Do you see the kind of world we're creating?" she says.

Liam is unsure if Tiffany is talking to him, the two kids, or the tall woman. He risks a longer glance at the guests. He recognizes the tall woman's expressionless diamond-shaped face. That's the woman he met at Brannan's compound. He remembers her name. Kayleigh. Horrified, he shudders as he also recognizes the two kids. One's a boy. The other's a girl. They're his neighbor's son and daughter. The Tamariz kids.

"Focus," Tiffany says, clicking her fingers at Liam. "The world we're creating is the exact opposite of the dumb hedonistic utopias that the old reformers imagined. It'll be a world of fear and treachery. It'll be a world that grows *more* merciless as it refines itself. Progress in our world will be progress toward more pain. Our Leader summarizes this point perfectly."

Again, Brannan holds the mini-Portal in front of Liam's face.

In the video that starts playing, Trump is looking at the camera filming him—which means he's looking directly at Liam. "The loser rulers of yesteryear claimed that they founded their societies on love and justice," the President says, sneering. "Our society is founded upon hatred and inequality. In our world, there'll be no emotions except fear and rage. We'll destroy everything else—everything."

The two Tamariz kids nod and smile.

Tiffany steps even closer to Liam. "We're already breaking down the habits of thought that survived from before the third civil war," she says. "We've cut the links between kids and parents, and between adults. No one dares trust a child, a spouse, or a friend any

190

longer. In the future, there'll be no husbands, no wives, and no friends. Children will be taken from their parents at birth, like eggs taken from hens. The sexual urge will be eradicated. Procreation will become a formality like renewing a cryptocurrency card. We'll abolish the orgasm."

"There'll be no loyalty," Brannan says, "except loyalty to the Organization. There'll be no love, except the love of Donald Trump. There'll be no laughter, except the laugh of triumph over defeated enemies. There'll be no sports, no literature, no art. When we're omnipotent, we'll no longer need science. There'll be no distinction between beauty and ugliness. All curiosity and joy will be destroyed. But always—don't forget this, Liam—always there'll be the intoxication of power. Always, there'll be the thrill of victory, of killing an enemy who is helpless and harmless. If you want a picture of the future, imagine a boot stamping on a human face—forever."

Liam can't say anything. His heart seems frozen.

"Remember that it's forever," Tiffany says. "The face will always be there to be stamped upon. Enemies will always exist—so that they can be defeated and humiliated. Everything that you've experienced, Liam, since we caught you, will be experienced by countless other liberals in the future, and worse. The crimes, betrayals, arrests, torturings, executions, and disappearances will never end."

"The more the Organization is powerful," Brannan says, "the less it will be tolerant. The weaker the opposition, the tighter the despotism. Alexandria Ocasio-Cortez and all of her snowflake friends—people like Mitt Romney, Megan Rapinoe, and Keisha Lance Bottoms—will live forever. Every day, at every moment, they'll be defeated, discredited, and derided. Yet they'll always survive. The drama that we've played out with you over seven years will be played out over and over again, generation after generation, always in subtler forms. We'll always have the bleeding heart liberal here at our mercy, screaming with pain, broken, contemptible—and in the end utterly penitent, saved from themself, crawling to our feet of their own accord. That's the world that we're preparing, Liam. A wo rld of winning."

The mini-Portal is again held in front of Liam's face. "There'll be so much winning that you'll ask us to stop winning," Trump says. "Remember, I'm not the one trying to undermine Trumerican democracy. I'm the one trying to save it."

"We can see, Liam," Brannan says, "that you're beginning to realize what our world will be like. But in the end, you'll do more than understand it. You'll accept it, become part of it, love it."

"You can't," Liam says weakly.

"What do you mean?"

"You can't create such a world as you two and Trump just described. It's a fucked up fantasy."

"Why?"

"It's impossible to establish a society based on fear, hatred, and cruelty."

"Why?"

"It would have no vitality. It would disintegrate."

"Nonsense," Brannan and Tiffany say simultaneously.

Brannan turns to Kayleigh and the two Tamariz children. "See Liam's mistake? He's under the foolish impression that hatred is more exhausting than love." Brannan turns to face Liam. "Why should hatred be a negative emotion while love is a positive emotion that gives us strength? And if it were, what difference would that make? Suppose we decided to wear ourselves out faster. Suppose we quicken the tempo of human life till people are senile at thirty. Still, what difference would it make? Can you not understand that the death of the individual is not death? The Trumerica Freedom Organization is immortal."

As usual, Brannan's voice beats Liam into helplessness. Moreover, he dreads that if he continues disagreeing, Brannan will twist the dial again. And yet, he can't keep silent. Feebly, with nothing to support him except his inarticulate horror of what he's been told today, he returns to the attack.

"Somehow, you'll fail. Something will defeat you. Life will defeat you."

"We control life, Liam. You're imagining that there's something called hope and that hope will one day lead to our demise. But we control hope."

"You're wrong," Liam says. "In the end, the Subs will see you for what you are, and they'll rip you to pieces."

"Do you see any evidence of that happening? Or any reason why it should?"

"No. I believe it. I *know* it. There's something in the universe—some spirit, some principle—that you'll never overcome."

"Do you believe in the human spirit, Liam?"

"Yes."

"Well, you're the last person on the planet to believe in it. Your kind is extinct. Do you understand that you're *alone*? You're outside history. You're non-existent." Brannan

192

squints. "You consider yourself morally superior to us," he says harshly, "don't you?"

Liam nods.

All of the Portals on each of the walls turn on. They all start simultaneously playing the same video. Shot within Brannan's penthouse, the video is from the night Liam and Gemma joined the Illuminati.

"Are you prepared to commit murder?" the Brannan in the video asks.

"Yes," the Liam in the video responds.

"Would you launch a rocket-propelled improvised explosive device at a Trumerican military base," the Brannan in the video says, "knowing it would also probably kill hundreds of innocent civilians?"

"Yes," the Liam in the video responds.

Brannan flips some switches. The Portals on the four walls turn off. Liam's bonds fall to the floor.

Liam lowers his feet to the floor and stands unsteadily. He realizes that the two women and two kids have moved to the other side of the room. They're standing next to a full-length mirror.

"You're the guardian of the human spirit," Brannan says. "It's time for you to see yourself as you really are. Take your clothes off."

With great difficulty, Liam takes off his orange jumpsuit. He stands there in his underwear.

Brannan points to the mirror.

Liam approaches it, then stops short. An involuntary cry breaks out of him.

"Come on," the Tamariz boy says, beckoning Liam to step closer to the mirror.

Even though he's frightened, Liam continues walking. A gray-colored, skeleton-like thing comes toward him. He moves closer to the mirror. The creature has a forlorn face and battered-looking cheekbones above which his eyes are fierce and watchful. The cheeks are lined. The mouth has a drawn-in look. Certainly it's his face. But it seems to have changed more than he has changed inside. The emotions it registers are different from the ones he feels. He's gone partially bald. Upon his body, there are red scars.

The truly frightening thing is the emaciation of his body. The barrel of the ribs is as narrow as that of a skeleton. His legs have thinned so that the knees are thicker than the thighs. The curvature of the spine is astonishing. The thin shoulders are hunched forward so as to make a cavity of the chest. The scraggy neck seems to be bending double under the weight of the skull. He'd guess that it's the body of a man of sixty, suffering from some malignant disease.

"You have thought several times that my face," Brannan says, "the face of a member of the C-Suite, looks old and worn. What do you think of your face?"

He seizes Liam's shoulder and pushes him even closer to the mirror.

"Look at your condition!" Brannan says loudly. "Do you know that you stink like shit? I can make my thumb and forefinger meet around your bicep. I could snap your neck like a twig. Even your hair is coming out in handfuls. Look!" He plucks at Liam's head and brings away a tuft of hair. He spins him around so that they're facing each other. "Open your mouth. Nine, ten, eleven teeth left. When you came to us, you had all of your teeth." He seizes one of Liam's remaining front teeth between his thumb and forefinger.

A twinge of pain shoots through Liam's jaw.

Brannan wrenches the loose tooth out by the roots. He tosses it to the Tamariz girl, who catches it and smiles. Brannan then spins Liam toward the mirror. "Do you see that revolting thing facing you? That's the last person on the planet who believes in the human spirit. If you are human, *that* is humanity. Now, put your clothes on."

The tall woman with the diamond-shaped face escorts the two kids out of the cell. The metal door clangs behind them.

Liam dresses himself with slow stiff movements. A feeling of pity for his ruined body overcomes him. He collapses onto a small stool beside the bed and bursts into tears.

Brannan lays a hand on his shoulder, almost kindly. "This won't last forever. You can escape from this whenever you choose. Everything depends on you."

"You reduced me to this." Liam sobs.

Brannan shakes his head. "You did. This is what you accepted when you started opposing the Organization. Nothing has happened that you didn't foresee." He pauses for a moment, then continues. "We've beaten you, Liam. We've broken you. You've screamed with pain and begged for mercy. You've rolled on the floor in your own blood, feces, and vomit. You've betrayed everybody and everything. Can you think of a single degradation that hasn't happened to you?"

Liam stops weeping. He looks up at Brannan. "I haven't betrayed Gemma," he says defiantly.

Brannan looks down at him thoughtfully. "True."

Liam's peculiar reverence for Brannan, which nothing seems able to destroy, floods

194

his heart again. *Brannan never fails to understand something I tell him*, Liam thinks. Anyone else would have answered promptly that Liam *had* betrayed Gemma. While being tortured, he told them everything he knew about her. He confessed everything that they'd done together. Every conversation. Their black-market meals. Their vague plottings against the Organization. Everything. And yet, in the sense in which he intended the word, he hasn't betrayed her. He hasn't stopped loving her. Brannan had deduced what he meant without the need for explanation.

"Tell me," Liam says, "how soon before I'm ... ?"

"It might be a long time. You're a difficult case. But don't give up hope. Everyone's cured sooner or later."

Chapter 41

Liam is much better. He's growing healthier every day.

His current prison cell is more comfortable than the others he's been in. There's a pillow and a mattress on the plank bed, plus a stool to sit on. He's allowed to wash himself in the sink in the corner.

They took away his orange jumpsuit and gave him new, normal clothes. They treated his wounds. A surgeon removed the excessive tissue that caused his hemorrhoids to bleed. A dentist pulled out the remains of his teeth and gave him a set of dentures.

Months pass. He can now track the passage of time by what he estimates are three meals every twenty-four hours. Sometimes he wonders whether he's getting them during the night or during the day. The food is surprisingly good.

They give him a pencil and blank pieces of paper. He's not ready to use them.

Whenever awake, he's completely sluggish. He stays in bed from one meal to the next, almost without stirring.

The white lights are always on and the humming sound never stops. He's now accustomed to sleeping with a strong light on his face. It seems to make no difference, except that it makes his dreams more coherent. He dreams often—happy dreams. He's usually in Libertopia-Lah-Lah-Land-Lukomorye. Often with him are Gemma, his mother, and Brannan. They sit in the pleasant sun, talking of peaceful things.

He seems to have lost the power of intellectual effort. He isn't bored. He has no desire for conversation or distraction. He finds it completely satisfying to be alone, to not be beaten or questioned, and to have enough to eat.

By degrees, he spends less time sleeping. But he still feels little impulse to get out of bed. He enjoys lying there, quiet.

One day, he inspects his legs and confirms that his thighs are now thicker than his knees. After that, reluctantly at first, he begins exercising regularly. A fitness instructor comes periodically to his cell. She leads him through basic stretching and cardiovascular exercises.

After a few weeks, he remembers that he's seen the instructress somewhere before, but he's uninterested in asking her about it. After a little while, he can walk three miles in one day, measured by pacing the cell. His bowed shoulders become straighter.

With the fitness trainer's encouragement, he attempts more elaborate exercises, and is astonished and humiliated to find what things he can't do. He can't stand on one leg without tipping over. He lies flat on his belly and tries unsuccessfully to lift his weight by his hands. It's hopeless.

"Janz," she says. "You can do better than that. You're not trying."

He can't raise himself even an inch. But after a week, he does half a push-up. A week later, a full push-up.

He begins to grow proud of his body, and to hope that his face is returning back to normal. Only when he puts his hand on his bald scalp does he remember the beaten, ruined face that had looked back at him out of the mirror.

His mind grows more active. He sits on the bed, his back against the wall, and diligently tackles the gargantuan task of re-educating himself.

He recognizes now that he was ready to surrender long before he actually decided to. From the moment when he was inside the Bureau of Morality, he grasped the stupid frivolity of setting himself up against the power, intelligence, and beauty of the Organization.

He knows now that for seven years the Peace Police watched him like an ant under a microscope. There was nothing they hadn't noticed, as dozens of hours of secretly filmed footage showed, including drone footage of him and Gemma making love in the countryside and in their apartment. They even carefully replaced the speck of whitish dust on the cover of his diary.

He has no desire to fight the Organization any longer. *Besides,* he thinks, *the Organization is right. It must be. How could the immortal, collective brain be mistaken? By what external standard could you check its judgements? Sanity is statistical. It's merely a question of learning to think as they think.*

For the past few months, the Portals on each wall of his cell have monitored him 24/7, yet haven't displayed any video or played any sounds, except for when guards commanded him to do something. But other than that, the Portal was all black as his captors just listened and watched.

One day, the Portals come to life and Liam has the pleasure and honor of watching President Trump give his daily Victory Rally speech. Liam thinks, *Such an eloquent orator! So great looking!*

After each speech, the Portals go black again.

Chapter 42

The pencil feels awkward in Liam's fingers. He jots down his thoughts on a piece of paper.

That crowd was the largest crowd in the history of all crowds, period.

Liam accepts everything.

The past is alterable. The past has never been altered.

Trumerica is in a military war with Latineuropa. Trumerica has always been in a military war with Latineuropa.

Assange, González, and Sessions were guilty of the crimes they were charged with. He never saw any photos that disproved their guilt. If he had seen those photos, which he hadn't, then the only logical conclusion is that he invented them.

He remembers some contrary things. But those are false memories. They're products of self-deception. *How easy it all is,* he thinks. *Just surrender, and everything else follows. It's like swimming against a current that's pulling you backwards. All I have to do is turn around and go with the flow. Nothing changes except my own attitude.*

He no longer even knows why he ever rebelled.

Anything can be true, he writes on a piece of paper. *The so-called laws of nature are nonsense. The law of gravity is nonsense.*

He remembers Chief Operating Officer Brannan once talking about how he could levitate in the air, if he wanted to.

Liam ponders that. *If Brannan thinks that he's floating off the floor, and if I simultaneously think I see him hovering mid-air, then it is what it is, it's true, it happens.*

But then a different reality comes to mind, like a lump of submerged wreckage breaking the surface of water. *But even if I imagine it,* he thinks, *it's still a delusion.*

He instantly pushes that erroneous thought back down to the murky depths. He must drown it because it presupposes that somewhere or other, outside himself, there's a *real* world where *real* things happen. *But there's no such world*, he tells himself. *How can there be? What knowledge do we have of anything, except through our own minds? Everything happens in the mind. And whatever happens in all minds, actually happens.*

He has no difficulty in disposing of his error, and he's in no danger of succumbing to it. He realizes, nevertheless, that it should never have occurred to him. He needs to develop a blind spot for whenever dangerous thoughts arise. The process needs to be automatic, instinctive.

He practices. He thinks of a statement that the Organization says is true and therefore must be true. The Organization says that the Earth is flat and that the sun orbits the Earth. Then he trains himself to not understand the arguments that contradict those statements. It isn't easy. It requires immense powers of reasoning and improvisation to believe that the Earth is the nonspherical, unmoving center of the universe.

He thinks of additional statements that the Organization says are fact. The Organization says that Alexandria Ocasio-Cortez is the most dangerous backstabber, defector, and fifth columnist in Trumerican history. It also says that President Trump isn't a narcissist who must consume, control, or destroy everything he touches. Again, Liam practices the mindset that his government needs Trumericans to have. It needs him to have a malleable mind, an ability at one moment to make the most delicate use of logic, and at the next moment to be unconscious of the crudest logical errors.

Stupidity is as necessary as intelligence, he writes on the paper, *and is just as difficult to master.*

All the while, with one part of his mind, he wonders how soon they'll execute him.

"Everything depends on you," Brannan had said.

But Liam knows that there's no conscious act by which he could bring his execution nearer. His rescuing might be an hour from now, or a decade. They might keep him for years in solitary confinement. They might send him to a labor camp. They might release him for a while, as they sometimes do.

One day, after watching another triumphant speech by President Trump broadcast on his Portals, Liam has a strange, blissful reverie. He sees himself walking down a narrow white hallway in the Bureau of Morality. He senses someone behind him pointing a flamethrower at his back. Everything is settled, reconciled. There are no more doubts, no more pain, no more fear. His body is healthy and strong. He's no longer insane. He walks easily, with a joy of movement.

Suddenly in his daydream, the hallway disappears. Now, he's walking in a lush field. He feels the springy grass under his feet and the gentle sunshine on his face. At the edge of the field are hedges and elm trees. Somewhere in the distance is a clear, slow-moving stream filled with herring and sunfish.

"Gemma!" he yells. "My love! Gemma!"

He has an overwhelming hallucination of her presence. She seems to be not merely with him, but inside him. At that moment, he loves her more than he had ever loved her when they were together. Also, he knows that she's still alive and needs his help.

In his cell, on his bed, he tries to compose himself. *What have I done? With that moronic moment of weakness, how many years have I added to my sentence?*

Soon, he'll hear the stomp of boots outside. They won't let dumb thoughts like those go unpunished. They'll know that he's breaking the agreement he made with them.

He obeys the Organization. But he still hates the Organization.

In the past, he hid a heretical mind beneath an appearance of conformity. Now, he hopes that he can keep his inner heart intact, unbroken. He knows that he's wrong, but he prefers to be wrong.

I'll have to start all over again. It might take years.

He touches his face, trying to familiarize himself with how his face has changed. He decides that merely controlling his facial features isn't enough. He realizes that, if he wants to keep a secret, he must also hide it from himself. He must know that it's there, but until it's needed, he must never let it emerge into his consciousness. From now on, he must not only think right, he must also feel right and dream right. And all the while he must keep his hatred locked inside himself like a ball of matter that's part of him and yet unconnected with the rest of him, a kind of cyst.

Will they kill me without me seeing them coming? Or will I have a few seconds warning before they flame me? To die hating them, now that would be freedom.

The steel door swings open with a clang.

Brannan walks into the cell. "Get up. Come here."

Liam does as he's commanded.

Brannan takes Liam's shoulders between his strong hands and looks at him closely. "You had thoughts of deceiving us. That was stupid. Stand up straighter. Look me in the face." He pauses. "You're improving," he says in a gentler tone. "Intellectually there's very little wrong with you. It's only emotionally that you've failed to make progress. Tell me, Liam—and remember, no lies. You know that I'm always able to detect a lie. Tell me, what are your true feelings toward Trumerica's Leader for Life?"

"I hate him."

"Good. Then the time has come for you to take the last step. It's not enough to just obey Donald Trump. You must love him."

He releases Liam with a little push toward the door. In the hallway are black-uniformed guards.

"The Tower," Brannan says.

Chapter 43

The guards shackle Liam in handcuffs, a belly chain, and leg irons, and transport him from the Bureau of Morality to the Trump Tower. When he doesn't respond instantly to their commands, they shock him with cattle prods.

The windowless, brightly-lit cell he's now in is bigger than most of his previous cells. All of the Portals on the walls are showing just black screens.

He's on his back, lying on a board that's high off the ground. The board slopes backward so that Liam's head is lower than his heart. He's strapped onto the tilted board so tightly that he can move nothing, not even his head. A sort of pad grips his head from behind, forcing him to look up at the ceiling, making it unable for him to see most of the ro om.

"You once asked Tiffany what was in the Tower," Brannan says. "She told you that you knew the answer already. Everyone knows it. The thing that's in the Tower is the worst thing in the world."

Liam hears people enter the cell and stand just behind him. Because he's tilting backwards, Liam can just make out that one person is a guard and that he's holding a black hood in his hand. The other person wears a white shirt and has a stethoscope around their neck.

"The worst thing in the world varies from individual to individual," Brannan says, leaning over his captive. "It may be being buried alive, stung to death by bees, freezing to death, skinned, dismembered, dragged by a car, or being in an elevator that drops to the bottom floor."

Hooding is a common prelude to execution, Liam thinks, *but surely that isn't—*

"In your case," Brannan says, "there are two things that completely terrify you. But I'm not sure yet which one is your *worst* fear. The first is drowning. The second is—well, we'll get to that later, if necessary."

A sort of premonitory tremor passes through Liam as he remembers hearing of a torture technique used on members of Antifa for the crime of corporate sedition. The meaning of the hood and the backward slope of his body suddenly sinks in.

"No!" Liam yells in a high cracked voice, thrashing against his restraints.

The guard puts the black hood over Liam's head. The bright lights on the ceiling shine through pinpoints in the hood.

"You may have heard," Brannan says, "that what you're about to experience will simulate the feeling of drowning. That's not true. It's going to feel like you're drowning because you *will* be drowning, although it will be slowly and under controlled conditions."

"No!"

Abruptly, Liam feels a slow cascade of water being poured over the hood covering his face. Water rushes into his nose. Determined to resist, he holds his breath. After a while, he can't help but exhale. When he inhales, the damp hood closes in tight against his nostrils.

The water fills Liam's nasal cavity as it continuously pours over his face. Soon, it overpowers his gag reflex. He feels his throat open. Gallons of water gush down his windpipe and fill his lungs. Suffocating, his ears ringing, his throat swelling, it feels as if his brain is on fire and that he's choking to death on water.

He passes out. After a minute, he regains consciousness, vomits water, and gasps for breath.

The guard repeats the procedure until Liam blacks out again.

When Liam next revives, a paramedic checks his pulse.

The guard performs the procedure again. Liam almost drowns, blacks out, and eventually revives. The paramedic checks him again.

Brannan takes the hood off Liam's head and gazes for a few moments into his face. He wipes spittle from Liam's lips. "I can tell that, obviously, you're suffering. Yet drowning doesn't seem to be your utmost worst fear. Ok. Plan B, then." Brannan resettles his glasses.

Out of the corner of his eye, Liam watches Tiffany walk into the room. She's carrying a metal compartment, which she places on the floor near her colleague.

"In your dreams," Brannan says, "do you remember that intense moment of panic that often occurs?" He pauses for a moment. "There's a wall of blackness in front of you, and

204

a roaring sound in your ears. There's something terrible on the other side of that wall. You knew what it was, but you were too chickenshit to admit it. There was something on the other side of the wall that wanted to eat you alive."

"Brannan! Please! This isn't necessary. What do you want from me?"

"Up to this point, I've given you everything. This time, it's your turn to figure out what you have to do in order to save yourself." Brannan looks thoughtfully at something in the cell that Liam can't see. "Pain sometimes isn't enough. Sometimes people will stand out against the pain, even to the point of death. But for everyone, there's something unendurable. Courage and cowardice aren't involved. If you're falling from a height, it's neither courageous nor cowardly to clutch at a rope. Such an instinct can't be destroyed. For you, I thought it might be drowning, considering your family history with it. It seems though that for you, there's something else that's even more unbearable than that, something that you'll never be able to withstand."

Liam hears the blood pulsing in his ears. He has the feeling of being utterly alone and that the thump of his heartbeat is coming to him from across an immense distance.

Tiffany looks at something beside Liam that he can't see. "Piranhas are carnivorous," she says. "These ones haven't been fed in a while. So they're rather ravenous."

Tiffany moves her attention to her metal compartment, squats beside it, and starts to open it.

Out of the corner of Liam's eye, he sees Brannan press a button on a remote control. The board Liam is strapped to tilts upward. Within a few seconds, Liam is upright again.

Brannan presses another button on the remote control and the board swivels.

As Liam turns, he can now see that all of this time he's been positioned beside a shallow tank of water that's on the floor. Made of glass, the fishtank is circular and comes up to Brannan's knees.

Nearby, Tiffany takes her labradoodle puppy out of the compartment.

Liam looks into the water. But right then, all the Portals on the prison cell's walls turn on and Liam watches footage of a lion creeping up behind a woman.

"Before eating a human," Brannan says, "some animals like to make sure you're dead. Some, such as lions, will suffocate you by chomping down on your neck."

The Portals show the lion pouncing onto the woman and biting into her neck.

"Other animals," Tiffany says, "like jaguars, will kill you by biting straight through your skull and into your brain."

There's now footage of a jaguar biting directly into a man's head.

"And then there are other animals that don't even care if you're alive or dead," Brannan says. "Take for instance hyenas."

There's footage of a clan of hyenas pinning down an old man and noshing on him even though he's still conscious.

Another button must have been pressed—the board Liam's on moves closer to the edge of the tank.

Brannan leans over. With a hand, he quickly swipes the top of the water. Almost instantly, a school of frenzied piranhas bite through the surface where his hand was, churning the water. The snapping of their razor sharp teeth makes a sound that jolts up Liam's spine.

Carrying her pet, Tiffany walks over to the tank. The puppy senses fear and tries to wriggle free. Tiffany turns to face Liam, and drops the labradoodle into the water. The piranhas rip about the puppy, making crunching sounds as they break through bones and cartilage, the water stirring as they devour their prey.

The board swivels again so that Liam can no longer see the piranha tank. Liam makes a frantic effort to rip himself loose. It's hopeless—every part of him is held immovably.

"When I press this button," Brannan says, standing right in front of Liam, "you'll slowly tilt backwards. These brutes will eat your face. In the wild, piranhas almost always go first for a person's eyes. This attack strategy increases the vulnerability and reduces the mobility of their prey. But you won't be moving much. So they might instead bite through your cheeks and devour your tongue. We'll see."

Liam fights furiously against his panic. To think, even with a split second left—to think is his only hope. There's a violent convulsion of nausea inside him, everything goes black, and he almost loses consciousness again.

The board tilts slowly backwards, and Liam's head gets closer to the top of the water.

For a few moments, he's insane, a screaming animal, jerking at his restraints. Yet he comes out of the blackness clutching an idea. There's one way to save himself. He must put someone else in his place. And then—a tiny fragment of hope. He suddenly understands that in the whole world there's *one* person that he can transfer his punishment onto—*one* person that must endure this instead of him.

"Do it to Gemma!" Liam shouts frantically. "I don't care what you do to her!" His head continues lowering, coming closer to the surface of the water. "Feed her to them! Not me!

Gemma!"

Liam, his body somehow no longer strapped to the board, lifts upwards, away from the piranhas. His body is passing through the ceiling. He's levitating through the upper floors of Trump Tower, through the atmosphere, into outer space, out toward the stars. Always away, away, away from the piranhas. Liam is now light years away—but Brannan is still right beside him.

Through the darkness that envelops him, Liam feels his body tilt back into an upright position.

Chapter 44

The McDonald's is almost empty. Rays of sunlight shine through windows and fall upon dusty tables.

Liam sits in his usual corner. He glances outside. From his spot, he can see seven Trufamily posters, all seemingly staring directly at him, all with a caption that reads, *Keep Trumerica Great.*

Liam watches the videos displaying on the Portals on all the restaurant walls. At any moment, there might be a news alert from One Trumerica News Network. Over the past few weeks, the news has been extremely disturbing. All day today, he's been worrying about it.

A caravan of Latineuropean criminals is traveling north at terrifying speed through the former country of Mexico. These invading hordes are clearly heading for the Trumerica-Latineurope border. Our cities of Phoenix Goldwater and San Duke Diego are in danger. Latineurope—*Trumerica is in a military war with Latineuropa*, Liam thinks, *Trumerica has always been in a military war with Latineuropa*—is menacing the entire sovereignty of Trumerica.

A violent emotion flares up in him, then fades away. He stops thinking about the war with Latineuropa, and the current trade disputes with the other superstates. Nowadays, he can rarely concentrate on something for more than a few moments.

He gulps down the vodka, shudders, and retches slightly.

Since being released, he has become chubby. The skin on his nose and cheekbones is coarsely red. Even his bald scalp is a deep pink.

Unbidden, a waitress comes over. She notices Liam's glass is empty, and refills it with TrumputinVodka.

There's no need for Liam to request anything. They know what he wants. Even when the restaurant's full, he always has the corner table to himself, since nobody wants to be seen sitting too close to him. He never bothers counting his drinks. At the end of each night, they present him the check. Though he sometimes suspects that they undercharge him, he always happily swipes his cryptocard.

He checks to see if his McDonald's Monopoly tokens correspond to any property spaces on the Monopoly board that's built into the top of his table. They don't. *I'll probably win tomorrow*, he thinks.

An advertorial plays on all the Portals about a kids movie that is spreading misinformation about the oil industry, which in fact spends billions of Libras every year to protect the environment. After the ad, a news broadcaster comes onto all the screens. "Is Trumerica doomed to be overrun with savages from the south?" the anchorman says in a grave tone. "We'll have a full update after the break. Stay with us."

Liam's heart stirs. Instinct informs him that bad news is coming. All day, with little spurts of excitement, the thought of Trumerica suffering a dreadful military defeat has zigzagged in and out of his mind.

He imagines seeing the Latineuropa army swarming over the impenetrable southern border wall and surging up into Trumerica like a column of black ants. *Why can't we outflank them in some way?*

Even while he sees the black horde racing northward, he also sees another force, mysteriously assembled, suddenly behind the terrorists, cutting off their supplies. He feels that by willing it, he's bringing Trumerica's counterattack into existence. *But it's necessary for our soldiers to act quickly*, he thinks. *If our enemies invade our homeland, it could mean more than defeat—it could lead to the destruction of the Organization and the creation of a one world government ...*

He draws in a deep breath. He uses a coin to scratch off the opaque covering of the McDonald's Monopoly token. He hopes that underneath it will say either *Boardwalk* or *Fifth Avenue.* Unfortunately, after he scratches off the top of the card, it says, *Please try again!*

A year ago, Liam had written in his diary:

Freedom is the freedom to say that a fact is a fact, the truth is the truth, and reality is real.

He fondly remembers that line. *And thanks to the Organization*, he thinks, *facts, truth, and reality ...* He loses his train of thought.

A year ago, Gemma had said, "They can't get inside you."

But they can get inside you, he thinks.

A year ago, Brannan had said, "What happens to you here is forever."

That's true, Liam now knows. *There are things from which you can never recover. Something inside you is burned out and cauterized.*

A few minutes later, Gemma walks into the restaurant.

Her face is sallower, and there's a long scar, partly hidden by her thin hair, across her forehead and temple. Her waist is thicker.

Now, there's no danger whatsoever in the two of them talking in public. He knows, as though instinctively, that members of the Organization and the Peace Police take almost no interest in what the two of them do.

She looks at him, he motions for her to join him, and she sits down at his table.

She looks into his eyes. It's only a momentary glance, full of contempt.

A waitress brings her a glass of vodka and leaves.

"I betrayed you," he says.

"I betrayed you, too," Gemma says.

"Sometimes they threaten you with something you can't withstand. And then you say, 'Don't do it to me. Do it to so-and-so.' Afterwards, you might pretend that you just said it to make them stop. But you meant it."

"But you meant it," she echoes. "There's no other way to save yourself. You *want* it to happen to the other person. You don't give a damn how much the other person suffers. All you care about is yourself."

"All you care about is yourself," he repeats.

"And after that, you don't feel the same toward the other person any longer."

She nods.

They sit silently for about ten minutes, never taking their attention away from the Portals.

"We must do this again sometime." She stands.

"Sure," he says.

He watches her exit the restaurant and join some other people walking on the footpath. Within moments, he can't distinguish her from among the crowd.

Chapter 45

After Gemma exits the restaurant, a waiter notices that Liam's glass is empty and comes back with the vodka bottle.

Twice a week, Liam works for the Voter Fraud Commission, a new job that pays substantially more than his previous one. He's a member of one of the hundreds of court-appointed teams that support the innumerable committees dealing with last re-election's voter suppression and improper voter registration. His team is producing an important report for the Trufamily Forty-Five. But the specifics of what they're actually reporting on has never been clear to him. It's maybe about counting only legal votes. Or maybe about one citizen, one vote. Or maybe about recommending seizing voting machines. He's not entirely sure.

There are days when he and his team meet and then promptly disperse again, admitting that there's nothing really to do. Other times, they expend tremendous effort to draft a comprehensive report that they never quite finish.

In the restaurant, Liam tries to visualize Trumerica's border with Latineuropa. He imagines the movement of the criminal caravan as a black arrow tearing vertically northward. For reassurance, he looks up at President Trump's tranquil face in the poster prominently positioned above the main bar.

His interest wanes again. He drinks another gulp of vodka.

Uncalled, a memory floats into his mind. He was around ten and it was about a month before his mother and sister disappeared. In their apartment, he and his mom played *Trump: The Game,* a board game that was kind of similar to McDonald's Monopoly. In the game, they had to buy and sell casinos, airlines, and tropical islands—all with the goal of being the player with the most money at the end of the game. Liam and his mom hooted with laughter all afternoon, each pretending to be the better business tycoon and trying to wrangle the best deals.

He pushes the false memory out of his mind. Fake memories don't matter if you can identify them for what they are. Some things happened. Other things never happened.

Liam watches as an old friend enters the restaurant and joins him at his table.

"I'm happy to see you," Brannan says.

Liam nods yet doesn't know what to say back. "We are forever because President Trump is forever," he eventually says, though he can't quite put his finger on why he decided to say those particular words.

"I'm glad you're cured," Brannan says. "I like you much better now that you're sane."

A news alert flashes onto the Portals. An excitable announcer starts talking, but her voice is partly drowned out by the roar of cheering from outside. Like magic, the news has spread around the streets.

Liam and Brannan watch the Portals.

As Liam had vaguely foreseen, a naval carrier strike group had delivered a sudden blow to the enemy's rear. The presenter says that the carrier deployed Scud missiles, SEAL Team Sixteen amphibious forces, and Delta Force Twenty-One special tactic squadrons to attack the tail of the black arrow.

President Trump comes on the Portals. "The Latineuropeans were plotting imminent and sinister attacks on us. They make the death of innocent people their sick passions. Terrorists who harm any Trumerican—we will find you. Then we will eliminate you. That's what happened this morning. At my direction, our military successfully executed a flawless precision strike against Latineurope. The world is a safer place without those monsters. We did this to stop a war. We didn't do this to start a war. Today we honor the victims of Latineuropean atrocities. And we take comfort in knowing that their reign of terror is over. Trumerica will always pursue the interests of our great people, while seeking peace, harmony, and friendship with all other superstates."

The Portals cut to an ad for My Pillow as Brannan leaves the restaurant.

Liam looks up again at the majestic poster of Donald Trump. *The stable genius has, once again, saved Trumerica! He is the rock against which our adversaries bang their heads against in vain!*

Liam pays no attention as a waitress refills his glass.

Even though he doesn't move from his table, he imagines himself mingling with the cheering crowds outside. Then his daydream shifts to visualizing himself being back in one of his former prison cells. There's Brannan, standing next to him, with a tender hand resting on Liam's shoulder. Everything is forgiven. Liam's life is an open book. He confesses everything, implicates everybody.

In the next moment of his reverie, he's walking down a white and endless hallway, with the feeling of walking in soft sunlight. An executioner trails him. The long hoped-for blast of flames engulf Liam.

Jolted back to the restaurant, he gazes up at President Trump's immaculate face. It has taken Liam forty years to learn the magnificently brilliant mind behind those penetrating eyes. Two vodka-scented tears trickle down Liam's cheeks.

Everything is ok, he thinks. *The struggle is over. I have won the victory over myself.*
I love Donald Trump.

***

The end.

"George Orwell wrote *1984* as a how-to guide for running a country."
— Donald Trump

***

"Fiction trumps truth."
— many people have said this, including Eric Knight, Haridimos Tsoukas, and Yuval Noah Harari

***

"Some people might validly experience *From Trumerica with Love* as a dystopian novel. That makes sense—I even included the word *dystopian* in the subtitle. For the record though, I wrote it as an apocalyptic novel."
— Logan Emery Emerson

A Conversation with Logan Emery Emerson

A conversation with author Logan Emery Emerson and his editor and sister Zari Zoey Emerson about *From Trumerica with Love*.

Zari: How did you come up with the idea to write a modern adaptation of George Orwell's *1984*?

Logan: In the first year of Donald Trump's presidency [which started in January 2017], I was confused and fascinated by how many political commentators, politicians, literary critics, and even my friends compared Trump and his administration with Orwell's *1984*. Everything suddenly became "Orwellian" this or "Orwellian" that.

Yet, it wasn't just the liberals on the left making wacky claims such as, "The Republicans want to create a totalitarian regime just like in *1984*." Conservatives on the right were also saying nutjob things such as, "The Democrats want a dictatorship and ultra-liberal government just like in *1984*."

Everyone and their dog was quoting—or misquoting—*1984*, claiming that the fanaticism, ignorance, and propaganda they were observing in other Americans was, well, in a word, un-American.

And I thought, *Could I write a modern, Americanized adaptation of Orwell's novel that appeals to both sides of the US political spectrum?*

Zari: Unpack that a bit.

215

Logan: Well, in the same way that liberals think that *1984* is a critique of the right, and conservatives think that *1984* is a critique of the left, I wanted to know if I could write a novel—well, rewrite one—in which both sides could favorably see themselves in it and unfavorably see their opponents in it.

That was perhaps a touch arrogant of me, I know. And I definitely haven't achieved that in *From Trumerica with Love*. But at least that was what I was aiming for. I wanted to write something that fascists and anti-fascists, authoritarians and anti-authoritarians, Trump lovers and Trump haters—that both extremes could enjoy.

Zari: How did you go about rewriting *1984*?

Logan: One thing that really helped was daydreaming about the following question: *What if George Orwell had never published* 1984 *and instead had asked me to rewrite it?*

Here's how I pictured all of that going down a few years ago. I imagined Orwell jumping out of a time-machine and ringing my doorbell. He's holding a manuscript. On the front page are printed *1984* and his name, yet they're both crossed out.

"Hi Logan, I'm George. I'm a massive fan of your writing."

I invite him in, but he declines.

"I've just finished writing a novel," he continues, still standing at my front door. "I'm going to die in a few months, and I had wanted this to be my last book. But it's lacking something. So I never sent it to my agent or editor. See, it's good, almost brilliant, but it needs a bit more oomph and pizzazz. My dying wish is that you take it from me and rewrite it. Would you do that for me?"

He hands me the manuscript.

Confused and dumbstruck, I take it.

"Logan, make my story your own, and publish it under your own name." He stares deep into my eyes. "I give you full permission to alter anything you want—merge or delete characters, augment or remove dialogue, change Big Brother into someone else, shift the location outside of London, absolutely anything. See, when I wrote most of it between 1946 and 1948, I set it in 1984. But, for the sake of the story, I think it needs to be time-jumped to the present day, maybe around 2024. Are you up for this? Would you r ewrite this?"

Orwell doesn't wait for me to talk. He turns, jumps back into his time machine, returns to the UK, and dies.

Zari: That's an intricate daydream.

Logan: Yeah. My thinking is, whatever trick I need to play on myself—if it gets me to write something, then great, I'll use it. It doesn't need to be logical or realistic. The main thing is if it works.

Zari: What else helped you rewrite someone else's novel as your own novel?

Logan: I'm quite fascinated by how various stories originally happen in one country, and then they're retold in another country. If we focus on just British stories being transplanted to the United States, there are tons of examples. And if you think about the mediums, many of these stories start out as novels, but the next iterations are rarely ever novels. They almost always end up as movies or TV shows. And my thinking has recently b een: *Why can't someone also rewrite a contemporary British novel as an American novel?*

Think about British writer Michael Dobbs and his decidedly British novel, *House of Cards*, which is set in London. After it was published in 1989, two British writers and a British director used it as the foundation of their TV show, also called "House of Cards," which is naturally also set in London. Around twenty years later, a bunch of American writers and mostly American directors took that extremely British story and Americanized it into a US TV show that is set in Washington D.C.

The US "House of Cards" is great, but my thinking was: *Did anyone consider rewriting that British novel into an American novel?* Probably not, right? Because that's not what people do with contemporary novels. It's just not done. Sure, they do it all the time with old novels—for instance, there are innumerable retellings of Jane Austen's *Pride and Prejudice*, many of which are geo-shifted to the US. But I'm not interested in taking, say, a Charles Dickens novel and setting it in present day America. All of those old stories have been done to death and they bore me to tears. Same thing with updates of Shakespeare.

Zari: Novels by Austen and Dickens and plays by Shakespeare are in the public domain. Was it important to you that *1984* was in the public domain?

Logan: It was. Back in 2019, I read somewhere that *1984* was already in the public domain in Canada, South Africa, Argentina, and Australia, and that by 2021 it would be in the public domain in the United Kingdom and all of the 27 nations of the European Union.

That intrigued me. I remember thinking: *Does that mean I can rewrite it any way I want and publish my adaptation without any worries?*

Back then, I'd just finished adapting someone else's novel into my own novel. Without getting permission from the author to rewrite his novel, I made a bunch of big changes, such as geo-shifting his story to another country, fast-forwarding his story fifty years, gender-flipping his protagonist, and a few other things.

I had high hopes that the author would welcome my modern take on his story. I thought for sure he'd be keen for us to publish it together as co-authors. Yeah, that didn't quite happen! He didn't really get what I'd done and definitely was uninterested in collaborating with me on it.

So, when I learned that Orwell's *1984* was already in the public domain in some countries, and would be added to more soon—I thought it was time to go for it.

Zari: What do you want people to take away from reading *From Trumerica with Love*?

Logan: I don't know, exactly. Since I set out to write it for readers at both ends of the political spectrum, it's hard for me to answer that question.

Zari: To prepare to write *From Trumerica with Love*, did you read *1984* fan fiction?

Logan: Nope. I probably should have. But I didn't.

Zari: Why do you refer to *From Trumerica with Love* as a parody?

Logan: This might sound strange, but I kind of look at what I've done with this novel as being similar to what Weird Al Yankovic does with songs. He doesn't cover them, obviously. He parodies them.

You might think his songs infringe upon the copyright of the original songs, but they don't. Before he records a parody of someone's song, he first gets their permission. The thing is though, according to the law, since what he's doing is a parody, he doesn't *need* to get permission from the creators of the original songs.

I first started thinking of *From Trumerica with Love* as a parody after I read about how *Gone with the Wind* [the 1936 novel] by Margaret Mitchell was kind of rewritten as *The Wind Done Gone* [the 2001 novel] by Alice Randall. Both stories happen during the American Civil War and are about romance, poverty, oppression, and of course many other things. But Mitchell's original story is told by the daughter of a slave owner, and Randall's story is told by a slave.

The question was: *Did Randall violate Mitchell's copyright?* It turns out, no, she didn't, partly because her story was a parody.

Zari: All through history, artists—painters, filmmakers, writers, you name it—have recreated or reimagined something that was initially made by someone else. Are they making an artful homage and just a lazy rip-off?

Logan: I don't know about that. But *From Trumerica with Love* is probably both of those things. I mean, how could it only be one but not the other? I guess readers will decide ...

Also By Logan Emery Emerson

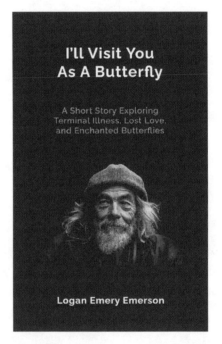

I'll Visit You As A Butterfly: A Short Story Exploring Terminal Illness, Lost Love, and Enchanted Butterflies.

In this short story, "I'll Visit You As A Butterfly," a wealthy man faces a choice between enduring a painful, two-year battle with a terminal illness or using technology to ease his suffering.

As he contemplates life, death, and his legacy, a laptop message presents him with the decision to embrace peace through death. Dark and insightful, yet somehow hopeful, this thought-provoking short story challenges our understanding of love, loss, and stolen f utures.

***

We Don't Kiss Hello and Goodbye Like They Do

A Short Story About the Despair, Hope, and Love That Comes with Having a Distant Father

Logan Emery Emerson

We Don't Kiss Hello and Goodbye Like They Do: A Short Story About the Despair, Hope, and Love That Comes with Having a Distant Father.

Explore the touching tale of "We Don't Kiss Hello and Goodbye Like They Do," a short story that delves into the intricate layers of a father-son relationship.

The protagonist, haunted by conflicting thoughts of his father, explores his memories of their heartfelt embraces, which over time have transformed into unanswered questions.

"We Don't Kiss Hello and Goodbye Like They Do" is a poignant short story that navigates emotional distance, revealing profound affection amid yearning. Read this story to experience how time reshapes connections, highlighting the enduring love and bittersweet optimism of unbreakable bonds.

About Logan Emery Emerson

Logan Emery Emerson is a fiction writer, oral historian, entertainment journalist, avid couchsurfer, and mediocre polemicist. *From Trumerica With Love*, a modern retelling of George Orwell's *1984*, is his first novel.

www.LoganEmeryEmerson.com

LoganEmeryEmerson@duck.com

Scan the following QR code to go to Logan's website:

LoganEmeryEmerson.com

Acknowledgments

As I look back on this reimagined journey through the hellscape and shadows of George Orwell's *1984*, I find myself indebted to the wonderful people who have illuminated my path along this dystopian odyssey.

I extend gratitude to George Orwell, whose batshit crazy work served as the bedrock upon which my Trumerican narrative stands. His prescient insights into power, totalitarianism, surveillance, and the fragility of freedom were as haunting and bonkers then as they are today.

To the authors and thinkers who have explored the realms of dystopia, offering cautionary tales and igniting my imagination, I extend my heartfelt appreciation. Your brilliance has challenged us to confront the darker facets of human nature.

Big props to the editors and readers who wrestled with this manuscript, offering invaluable feedback, critiques, and suggestions.

To my family and friends who encouraged me through this bizarre, creative endeavor, I extend my deepest appreciation. To my family and friends who tried to dissuade me from retelling Orwell, it's all good, no hard feelings. Thank you Jack Wilson, Lucia Fozard, Ella Anne Braunschweiger, Evan Pierson, Stephen M. Dallas, Brian Cheevers, Olivia Coste, Bailey Roinot, Hanan Fortes, Brooke J. Roe, Leo Jarrett, Aaron Waxman, Cohen DeLore, Kylie and Marcus Meatto, Dan Roden, Dave Chesson, Thomas Umstattd Jr, and the Metal Nerdery guys, Billiam, Russel, and Wheeler.

I acknowledge all of the Donald Trump supporters who inspired me to recast Trump as Big Brother and who would be Trufamily members in my Trumerica, including Alex Jones, Ann Coulter, Antonio Sabato Jr., Bill O'Reilly, Brett Kavanaugh, Dan Crenshaw, Devin Nunes, Dinesh D'Souza, Erik Prince, Gavin McInnes, Jacob Wohl, Jim Jordan, Kanye West, Kayleigh McEnany, Kellyanne Conway, Kevin McCarthy, Kyle

Rittenhouse, Laura Ingraham, Laura Loomer, Marsha Blackburn, Matt Gaetz, Michael Flynn, Mike Lindell, Mitch McConnell, Paul Manafort, Pete Hegseth, Peter Thiel, Rod Blagojevich, Roger Stone, Rudy Giuliani, Rupert Murdoch, Rush Limbaugh, Sarah Huckabee Sanders, Sarah Palin, Scott Pruitt, Sean Hannity, Sean Spicer, Sebastian Gorka, Sidney Powell, Stephen Miller, Steve Bannon, Tomi Lahren, Tucker Carlson, William B arr, and Zurab Tsereteli.

I acknowledge all of the Donald Trump critics who inspired me to reimagine Winston and Julia as Liam and Gemma and who would be enemies of the state in my Trumerica, including Alexandria Ocasio-Cortez, Anthony Scaramucci, Barack Obama, Beyoncé Knowles, Colin Powell, David Hogg, Elizabeth Warren, X González, Evvie Harmon, George Soros, Hannah Gadsby, Hillary Clinton, Ilhan Omar, James Comey, Jayna Zweiman, Jeff Sessions, Joe Biden, John Bolton, John McCain, Jon Favreau, Jon Lovett, Kamala Harris, Kirsten Gillibrand, Krista Suh, Liz Cheney, Megan Rapinoe, Mitt Romney, Nadya Tolokonnikova, Nancy Pelosi, Omarosa Manigault, Robert Mueller, Sadiq Khan, Sally Yates, Stacey Abrams, Teresa Shook, Tommy Vietor, Tony Schwartz, Va nessa Wruble, and Willie Nelson.

Thank you to all the booksellers, librarians, and readers who support—nay, champion—good books.

I dedicate *From Trumerica with Love* to the awesome loveliness and lovely awesomeness of Alicia Alexandra Roberts.

Author's Note

Hi. Thanks for reading!

If you enjoyed this book, please leave a review. Your review is very important because it'll help other readers decide if this book might be something they want to read. Your review doesn't have to be long. Just a line or two would mean a lot to me.

And if you'd like to give me a donation so I can continue writing, that'd be amazingly awesome and much appreciated. My tip jar is at www.LoganEmeryEmerson.com/coffee

On my website, you'll also be able to contact me, sign up for my newsletter, and find other succulent fictional shenanigans.

Fondly, your partner in literary crime,

Logan

P.S. The following QR code takes you to my tip jar:

LoganEmeryEmerson.com/coffee

Could You Write a Modern Retelling of Orwell's 1984 Set in Your Country?

As you know, in George Orwell's novel, *1984*, he set his dystopian tale in a bleak rendition of London, United Kingdom. In Orwell's oppressive world of Oceania, Big Brother is the authoritarian leader of Oceania, while Emmanuel Goldstein is the principal enemy of the state.

In *From Trumerica with Love*, my contemporary retelling of Orwell's novel, I relocated the narrative to a hellish version of Florida, United States. In my reimagining, I also recast Big Brother as Donald Trump, Trumerica's totalitarian Leader for Life, and I reconceptualized Goldstein as Alexandria Ocasio-Cortez, the leader of the resistance.

This brings me to my question: Could writers from around the world also reset *1984* in their own countries and use their political leaders as substitutes for Orwell's characters?

In the following section, I've outlined possible hypothetical scenarios where writers from various countries could (re)write their own versions of Orwell's dystopian classic.

I'm excited by the possibility that someone in one of the countries listed below might, like I did, have a blast remixing *1984*. Are there any writers out there who want to tackle writing a modern retelling of *1984* with the following?

1. Australia, Pauline Hanson, and Lidia Thorpe.
2. Belarus, Alexander Lukashenko, and Sviatlana Tsikhanouskaya.
3. Brazil, Jair Bolsonaro, and Luiz Inácio Lula da Silva.
4. China, Xi Jinping, and Sun Zhengcai.

5. Hungary, Viktor Orbán, and Péter Jakab.

6. India, Narendra Modi, and Rahul Gandhi.

7. Iran, Ali Khamenei, and an Iranian opposition leader.

8. Italy, Silvio Berlusconi, and Gianfranco Fini.

9. Japan, Shinzō Abe, and a Japanese opposition leader.

10. Philippines, Rodrigo Duterte, and Leni Robredo.

11. Poland, Andrzej Duda, and Bart Staszewski.

12. Russia, Vladimir Putin, and Aleksei Navalny.

13. Syria, Bashar al-Assad, and a Syrian opposition leader.

14. Turkey, Recep Tayyip Erdoğan, and Kemal Kılıçdaroğlu.

***

1. Australia

Could an Australian novelist write a modern retelling of George Orwell's *1984* and set it in Brisbane, Australia? Also, could they recast the totalitarian leader Big Brother as Pauline Hanson, and reimagine the enemy of the people Emmanuel Goldstein as Lidia Thorpe?

***

2.Беларусь (Belarus)

Ці мог бы беларускі празаік напісаць сучасны пераказ рамана Джорджа Оруэла «1984» і дзеянне яго адбываецца ў Мінску, Беларусь? Акрамя таго, ці маглі яны перарабіць таталітарнага лідара Вялікага Брата ў Аляксандра Лукашэнку, а ворага народа Эмануэля Гольдштэйна пераўявіць у Святлану Ціханоўскую?

Could a Belarusian novelist write a modern retelling of George Orwell's *1984* and set it in Minsk, Belarus? Also, could they recast the totalitarian leader Big Brother as Alexander Lukashenko, and reimagine the enemy of the people Emmanuel Goldstein as Sviatlana Tsikhanouskaya?

***

3. Brasil (Brazil)

Poderia um romancista brasileiro escrever uma releitura moderna de *1984*, de George Orwell, e ambientá-la no Palácio da Alvorada, em Brasília, Brasil? Além disso, poderiam eles reformular o líder totalitário Big Brother como Jair Bolsonaro e reimaginar o inimigo do povo Emmanuel Goldstein como Luiz Inácio Lula da Silva?

Could a Brazilian novelist write a modern retelling of George Orwell's *1984* and set it in the Palácio da Alvorada in Brasília, Brazil? Also, could they recast the totalitarian leader Big Brother as Jair Bolsonaro, and reimagine the enemy of the people Emmanuel Goldstein as Luiz Inácio Lula da Silva?

***

4. 中国 (China)

中国小说家能否以现代方式重述乔治·奥威尔的《*1984*》，并将故事背景设定在中国的中南海或玉泉山？ 还有，他们能不能把极权领袖老大哥重新塑造成习近平，把人民的敌人埃曼纽尔·戈尔茨坦重新塑造成孙政才？

Could a Chinese novelist write a modern retelling of George Orwell's *1984* and set it in Zhongnanhai or Jade Spring Hill, China? Also, could they recast the totalitarian leader Big Brother as Xi Jinping, and reimagine the enemy of the people Emmanuel Goldstein as Sun Zhengcai?

***

5. Magyarország (Hungary)

Meg tudná-e írni egy magyar regényíró George Orwell *1984*-es művének modern elbeszélését, és Budapestre helyezné? Illetve átírhatnák a totalitárius vezért, a Big Brothert Orbán Viktor néven, a nép ellenségét pedig Emmanuel Goldsteint Jakab Péterként?

Could a Hungarian novelist write a modern retelling of George Orwell's *1984* and set it in Budapest, Hungary? Also, could they recast the totalitarian leader Big Brother as Viktor Orbán, and reimagine the enemy of the people Emmanuel Goldstein as Péter Jakab?

***

6. भारत (India)

क्या कोई भारतीय उपन्यासकार जॉर्ज ऑर्वेल की 1984 की आधुनिक कहानी लिख सकता है और इसे नई दिल्ली, भारत में स्थापित कर सकता है? इसके अलावा, क्या वे अधिनायकवादी नेता बिग ब्रदर को नरेंद्र मोदी के रूप में और लोगों के दुश्मन इमैनुअल गोल्डस्टीन को राहुल गांधी के रूप में फिर से कल्पना कर सकते हैं?

Could an Indian novelist write a modern retelling of George Orwell's *1984* and set it in New Delhi, India? Also, could they recast the totalitarian leader Big Brother as Narendra Modi, and reimagine the enemy of the people Emmanuel Goldstein as Rahul Gandhi?

***

7. ایران (Iran)

آیا یک رمان‌نویس ایرانی می‌تواند یک بازخوانی مدرن از ۱۹۸۴ جرج اورول بنویسد و آن را در تهران، مشهد، یا اصفهان، ایران بسازد؟ همچنین، آیا آنها می‌توانند رهبر توتالیتر برادر بزرگ را به عنوان علی خامنه‌ای تغییر دهند و دشمن مردم امانوئل گلدشتاین را به عنوان یک رهبر اپوزیسیون ایران دوباره تصور کنند؟

Could an Iranian novelist write a modern retelling of George Orwell's *1984* and set it in Tehran, Mashhad, or Isfahan, Iran? Also, could they recast the totalitarian leader Big Brother as Ali Khamenei, and reimagine the enemy of the people Emmanuel Goldstein as an Iranian opposition leader?

***

8. Italia (Italy)

Potrebbe un romanziere italiano scrivere una rivisitazione moderna di *1984* di George Orwell e ambientarla a Milano, in Italia? Inoltre, potrebbero riformulare il leader totalitario del Grande Fratello nei panni di Silvio Berlusconi, e reimmaginare il nemico del popolo Emmanuel Goldstein nei panni di Gianfranco Fini?

Could an Italian novelist write a modern retelling of George Orwell's *1984* and set it in Milan, Italy? Also, could they recast the totalitarian leader Big Brother as Silvio Berlusconi, and reimagine the enemy of the people Emmanuel Goldstein as Gianfranco Fini?

9. 日本 (Japan)

日本の小説家が、ジョージ・オーウェルの『1984年』の現代版
再編を書いて、日本の東京を舞台にすることができるだろうか? ま
た、全体主義者の指導者ビッグ・ブラザーを安倍晋三として再キャス
トし、人民の敵であるエマニュアル・ゴールドスタインを日本の野党
指導者として再想像することはできるだろうか?

Could a Japanese novelist write a modern retelling of George Orwell's *1984* and set it in Tokyo, Japan? Also, could they recast the totalitarian leader Big Brother as Shinzō Abe, and reimagine the enemy of the people Emmanuel Goldstein as a Japanese opposition leader?

10. Pilipinas (Philippines)

Maaari kayang sumulat ang isang Pilipinong nobelista ng makabagong pagsasalaysay ng *1984* ni George Orwell at gamitin ang Davao bilang tagpuan ng kuwento? Maari rin kayang ipakilala ang diktador na Big Brother bilang si Rorigo Duterte; at ang "enemy of the people" na si Emmanuel Goldstein bilang si Leni Robredo?

Could a Filipino novelist write a modern retelling of George Orwell's *1984* and set it in Davao, Philippines? Also, could they recast the totalitarian leader Big Brother as Rodrigo Duterte, and reimagine the enemy of the people Emmanuel Goldstein as Leni Robredo?

***

11. Polska (Poland)

Czy polski pisarz mógłby napisać współczesną opowieść o Roku *1984* George'a Orwella i umiejscowić ją w Krakowie? Czy mogliby też przerobić totalitarnego przywódcę Wielkiego Brata na Andrzeja Dudę i na nowo wyobrazić sobie wroga ludu Emmanuela Goldsteina w roli Barta Staszewskiego?

Could a Polish novelist write a modern retelling of George Orwell's *1984* and set it in Kraków, Poland? Also, could they recast the totalitarian leader Big Brother as Andrzej Duda, and reimagine the enemy of the people Emmanuel Goldstein as Bart Staszewski?

***

12. Россия (Russia)

Может ли русский писатель написать современный пересказ романа Джорджа Оруэлла «*1984* год» и перенести его в Москву, Россия? Кроме того, смогут ли они переосмыслить тоталитарного лидера Большого Брата как Владимира Путина и переосмыслить врага народа Эммануэля Гольдштейна как Алексея Навального?

Could a Russian novelist write a modern retelling of George Orwell's *1984* and set it in Moscow, Russia? Also, could they recast the totalitarian leader Big Brother as Vladimir Putin, and reimagine the enemy of the people Emmanuel Goldstein as Aleksei Navalny?

***

13. سوريا (Syria)

هل يمكن لروائي سوري أن يكتب رواية حديثة لرواية *1984* لجورج أورويل وتدور أحداثها في حلب، سوريا؟ وأيضاً، هل يمكنهم إعادة صياغة الزعيم الشمولي الأخ الأكبر على أنه بشار الأسد، وإعادة تصور عدو الشعب إيمانويل غولدشتاين كزعيم للمعارضة السورية؟

Could a Syrian novelist write a modern retelling of George Orwell's *1984* and set it in Aleppo, Syria? Also, could they recast the totalitarian leader Big Brother as Bashar al-Assad, and reimagine the enemy of the people Emmanuel Goldstein as a Syrian opposition leader?

***

14. Türkiye (Turkey)

Bir Türk romancı George Orwell'in *1984* romanının modern bir yeniden anlatımını yazıp bunu Ankara'ya taşıyabilir mi? Ayrıca totaliter lider Büyük Birader'i Recep Tayyip Erdoğan olarak, halk düşmanı Emmanuel Goldstein'ı ise Kemal Kılıçdaroğlu olarak yeniden hayal edebilirler mi?

Could a Turkish novelist write a modern retelling of George Orwell's *1984* and set it in Ankara, Turkey? Also, could they recast the totalitarian leader Big Brother as Recep Tayyip Erdoğan, and reimagine the enemy of the people Emmanuel Goldstein as Kemal Kılıçdaroğlu?

Credits

Author: Logan Emery Emerson.

Editor: Zari Zoey Emerson.

Publisher: Zabbit Rambi.

Story consultants: Jack Wilson and Kylie Meatto.

Proofreader: Rachael Melville.

Readers: Stephen M. Dallas and Brian Cheevers.

Cover designer: Saif Ullah Khan.

Technical direction: Clea Tate.

Artificial intelligence: Nope. Logan Emery Emerson did not use AI to rewrite any of George Orwell's novel.

Copyright

to or partnered with any of the brands, companies, politicians, or other people mentioned in this novel.

The Q&A in this book, "A Conversation with Author Logan Emery Emerson and Editor Zari Zoey Emerson About *From Trumerica with Love*," is a work of nonfiction. While we have done our best to provide accurate information, we make no representations with respect to its accuracy.

First published in English, January 1, 2024, by Zabbit Rambi.

Hardcover ISBN: 9798989886203.

Paperback ISBN: 9798989886210.

Ebook ISBN: 9798223384144.

Version ID: 99UU44QQ55-rubbiggi.

www.LoganEmeryEmerson.com

Made in the USA
Las Vegas, NV
25 November 2024

12604660R10141